THE DUKE'S DISCOVERY:

A REGENCY REPUTATIONS NOVEL

BY

RACHEL ROWAN
AUTHOR OF "ENTITLED LOVE"

Please visit www.rachelrowan.com to sign up to Rachel Rowan's newsletter and for more information on her books.

Editing by Chrisandra's Corrections

Cover design by GetCovers

The Duke's Discovery

Published 2025

1st Edition

Copyright © Rachel Rowan 2025

The right of Rachel Rowan to be identified as the author of this work has been asserted in accordance with sections 77 and 78 of the Copyright Designs and Patents Act 1988.

This book is a work of fiction. The characters and events in this book are fictitious and any resemblance to actual persons, living or dead, is purely coincidental and not intended by the author.

No part of this book may be reproduced in any form or by any electronic or mechanical means, including information storage and retrieval systems, without written permission from the author, except for the use of brief quotations in a book review.

To my husband, without whom none of this would be possible.

"The world, we know, is mightily influenced by reputation..."

— James Fordyce, *Sermons to Young Women* (1766)

One

Lucian Grey, second Duke of Cumbria, met the dowager duchess's astonishment with a smile.

"Yes, dearest Mother, I really am being serious."

"But...who is the girl? For I love her already, indeed I do, and yet I haven't heard a word of you taking an interest in any lady—"

"No matter how hard you listened for the gossip of it?" he suggested, smiling again.

The dowager duchess wasn't one to be easily embarrassed, so she didn't colour, but instead gave her son a scolding look. It worked on him about as well at four-and-thirty as it had ever done. That is to say, not at all. She rearranged her skirts in a flouncing manner on the pink and cream sofa in the saloon at Cumbria House, before again fixing her eye on him. He met her look calmly. She was as able to take a joke as him, and just as likely to choose amusement over irritation. As he'd known she would, she gave up her lofty reproach and laughed.

"Yes. Listened until my ears hurt. And who can blame me? You, a confirmed bachelor for all that I can see, and—"

"Bringing the dukedom to an early close after a scant two generations." He adopted a woeful expression. "And breaking my poor grandchildless mother's heart into the bargain. I know, I know. What an undutiful son."

She twinkled, her scarcely wrinkled cheek displaying the dimple that had no doubt won his father's heart many years ago. "I should've known you had an ace up your sleeve."

He feigned astonishment. "Cheat at cards? Never!"

"You know what I mean. You always do play your cards close to your chest, but I know you're never...never caught napping."

"Are you revealing yourself to have turned gamester, Mother? All these expressions...!"

She gave him an unimpressed look. "Very well, to be more blunt, you like to shroud your life in mystery just...just as a villain in a novel shrouds himself in the blackest of cloaks."

"Awful," he protested, laughing. "No, say I do not."

"And you never say anything if you do not think it's going to astonish the room, or, at least make you look ten times as clever as everyone in it!"

"A poppycock," he mourned. "I'm the veriest poppycock."

"Oh, nonsense. How did we even get onto this? You've done it again—diverted the topic away from your real news when we were barely started, and I didn't even feel the pull of the rein. Abominable, evasive man."

"Disappointing, undutiful poppycock I may be, but you'll allow I know how to handle the reins."

"Oh, do stop funning me and be serious."

"I'm being perfectly serious. Buxton himself once commended my skill, and if I hadn't been so blinded by his striped waistcoat, I might've let the praise go to my head."

"Lucian! You just informed me you were to be married!"

"So I did!"

But he relented, got up, kissed his mother's head in apology, then returned to his seat. He crossed his legs and adopted a more serious expression—one that was instantly belied by him saying, "I am ready for my interrogation."

She pursed her lips but abandoned the desire to remonstrate

further, too tempted, he knew, by his news.

"Well! Who is she? And when did you become engaged? We must put it in the paper."

"To answer the first: she is Miss Parling. Miss Jane Parling, the eldest daughter. To answer the second: I haven't."

His mother's lips opened on a silent "P", the rest of the name being stolen by confusion. "You haven't? Haven't what?"

"Become engaged."

"But you told me you were to be married!"

"And so I shall be. But I consider it prudent, even polite, to ask the lady first. Her father, too, I suspect."

"Oh, Lucian, will you please be serious? I cannot bear you to joke on this matter. And the Parlings... They're a very good sort of family, to be sure, and your papa was very fond of Mr Parling, indeed, considered himself quite in the gentleman's debt, but they are... I mean to say...it is not...not what one would call a great match?"

"No need to say it with that note of uncertainty. You know as well as I that the Parlings have no fortune. Miss Parling's dowry is one thousand. Parling's estate brings him three or four at best. And I *could* have had Miss Abernathy with her forty thousand, or even that celebrated heiress, Lady Lloyd; but no, I decided two years ago on her London debut that Miss Parling would do, and I've had no reason to change my mind since. We do not need the money. And there can be no other objection to the lady."

His mother looked troubled. "I've known you were never *romantic*, but I cannot quite like this...this matter-of-fact way of talking. And you know better of me than to think money my chief concern."

"Not your *chief* concern, no," he said, smiling.

"Don't make me feel petty for the very natural respect I have for our standing. You're a duke. And Miss Parling..."

"Is a countrified little no one. But let me advertise my chosen one to you and see if I can't convince you. You, yourself, acknowledge that they're a good family. Perfectly genteel, an old name, entirely respectable. Mr Parling is a man of good sense, and was, as you also acknowledge, one of my father's closest friends in their youth. From my brief acquaintance with the lady herself, I know her to be of good understanding, impeccable manners, biddable, calm, and sensible. A lady, in short, who would never cause the least embarrassment to our name. And, my final, and you'll allow, most unassailable argument: she is the most beautiful creature I ever saw."

He said the last part smiling, but his mother didn't return his humour.

"That's what it is?" she asked quietly. "A pretty face?"

"An astonishingly beautiful one. The distinction is important."

His mother's frown deepened. "It's hardly a secret you're an aesthete, but in the matter of choosing a wife..." She trailed off, sighing. "When did you last see the girl?"

"Two years ago, on her debut."

"And had you much conversation?"

"Oh, at least a full ten minutes. And the length of a country dance."

"She is now how old?"

"Almost one-and-twenty, I believe."

"I suppose that's a decent age, at least. She's no schoolgirl. And if she is still unmarried..."

"Then a proposal must be welcome?" he suggested, eyes twinkling.

His mother shook her head. "Odious. That's what you presume, is it? This girl will say yes to you, basically a stranger, merely for the asking?"

"You're forgetting I'm the son of her father's oldest friend. And considered a tolerable catch."

"Oh, tolerable, yes! A mere duke!"

He tugged at his impeccable coat sleeves, assuming an expression of wounded pride. "I was thinking more of my person, Mama."

She tutted. "Don't think my motherly pride is going to puff you up. You're no beauty, Lucian, your face is too hard for that, but you're handsome enough."

He leant forward. "Not an ogre, pray?"

She gave in and laughed, shaking her head as though she smiled against her will. "As if you're unaware of the caps that have been set at you since even before you left Oxford. When I think of all those girls... Half of them I did my best to keep away from you and half I did my best to throw in your path, and you didn't so much as notice a single one of them. Oh, the times I've despaired of ever seeing you happily settled. And it turns out I needn't have troubled myself at all."

"Mother," he chided softly, "have I ever given you cause to think I was not perfectly capable of managing my own affairs?"

"No," she admitted with a sigh. Then she fixed him with a thoughtful look. "Until now."

"You do not approve."

"I suppose I can have no objection to the girl. Your arguments are sound enough. But...you do know a pretty face doesn't last forever?"

"Oh, quite," he agreed, adding very earnestly, "And if, when I arrive at Rowlands, I find the fair Miss Parling has turned sallow or stout, I promise to swerve. I give you my word."

She huffed. "That is *not* what I meant. Lucian...you don't love the girl, that much is clear."

"Yes, but I've never been in any danger of succumbing to that. I'm sadly not built for it, you know."

"I had the great fortune to be very happily married," she said, wisely ignoring this. "And even without love, a happy marriage needs...friendship. Mutual respect. This quiet, biddable, meek country mouse you describe... You'll be bored within a year."

"You underestimate me. It will probably be a week."

She alarmed him then by looking suddenly close to tears. He got up and knelt at her feet, taking her hands in his. "You know as well as I that I'm never going to be romantic. Give me a sensible, respectable girl, and I'll make her a duchess and exert myself to make her happy. And my own happiness will come from having done my duty to my name and my title. And to you."

Whether Lucian would have ever been fond of sailing if left to his own inclinations, he was unsure. He'd certainly spent a great deal of his youth playing around in small boats on the lake at Thornley, his main seat in the Lake District and his childhood home. But the purchase and use of his private triple-masted yacht was a necessity of his work, not the prompting of his heart. Indeed, almost everything Lucian did was prompted by his work.

Even his marriage proposal.

He frowned into the frigid February wind that blew relentlessly from the sea and through the Portsmouth dockyard. But the breeze was welcome to him, despite his expression. He had the grimy, regretful feeling of an overindulged man, though he'd drunk little enough the evening before, and the single glass of brandy he'd taken alone in his guest room after retiring for the night had been drunk sombrely and slowly.

Yesterday evening, he'd offered his hand.

He'd written to Parling, arranging his visit, albeit not his reason for it, and was welcomed very cordially, travelling from

London with his usual mixture of expediency and comfort to arrive at Rowlands in time for dinner.

Situated in Hampshire, the Parlings' house was only six or seven miles from Portsmouth. The bitter promptings of his late-night brandy had suggested this neat efficiency was yet another reason for choosing Miss Jane Parling. How convenient, to find the perfect bride so close to his ship's current anchorage, with business due to take him from England's shore in the morning! He *did* like to run his life with efficiency. At least in the small areas where he was still master of it.

It was gratifying, then, to discover Miss Parling's beauty hadn't diminished one iota in the last two years. Asking Parling for her hand over port, not long after the ladies had left the dining room, had been a rare miscalculation, almost causing his prospective father-in-law's demise. But, after hastily patting the choking man on the back and offering a handkerchief to mop up the spillage, his suit was permitted. Lucian then exchanged dining room for library, where the fair one was shortly escorted by her somewhat dazed papa.

So far, so efficient. He suppressed a rueful smile as he climbed down into the waiting rowboat and gave the nod. The men took up the oars and began their fight across the choppy waters to where his boat waited, a looming hulk, dark with the sun behind it, and all the gilded decor on her sides dulled to invisibility. The sails were already being run up, snatching hungrily at the same biting wind that stung his narrowed eyes. Good. For once, he was almost eager to leave England.

She'd curtsied, his bride-to-be, blushing prettily at being left alone with him. She'd stammered some polite nothings in an ethereal haze of alabaster skin, silver-blonde hair, and silver-blue skirts. He'd asked her to marry him. She'd looked very faint. He'd taken her hand and helped her to a chair.

"Indeed I... I... Sir—forgive me, I mean, Your Grace..."

Thinking ruefully of his mother—not ideal given the circumstances—he'd then gone down on one knee and attempted the role of gallant lover. "It's a shock, I know." But he'd pleaded his case, pressing the trembling fingers and softly repeating his offer.

"You...you do me g-g-great honour," had been her reply, a red flush scalding her swan-like neck. Then she'd abruptly stood and fled the room.

He'd stood too, albeit much more slowly. Hands clasped behind his back, he'd looked into the scanty fire struggling in the grate, a clock ticking loudly somewhere in the corner behind him, and reminded himself he was no romantic.

He wasn't allowed to be.

On board, Lucian climbed down into his cabin, glad to escape the cold, slapping water. He found his man there, laying out his writing tools on the small desk.

Taking off his hat and overcoat, Lucian shivered from his blustery journey. "Tell me you safely stowed that crate of Burgundy."

Willsly looked up and grinned. "Be more than my life's worth if I forgot that, Your Grace."

"As always, Willsly, I'm gratified to find you so cognisant of your duties."

The man chuckled, showing little of the reserve one might expect to find between a valet and such an employer. But Willsly had been in Lucian's employ for a decade, had saved his life on at least two occasions—four, if you believed Willsly—and was one of only a handful of people alive who knew the reality of Lucian's work for the Crown. Indeed, he was only a valet in one of his many guises. Brawler, horseman, marksman, lockpick... Lucian had yet to find an end to the man's talents.

"Gander over there, Your Grace, and you'll see just how well I know my duties."

Lucian looked at the side table indicated, spotting the decanted bottle and waiting glass. "Good Lord. Have I grown so predictable?"

Willsly grinned again. "Dare say it happens to us all as we get older." He was eight years younger and increasingly fond of bringing up the fact. "Getting settled in your ways, like."

Lucian feigned giving him a cuff round the ear, laughing. "Go settle yourself elsewhere, Will. Like the bilge. I have work to do."

"I know it." Willsly gave a smug look at the writing desk he'd just prepared. "Not to say you're getting predictable or naught..."

"Out," commanded Lucian, pointing to the door.

The man went, grinning, and closed the door behind him.

Lucian removed his coat, rolled up his sleeves to save them from ink, and poured himself a glass of wine before sitting at his desk. The ship was gently rocking, but the noise of its imminent departure came loud and chaotic from the deck above, the rigging being hauled, the anchor chain like thunder. His window looked to port, where he could see the distant harbour across the grey water. The sharp breeze tore white crests from the restless sea, but he was glad of it. It blew in their favour.

Taking a key from his person, he unlocked the small chest on his desk and began sorting through the correspondence inside.

He'd been reading for some time, and they were well under way, when a faint noise made him look up. Even at sea the ship was a noisy place, creaking and groaning, but the sound, a faint scratching, had seemed to come from inside his cabin. Mice. Rats. Suppressing a grimace, Lucian put the thought from his mind and sipped his wine, looking out through the window and seeing nothing but sea, the coast of England already an hour or two behind them. They would not head north from the Channel towards Ireland as their official manifest had said, but south.

He was in the motion of putting his glass back down when he heard a voice. A woman's voice, faint but so unexpected that he jumped, spilling his wine over his shirt and cursing at the mess even as he stood and turned quickly to face the room.

"Help! Hello? Please…"

The scratching again. And a tapping, louder.

"Hello? Please. Please, I'm trapped!"

It was coming from his large travelling trunk. Lucian stared at it, hairs prickling up the back of his neck, before he gave himself a shake and strode across the cabin to where it lay to the side of the door. Fingers hasty on the buckles, he flung back the lid and stepped back, heart thumping.

There was a woman inside. A tiny, scrawny, pale, dishevelled chit of a girl, looking very crumpled and rather shaky as she sat up stiffly from the confines of the trunk.

Pale grey eyes fixed on him, and she blinked, squinting against the light.

"Oh, thank goodness," she said. "It's you at last."

Two

THE DUKE OF CUMBRIA stared at her before recovering his composure with a speed Hester would've acknowledged to be admirable, if she hadn't been too cramped and sore to appreciate it. She glanced around the room, finding, as she'd feared from the disorientating rocking, that she seemed to be on a boat.

"Oh...! Where am I?"

"Where?" repeated the duke. "I think *who* is the more pressing question. *Who* are you? And *how* did you come to be in my trunk?"

"And *why*?" The words tumbled from her still reeling brain. "And *what* do I want?"

"Yes." The duke sounded as stony as he looked. "All excellent questions. I'm hoping for equally excellent answers."

She nodded, still trying to get her breath back. It had been stuffy in the trunk. *Not just stuffy,* the quietly panicking part of her brain insisted, but terrifying, breathless. She pushed the unhelpful voice away and gripped the sides of the trunk, trying to lift herself to a standing position. Her legs failed to cooperate.

The duke was still staring at her. Now his eyes narrowed. "You look familiar."

"Well, yes. We dined together last night. I'm Hester Littleton. That answers your first question—the *who*."

"Parling's ward," he said slowly, apparently still trying to place her. She could hardly blame him for not noticing her yesterday. No one did when Jane was around. Or, indeed, any of the Miss Parlings.

"That's it," she said. "Or I was his ward. Technically, I'm not anymore, now I'm of age." She tried to strengthen her grip on the sides of the trunk, but her muscles were too busy jittering and shuddering to comply. "I say...I don't suppose you'd help me out of here? It's rather embarrassing, but I'm strangely weak."

A grim smile cracked his stony facade. "Was it the lack of air, or the being stuck curled up for hours, do you think?"

Despite his sarcasm, he came over and hauled her to her feet—not roughly, but not delicately either. He offered her his hand for support, and she took it gratefully as she lifted first one trembling leg over the wall of the trunk, then the other. Her skirts revealed her calf as she did so, but the duke took no more notice of that than he had her entire presence last night.

He dropped her arm and stepped back, pulling over a chair and commanding her to sit. Then he poured a glass of wine and handed it to her. She sipped, willing her hand to stop shaking, and found it to be a rather excellent Burgundy—hard to come by these days. Her eyes alighted on a large stain of what she supposed to be the same wine on his shirt.

"Forgive my appearance," said the duke. His eyes were very dark, but dry as flint. "I wasn't expecting visitors—being surrounded by miles of seawater. Remiss of me, no doubt."

"Oh dear. Have we left port?"

"Some time ago."

"And when will we return?"

"In about four to eight weeks, weather dependant."

Her heart flipped, and she stood, almost spilling her own wine. "But...but we must turn back. Please put me back ashore!"

The duke's stern mouth went entirely flat. He walked over to a writing desk and refilled his glass. "I'm afraid I cannot."

"But you have to! I can't stay here."

"I don't recommend going elsewhere. Unless... Do you happen to be a merwoman?"

"No!"

"Then I would suggest remaining aboard."

Her mouth hung open before she shut it with a resolute snap, determined not to look quite as foolish as she undoubtedly appeared. The attempt was ruined, however, by the unavoidable glance she gave the cabin, as though some escape route might materialise in a hidden corner.

"My second question remains unanswered, Miss Littleton. How did you come to be in my trunk?" He casually swirled his wine—the casualness deceptive, unnervingly so. "You're fleeing the country, perhaps?"

"No, not at all—"

"A game of hide-and-seek gone disastrously wrong?"

"No, I—"

"A delusional state in which you mistook yourself for an item of linen?"

"I—" But she broke off as his words hit home, her lips quirking despite herself.

The duke put down his wine and folded his arms.

"An answer, if you please, Miss Littleton."

"I didn't intend to get in the trunk at all. It was a moment of...panic."

"Panic."

"I was waiting for you in your room, you see."

She was fairly sure it was only good breeding and iron-willed self-control that kept his face impassive at that shocking statement. "I'm afraid, Miss Littleton, that I entirely fail to *see*."

"I needed to talk to you. But downstairs you were always with

Mr Parling, or...or Jane. I couldn't find a moment to speak with you privately. Please forgive the impudence. The...the impropriety. I never would've stooped to such desperate means if it were not a matter of utmost urgency."

"Go on," he commanded.

"So... So... I was waiting for you, needing to speak to you before you departed, when I heard voices outside. Two of the footmen. I panicked and hid in the trunk—it was open, you see, waiting to be packed. I drew the lid shut, meaning only to hide until they had gone, but, seeing the lid shut, they must have assumed it was packed. They locked it, carried it downstairs, placed it on the wagon and..." She gave a small shrug. "As you see. Here I am."

"But why wait until now to make your presence known?"

"I...ah...I fear I fell asleep."

"Oh, yes, I can see how it must have been a very soothing experience. The gentle rocking of the luggage wagon as you slowly suffocated."

"Well, yes," she admitted, cheeks hot. "Perhaps I fainted. Or passed out. Or something of the kind."

"And it didn't occur to you to shout for help when the trunk was first locked?"

"I was afraid to be found hiding in your room. It would have been...a scandal."

"Quite," he agreed. "Almost as bad as being found in my cabin on a ship bound for Portugal."

"Portugal!" she gasped. "But...but...the war! And so far!"

He didn't respond to that, instead fixing her with his dark eyes, very serious now.

"You've answered the *who*, and the *how*, Miss Littleton. Now pray answer the *why*."

She swallowed. The man she'd met last night, tall and well-dressed in his impeccably tailored dark coat, had seemed somewhat imposing. But she'd done no more than curtsy to him when they were introduced, then sit and observe as he made very elegant and polite conversation with everyone else.

True, he was a duke, and everyone had treated him with great deference—Georgina and Elizabeth, the two younger Miss Parlings, had been reduced to wide-eyed awe in the duke's presence and breathless giddiness when not. But Jane, meeting him with her usual calm politeness, had steadily grown more pale and quiet as his attentions to her grew more marked. Not that he was encroaching—he merely spoke to her more, asked her opinions more, looked at her more often than he did the others. But it was enough to make Mrs Parling look at Jane, and then at her husband, with a significant lift of her eyebrows. Hester, in her usual way, had observed it all. And Jane's tearful flight to the room they shared had confirmed it. The duke wanted her. It was a disaster. And little but her loyal defence of the two people closest to her heart had been in Hester's mind until now.

But *this* man, *this* duke, even without the fine coat, even with a stain on his shirt and his sleeves pushed up forearms as corded as a common labourer, was a far more terrifying prospect than the well-mannered gentleman she'd watched over dinner last night. It was his eyes, almost black, the set to his jaw. The implacable will. So Hester swallowed but lifted her chin.

"For Jane," she told him. "To beg you to retract your offer. You must not ask for her."

"And still I'm ignorant as to the *why*."

"Because she is already engaged! She is to marry Charles. They have loved each other for years!"

The duke looked at her for a moment.

"And who, if you'll forgive me for my endless curiosity, is Charles?"

"My brother. Charles Littleton."

A knock at the door stopped whatever the duke's reply might

have been, and Hester found she was relieved to have him look away and stride to open it. But her relief was short-lived. Her existence on board was about to be discovered. How could it be explained? Or hidden? It was impossible.

"Ah, Willsly," said the duke, opening the door, but not stepping back, holding it at an angle that prevented the newcomer from catching sight of her. "Just the man I wanted."

"Is that so, Your Grace?" The man had a somewhat coarse accent. A servant or sailor of some kind, Hester assumed.

"Now, my good man, will you agree that you have an uncommonly high degree of what might be called mettle?"

There was the smallest of pauses. "If you say so, Your Grace."

"I've seen you face mortar shells without flinching. You took a dagger to the thigh with the mildest of curses. And you'll recall how calm you were that time I was poisoned."

"Yes..." said the man with a mildly questioning note.

"Excellent. Recall all those moments of fortitude to mind as I introduce you to my newest acquaintance."

The duke stepped back, admitting a youngish man of stocky build, with a rough, tanned face, but dressed very neatly, albeit simply. The man—Willsly, the duke had called him—looked at her for a moment, face expressionless, as the duke closed, then locked, the door behind him.

Willsly bowed. "Pleased to meet you, ma'am."

Recalling herself, Hester stood and nodded.

"Don't let appearances deceive you, Willsly," said the duke. "This is my friend's...um...nephew. Harry, ah..." He cast around the room. "Trunkton. Yes. Harry Trunkton."

Willsly fought back a grin before agreeing, very blandly, "So it is."

Hester stared between the two men, caught between confusion and amusement. *Trunkton* did it for her. Glancing at the travelling trunk where she'd been trapped, she laughed, then clapped a hand over her mouth.

"An unruly youth, as you can see," said the duke. "Fond of all sorts of unwise larks. The latest being to stow himself away on board my ship for a taste of adventure. Thought we were sailing to Dover, somewhat shocked to learn his destination is the Peninsular."

Willsly nodded soberly. "Quite understandable, Your Grace."

"Of course, it's a complete disaster," said the duke. "Because by taking the place of my clothes within my trunk, the boy has deprived me of anything to wear."

Willsly took a step towards the yawning trunk and bleakly inspected the emptiness within. "This is indeed a dark day, Your Grace."

"I'm relieved you enter into my feelings. But it still begs the question of what is to be done. The captain will expect me at his table two hours hence."

His grave expression not faltering, Willsly said, "Reckon it's as well we have the other trunk, then."

"The other trunk! Willsly, I think this salvation almost exceeds the poisoning."

Willsly inclined his head, Hester watching the exchange in astonishment. They were mad, the pair of them.

"I suppose the young gentleman has nothing but what's on his back, though, Your Grace?"

"And that," said the duke, clapping a hand on his shoulder, "is why I'm so glad of your skill with a needle." He looked at Hester. "Are you any good at sewing Miss...ah...Harry?"

"Only...only the basics."

"Then you can help sew your own shirts." Turning back to Willsly, he said, "Find my most unattractive coat, if any such thing exists, and shirts, trousers. Begin to alter them for a youth of...Harry's dimensions."

Willsly gave her a measuring look, so entirely pragmatic she felt no unease at being studied so. He nodded.

"And bring the first outfit as quickly as you can. And some items for Harry to work on, because the poor boy has been well paid for his prank by discovering he's dreadfully afflicted by seasickness and won't be able to leave his cabin for quite some time."

Willsly nodded again, but, before turning to the door, glanced at his employer and said, "Speaking of cabins, Your Grace, where might the young master be staying? Reckon with the, ah, seasickness, you might be wanting to keep a close eye on him?"

"An excellent question, and why I'm so grateful to you for volunteering the use of your own room."

"My pleasure," murmured the imperturbable Willsly.

The man left to carry out his orders, and the duke walked over to his table, tidying away some letters in a small strongbox, which he then locked. He picked up his glass of wine and took a meditative sip, looking out of the small window. The late afternoon light that touched his sharp profile had an amber hue.

She sat down again, still feeling weak, her legs unused to bracing against the movement of the boat. "I understand what you're trying to do." The weakness in her voice matched that of her muscles, and she pushed the cowed, frightened feeling down. "But it won't work. Your man doesn't believe for a moment that I'm a boy."

"Of course he doesn't. He saw you in a dress, and he's no simpleton. I'll fill him in on the details later, for I don't keep secrets from Willsly. I trust him, quite literally, with my life. But we might convince the crew."

"I know I've no face, nor figure, and really am as scrawny as a schoolboy, but I can't believe they won't realise."

The duke gave her a considering look, his gaze passing briefly up and down her body as though looking for a hint of the feminine curves she knew he wouldn't find.

"People see what they expect to see. And you'll stay mostly out of sight."

"For weeks?"

"If the winds are favourable, we ought to reach Lisbon in fourteen days, or a little under. This is a fast ship, with a good crew."

"And then what happens?"

"I'll find you a lodging while I conduct my business. That should only take two or three days. Then we return in the same manner."

"But when I reach England? After being gone for so long?"

"We have time to think of that. I suspect…you were called away suddenly to a sick relative, took passage in my coach to catch the stage from Portsmouth—I left early, as you know, before anyone was down. The letter you left the Parlings went astray. You had no idea at all anyone was worried. If necessary, I will…convince Mr Parling that no questions are required."

Hester looked at him bluntly. "I'm ruined, Your Grace. There's no way around it."

The stoniness returned to his answering frown. "You are not ruined, Miss Littleton. I will not permit it. So if that was your real game by climbing into my trunk, you can forget it. I'll not allow you to catch yourself a duke."

Three

The look Miss Littleton gave him was so astonished it almost convinced him his suspicion was unfounded. Good. He hadn't wanted to believe it, but it was still prudent to check. He needed to allay any fears, or hopes, she might hold on *that* score.

Which meant it was time to act like an ass.

"I cannot marry you, Miss Littleton. And I will not, even if this deception fails and it appears to be the only way to save your name."

She flushed, bristling in her chair, as much with indignation as embarrassed offence. He spoke again before she could find her words.

"If marriage turns out to be your only recourse upon your return to England, I'll arrange it for you, find a suitable gentleman, and settle the whole."

"I do not wish to marry at all! I've never had any wish to marry—not you or anyone else!"

"Then I suggest you do your best to avoid discovery."

"I came to speak to you for Jane's sake. And my brother's. I had no thought of myself."

"Clearly."

"And you haven't yet answered my request." Despite the violent embarrassment colouring her face, her small, pointed chin lifted firmly. "I refuse to let this all have been in vain. Promise me you'll relinquish Jane."

"Oh, definitely," he said with a careless gesture. "I've no wish for a girl who doesn't want me. It would be beyond tiresome. So long as I can find someone equally beautiful, I'll give her up without hesitation."

It amazed him sometimes just how easy he found it, this guise of *unmitigated ass*. More worrying was that he quite enjoyed it. Though in this case, a very real bitterness added conviction to his act.

She stared at him, aghast. "Is that all you care about? Jane's beauty?"

"Not quite all. But I admit, it's of paramount importance."

"I knew it!"

"Ah, but you do not know my reason."

"I can guess it," she muttered in heavy disgust.

"I suspect not, but it does not matter, as I'm not about to tell you." He turned his desk chair to face hers and sat down on it, one elbow propped casually on the back. "I don't suppose you know any unattached young ladies who happen to be her equal?"

"There is no one her equal."

"That's unfortunate," he murmured. His tone was provocatively ironic, but it really *was* unfortunate. The girl had been just in Prinny's line, and exactly the sort of *nonpareil* that might secure the Regent's interest, and, hopefully, his forgiveness.

"Is Miss Parling really engaged to your brother? Her father made no mention of it when I sought his permission."

Miss Littleton busied herself for a moment, adjusting the lie of her skirt over her knee. "It is...a secret betrothal."

"Ah. Penniless, is he?"

"Yes," she said, anger rising again. "And nameless, and unimportant, and the child of Mrs Parling's old governess and Mr Parling's old solicitor—a complete nobody, just like me. But they *love* each other. Your Grace, you do not understand—"

"No, I dare say I don't."

"We grew up together, all of us. I am two years older than Jane, and Charles is two years older than me. When my parents married, Mr and Mrs Parling gave them the cottage on their grounds. They were very good friends, you see. My mother was Mrs Parling's—"

"Old governess. Yes, I'm paying attention."

"Not just her governess; she became her greatest friend too as Miss Watson—the young Mrs Parling, that is—grew beyond the age for a governess. Miss Watson brought her to Hampshire when she was married and—"

"That is where she met Mr Littleton, Mr Parling's solicitor."

"Yes."

"But one very important thing I don't understand."

"What?"

He smiled slightly. "How can you be two years older than Miss Parling? She is almost one-and-twenty. And you look far less than that."

"Oh." Miss Littleton gave a dismissive wave of her hand. "It's because I'm such an ugly, scrawny little thing, as I said."

Lucian blinked slightly at this easy dismissal of her attributes. Not that she was wrong—or not *entirely* wrong. She was very definitely little—that part was correct. But he wouldn't call her ugly. She wasn't unappealing, but her thin face was entirely unremarkable. There was an unfortunate scattering of faint freckles across her nose, though he found he couldn't hate them. As for scrawny... There were no bones sticking out, no hollow cheeks or sunken eyes. She was just very, very...petite.

"It's a great pity you're not bigger," he said.

"Yes, I've often thought so."

"I mean because then you wouldn't have fitted in my trunk, and we would've been saved this whole mess."

For the first time, she looked contrite.

"I suppose I've caused you an awful lot of trouble. I'm sorry."

"But you did it for *love*," he said grandly.

She gave a small laugh. "I suppose I did. But you needn't fear I'll be a burden on you, or at least no more than I can avoid given the circumstances. As you now realise, I'm no green girl but a grown woman, and I'm well used to taking care of myself."

"Is that so?" Lucian asked, sitting back, amused despite himself.

"Yes," replied Miss Littleton seriously. "I went away to a seminary when I was fourteen—that's when my parents died. And I paid my way by helping tutor the younger children and being a…a…general assistant of sorts to the other teachers."

"A drudge," he stated with sympathy.

She gave a surprised laugh. "Yes, a drudge! You guessed it. But it served me in good stead. Because when I left the school, I went to be a governess."

"At how old?"

"Eighteen."

He lifted his brows in surprise. "But I thought you were Parling's ward?"

"Of a kind. They took me and Charles in and clothed us, fed us, but they didn't have the money to do more. Charles sat in on Tom's lessons—Mr Thomas Parling, that is, Jane's elder brother. But he was always so far ahead of what Tom was learning, it didn't do him any good. Our parents were quite academic, you see. They gave me and my brother a very excellent education before they passed."

"Which, let me guess," he said, his irony tempered by warm amusement, "served you *in good stead?*"

She smiled. "Yes! I was the perfect governess. Unless they wanted instruction in the pianoforte, or watercolours, or how to embroider a screen. French and Italian are my better subjects." Her smile faded. "Charles ought to have gone to Oxford, but it was impossible. Instead, he joined the army."

"Not the most obvious alternative."

"No. But they were recruiting heavily. And it paid a wage. There was the chance of advancement—of becoming an officer."

"And being more eligible for Miss Parling?"

"Yes. But really...well...Mr and Mrs Parling were in favour of it, and he felt too much obligation to them to refuse."

"I see," said Lucian, feeling no need to voice the rest, for Miss Littleton's uneasy knowledge of it was clear. Suspecting the state of things between the penniless Charles and their most beautiful daughter, Mr and Mrs Parling had found it convenient for him to leave the country. Free from the familiar adoration of her childhood playmate, what might she achieve? A better match, surely. Even, hard as it was to believe, a duke!

His smile was rueful, a little grim.

"And where is your brother serving, do you know?"

Miss Littleton gave him a slanted smile. "Well...the Peninsular, as it happens."

"His regiment?"

"The 95th Rifles. Our local regiment, the 67th, were always being deployed to the West Indies or some such place, and Charles is no sailor; he hates the sea. It's why he didn't even think of the Navy."

Lucian only nodded, knowing the 95th had often been engaged in all the bloodiest battles. First in, last out. Excellent soldiers, but hard used.

Miss Littleton appeared to read his thoughts. "We've not heard from him in a very long time."

"No wonder." He made himself smile. "It's no place to send a letter from. But the tide is turning, Miss Littleton. Viscount Wellington will rout Marmont, never fear."

He stood up, wincing at hearing himself talk like one of the boneheaded armchair experts who knew nothing of the matter.

"Why do you go there?" she asked. "To Lisbon?"

"Oh, you know us dukes," he said airily. "Good for pretty diplomacy. I'm sure my presence will make someone feel important, or some such thing. Now," he said, moving to the door, "I must find Willsly and change for dinner. Lock the door behind me, if you please. We can't risk anyone seeing you before your transformation is complete."

By the time Lucian rose from dinner with his ship's captain, Miss Littleton had been installed in Willsly's vacated room, which was positioned next to his own cabin; the door to each accessed via the antechamber of his dressing room. She had also been provided with a hastily altered pair of long trousers and a shirt.

She opened the door to him thus attired, frowning apologetically, the room lit by a lantern on the wall behind her. "Mr Willsly is still working on the coat." She stood, looking awkward and self-conscious, as he shut the door behind himself and appraised her appearance. "I'm afraid I do not make a very good boy, Your Grace."

"You'd scarcely make a scarecrow in those rags. Deplorable tailoring."

"Willsly admitted it. Said haste was his byword on this first attempt and that he would do better on the next."

"And the man calls himself a valet. Butcher would be more appropriate, judging by what he's done to my shirt."

He lifted his eyes from the misshapen garment and found Miss Littleton blushing, in the act of turning away as though she wished to hide her embarrassment. For the first time, he recalled himself to the fact that she was a young maiden, scandalously dressed, and alone in a very small room with an unmarried man. He glanced away but found himself looking at the slim bare feet that poked out from the still overlong trousers.

"Did Willsly give you no stockings?"

"Yes, but they didn't fit."

"You must still wear them. You cannot go around dressed...like that."

"Of course."

She went to the narrow bed that was along the wooden wall and sat down on it, hastily pulling on a pair of—he identified them correctly—his own silk stockings.

"They go under—" he began helpfully.

"Yes. I know."

He kept quiet, until, the action completed, his gaze fell on the stockings. They fitted his own calves and feet like a glove but hung in a pathetically baggy manner from Miss Littleton's, ready to fall off at the slightest movement. He caught her eye. They both started laughing.

"Oh, I told you it was hopeless!" She pulled them off and threw them on the floor in disgust. "I'll ask Willsly for some cotton ones and alter them myself."

"See," he said. "Not hopeless at all. You have a solution to hand."

She sighed. "I cannot tie a neckcloth. I don't know how to walk or talk like a man. And my hair..." She put a hand to it and shook her head. "I suppose I shall wear a hat."

"Of course you will. You're a gentleman. But also, we'll cut it."

She looked at him in shock. "Cut it?"

There was a rap at the door. Willsly announced himself.

"Ah, and here are the tools I requested."

He let Willsly in. It was very crowded with three in the room. Lucian pressed himself against the wall as Willsly passed him, a towel over his arm and a jug of hot water in his hands. He put them down on the small table by the bed, then took a folded leather case from under his arm and put that down too.

"Shall I do it, Your Grace? I'm no expert, but I've cut your hair a fair few times now."

"Only in the most extreme circumstances," Lucian said grimly, making the man chuckle. "Thank you, but no. I take the deed and the consequences into my own hands."

Willsly bowed and left. Lucian once more turned the key in the lock. Miss Littleton watched him warily from where she sat on the bed.

"May I not just wear a hat?"

"And be discovered the moment you removed it? Besides, it wouldn't sit right with all that hair piled at the back of your head."

She touched it instinctively, looking pale. "I'm not a vain woman, or I've never thought myself so, but to lose my hair…"

"It will grow back."

"Not by the time I return to England."

"You could be a leader of fashion. Lady Caroline Lamb cut her hair short, if I recall."

"I'm not sure I should take Lady Lamb as a role model."

"No," he said, smiling. "True. But I mean to say, you'll not be the first woman to have short hair. There is a precedent. And I promise to buy you any number of fetching bonnets the moment we return to England."

His tone forced a laugh from her, then she sighed. "I must do it, for the sake of this ruse and all the trouble I've put you to on my behalf. As little as I wish to embroil myself in a scandal, I've also no wish to bring one down upon you."

She said it so humbly that much of the resentment he'd been

holding towards her melted away. It was true that her presence was nothing but a headache. He had a great deal of very important work to do during their journey—and more important work still when they finally reached Lisbon. He had little time or energy for the considerable problem she presented, although it was hardly the first time a mission had gone awry. In his line of work, one had to cultivate a certain degree of sangfroid.

And besides... "I feel I'll be more able to weather any scandal than you, Miss Littleton. Don't fret on my behalf."

She pressed her lips together, giving a short, resolute nod, though her expression remained troubled. "I really will try my best, Your Grace."

"As will I. Now..." He reached for the leather wallet and opened it, finding hairdressing scissors and combs tucked into the pockets inside. Willsly had also provided a small bar of soap. "I believe the cutting will be easier with wet hair. Are you able to wash it? Willsly has brought us hot water, and there's already a pitcher of cold here, and the washbasin. Shall I leave you?"

Still resolute, biting her lip and not meeting his eyes, she got up. "I'll be quick."

He stepped back from the table, letting her take his place. Then took another step back as, with her back to him, she began to remove the ribbon and pins from her hair.

She worked rapidly, though her shoulders were stiff, her movements jerky. He couldn't see her face, but her unease was clear in every line of her body. The air was taut with it.

"I'm as aware as you are, Miss Littleton," he said softly as she let her hair down around her thin, shirt-clad shoulders, "of the great impropriety of our current situation." There was a wave to the long and otherwise straight hair from where it had been twisted into its confining knot. Lamplight caught in the valleys of that wave like honey. "Over the next few weeks, we'll both find ourselves in situations mortifying to our sensibilities."

"Yes," she agreed unhappily, still with her back to him as she shook out the last of her hair and combed her fingers through it, pulling it forward over her shoulder.

"Given it's impossible to avoid, I'd suggest you not exhaust yourself by repining upon it. There's nothing that can be done except that which we must. Protecting your reputation so that you may return to England unblemished is paramount to us both. Whatever the humiliations and trials of your current situation, you take no blame from it in my eyes. And I promise you'll return to England as uninjured in fact as in spirit."

She was very still, listening, her shoulders high and stiff.

"I've no designs upon you, Miss Littleton," he promised gently. "I would be as a guardian to you while we journey together. A brother, an uncle. Will you trust me on this? Trust your protection to my care? You needn't blush for any unavoidable loss of your maidenly dignity while we endeavour to return you to your home. Don't add shame to your cares. You'll need to act and live and think as a man does to survive this. Can you do so?"

Her shoulders slumped, her head bowed. "Yes. I understand. You...you are right that I must forget almost every stricture I have learnt. I think you...you are wise."

"I don't know if I'm wise, but I speak from experience. There have been several occasions in my life when I've found myself in desperate situations and all the outward requirements of a gentleman have been impossible. But I've learnt that the only thing required to hold my head high when in society once more is to remember I always remained a gentleman on the inside. Just as you will still be a gentlewoman, Miss Littleton, no matter what disguises you must take."

She nodded again, then, glancing over her shoulder, she managed a smile. "That was a very elaborate way of persuading me to have my hair cut."

He chuckled, both of them knowing it was about much more

than that. But he appreciated the return to levity she offered him.

"So let's get on with it then," he commanded briskly, "while the water is still hot."

She poured both hot and cold water into the bowl, swirling them together with her hand, before gathering her hair and pulling it forwards as she bent her head over the bowl. It looked an awkward task. With a murmured, "Allow me," Lucian stepped behind her and took over, gathering her hair in one hand and pouring water from the basin over it with the other. He reached for the soap and lathered it, pushing his soapy fingers into her wet locks. He'd briefly caught the scent of something feminine, her usual soap, perhaps. But the men's soap he worked into her hair soon covered it, sandalwood replacing roses.

She stayed very still as he worked, though her breathing was audible, along with the slick sound of the lather, the wet rubbing of his fingers. He was a tall man, but slender, and he didn't normally feel gigantic, but the span of his fingers covered all the back of her skull, the bone feeling strangely small and fragile, the bare back of her neck slender as a reed. The overlarge shirt, open at the neck, was slipping from one of her shoulders.

He took a soap-scented breath and attempted to keep his mind firmly on the task. But when he reached for the jug, her bent over form was close enough to brush his front. She wore thin trousers. So did he. There was none of the usual mass of a lady's skirts. He felt the curve of a buttock skim over him and clenched his jaw as he rinsed her hair, irritated at the swell of lust he felt. And after the speech he'd just made! But he'd meant every word. It was only the base reaction of his body to a female's, so intimately close. It had nothing at all to do with intention or desire.

He finished rinsing her hair and stood away, handing her the towel.

She took it silently, and he dragged out the small wooden stool from under the washstand, bidding her to sit while he selected a comb and scissors from the leather pouch. Even rubbed dry, her hair was still wet enough to drip from the ends, soaking into the back of her shirt and turning the material translucent where it clung to the pale skin underneath. He snipped without comment until he leant forward to reach for a new handful of hair and realised the front of her shirt was almost as translucent as the back.

He caught his fingers with the scissors.

"Are you all right?" she asked, turning at his hiss of pain.

"Yes, yes," he assured her, cursing himself. It was as well he'd not resigned this task to Willsly. Or perhaps his man would've had more control than he appeared to, because his eyes dipped down once more before he could force them away. Miss Littleton was not entirely as scrawny as a schoolboy. Her breasts were very small but most definitely present, the nipples clear as day through the newly sheer fabric.

Refusing to look, he worked like Willsly had with the clothes: with more haste than skill. Until, recalling himself, he remembered the importance of his task to his charge's future comfort. He must make a decent go of this. Perhaps Brummell's finest Brutus lay out of reach, especially as Miss Littleton's hair was more straight than curling. And the Caesar or Titus seemed too brutally short. He opted for a less severe look, aiming for the romantic, trusting the sea air and salt spray to introduce the dishevelled wildness normally carefully cultivated by the skilled hands of a valet and a plentiful helping of pomade.

Besides. She could always wear a hat.

He gave her cropped hair one last comb through, keeping his eyes raised.

"There, Miss Littleton. I hope you'll forgive me for the massacre."

She laughed slightly, looking around in some dismay at the limp brown strands scattered all over the wooden floor. He'd never so much as begged a lady for a lock, and here he was, with a whole headful at his feet.

"What a mess," she said, beginning to brush more hair from her knees, her shoulders—then her chest, gasping and whirling away from him with her arms across her body as she realised.

Lucian retreated to the door. "Binding a neckcloth around yourself might work," he suggested, forcing any awkwardness from his voice; his own embarrassment would only worsen hers. "It would be better with the line of a man's clothing than attempting to wear your stays. I'll have some of mine brought to you."

He'd never thought himself a coward, but he was still relieved to flee.

Four

Hester had always been quietly pleased to believe herself a sensible, resilient female, not prone to vapours or dramatics. But as the door closed behind the duke, she was gripped by the violent urge to cast herself overboard and die in the cruel, icy waters rather than face him again.

She pressed the cold backs of her fingers to her burning cheeks, gave up the futile attempt to calm her blush, then strode rapidly up and down the tiny space until she slipped on the shorn, wet hair covering the floor.

Her eye caught on the cold suds in the basin as she grasped the small table to stop herself falling. For a brief moment she felt as starved for air as she'd been in the terrifying blackness of the trunk. The leather pouch still lay open, the scissors left on top. Oh God... His hands had been on her scalp and his breath on her neck and then...then...

She flung herself down on the bed, face hidden in her hands.

A knock at the door jerked her from her fever pitch of wretchedness.

"Mr Trunkton, sir?"

It was Willsly. And Lord, yes, she was Mr Trunkton, not a hysterically weeping female.

She dashed her tears away with an angry hand and pulled the rough blanket from the narrow bed, wrapping it around her shoulders. Her shirt was still very damp.

She opened the door a crack, conscious of her red-rimmed eyes, her shorn head, her strange, ill-fitting clothing—conscious, in short, of everything.

Willsly held a folded pile of clothing. He performed the usual servant trick of affecting not to notice his better's distress. "Another shirt for you, sir, that I've just about finished adjusting. And some others to try your hand at. I'll have a waistcoat for you by tomorrow morning, though the coat itself is giving me no end of trouble. And here are some neckcloths. His Grace says to come to his cabin when you're ready and he'll show you the art of tying 'em."

Noting her flinch at the mention of neckcloths, he quite understandably misinterpreted the reason for it and gave her a reassuring grin. "Don't worry, sir, reckon he's only going to teach you the Waterfall or something simple. He won't be expecting you to master the Mathematical or nothing like that. And he apologises for having no stocks, but he can't abide them. And rightly so. Cheap, nasty things." With that, he passed her the bundle of linen and bowed crisply, spoiling the effect with a wink before leaving her to her dismay.

She retreated into the room. The air felt very strange against her scalp, cut ends of hair tickling her nape in unaccustomed places as it dried. Willsly had left a small, cracked hand mirror among the furnishings of her room. She put the shirts and neckcloths on the bed and picked up the mirror instead, bracing herself as she lifted it.

Grey eyes—far wider and warier than usual. Skinny face. Pointed chin. The freckles! Still the freckles. If only *they* could be disguised too. And softly shaggy hair falling across her brow and to her ears, the same dull brown, a little darker from the water, but already drying now there was so little of it. She pushed her fingers into it this way and that, pulling it up and forwards in the style young men wore, and wishing, as she always did, that it was at least a *little* curly.

The truth of her unprepossessing image steadied her. She might have inadvertently exposed more of herself than she could ever have wished, but at least she could be sure the duke would think little of it. She was barely a woman at all, of entirely no interest to him, and he was a man of the world, undoubtedly experienced in...in such things.

Taken altogether, the event that to her had seemed so calamitous could have been nothing at all to him. Probably he'd already forgotten it. His summons suggested that he wished her to forget it too. It was much like the advice to remount one's horse soon after falling: face the unpleasant act before one had a chance to dwell on it.

Yes. She felt she was beginning to understand him. He would brush the whole incident aside and move swiftly on. She'd sensed it already in his cabin, something implacable in his nature. It might have been *him* driving the ship onwards through the uncaring ocean rather than the winds. And now she was caught up in it too. This mad plan to disguise her, so rapidly invented and executed. It was his will alone. His decision. He'd promised her she would be safe. In that moment, she believed him.

She redressed, managing to wind a neckcloth around her chest twice, with just enough room for a knot to secure it. The fact that it was *his* neckcloth, that it had once been around his throat and was now around one of her most intimate places, she told herself not to think of. These were *all* his clothes. It was no different. She pulled on the dry shirt—it fitted her a little better than her first—and hung the other over the stool to dry. With a nervous hand through her hair, she left her little room for the anteroom beyond and knocked on his cabin door.

"Yes?"

"It's me, Trunkton, Your Grace."

His "Come in" held only a faint trace of amusement, nothing at all of embarrassment or awkwardness. Telling herself that she would meet him likewise, she took a breath and stepped into the room.

Compared to the rooms at Rowlands—or those even grander ones she imagined he possessed in his various houses—the duke's cabin was very small. But it felt like luxury after the valet's windowless closet next door. She took a deep breath, aware of the strange sensation of the cloth around her chest, and stepped quickly to a side table, where she placed the remaining neckcloths Willsly had supplied.

The duke, who was sitting at his writing desk, had turned to the room and was looking her over, giving her hair an assessing look. "Yes. I think it will do."

"It feels very strange."

"I daresay it must." He tilted his head, giving her a different kind of assessment. "But you're holding up admirably, Miss Littleton, given the circumstances. Did you eat while I was at dinner? I forgot to enquire, but I did ask Willsly to bring you a tray."

"He did, yes, thank you. It was a very generous meal."

The duke smiled. "The kitchen thinks you're a young man and will feed you accordingly." His smile deepened. "I suppose they gave you a mug of beer. Did you enjoy it?"

She had to laugh. "I confess I sipped it. I was curious. Though perhaps I shouldn't admit it's not the first time I've tried it."

"Let me guess. Your brother Charles?"

"And Tom!"

He chuckled. "And thus incorrigible brothers—and their friends—have always corroded the fine work of their parents."

"I think without older brothers a girl's life would be very dull indeed," she said, smiling.

"Well, hopefully your experience of brothers will stand you in *good stead*. Breakfast, by the way, will be brought to your room on a tray—you'll not need to venture into the ship. And, as your first instruction in the art of young manhood, I grant you the knowledge that it's quite acceptable to receive your tray with your blanket pulled over your head and no word other than a grunt. It is even," he continued, a twinkle in his eye, "permissible to receive your breakfast by flinging a boot at the head of the man who brings it, accompanied by a curse. But I would beg you not, as these are my staff, and one must, I suppose, look to their comfort."

She was laughing by the time he'd finished, and he joined her, grinning as he stood up and went to the pile of neckcloths.

"Willsly made ominous references to something called the Mathematical," she said, still bubbling with amusement. Somehow, he'd done it—removed the awkwardness of their last encounter as though it had never been.

"Good Lord, no. I wouldn't inflict that on you. Nor the Oriental. Assure me, Mr Trunkton, that you have no pretensions to joining the dandy set. Don't make me regret what I've unleashed on the world."

"Well..." she teased, drawing out the word, "Willsly has promised me a waistcoat by the morning, and I was hoping it might be something rather dashing and bold..."

"Worse than a dandy! A fop!"

"Perhaps striped? Or floral!"

The duke groaned, putting a hand to his eyes. "As it will be drawn from my own wardrobe, at least I can be sure it'll be absolutely neither of those things."

Hester grinned. "And when we reach Lisbon, I'm hoping to supply myself with a large fob watch, some bejewelled seals, perhaps some rings, a Malacca cane..."

"Awful. No. I'll lock you in your quarters rather than have

you lay waste to a Portuguese trinket bazaar."

His smile echoed hers, humour dancing between them for a moment until he dropped his eyes to the neckcloth in his hand.

"To business, Miss Littleton. Harry. Trunkton. Do you know...you have far too many names."

"And Hester," she added helpfully.

His eyes briefly met hers. "No. It'll have to be Harry. I must get into good habits. Now. *Harry.* To business. And a serious business it is." His mock gravity made her laugh all over again. "The art of tying a neckcloth has sent many a man mad before his time. But we've established you're not to be a fop. A sober, serious young man you will be. Desirous of making amends for the rash actions that have brought you under my unwilling care. On your return to England, you mean to study hard. And...take orders."

"Orders!" She burst out laughing. "Oh no, please say not. I'd be a terrible vicar."

"Yes, Harry, orders. Your uncle and I quite agree. It's the only thing for a scapegrace like you."

She bowed her head, very contrite, and managed to mumble, "Yes, sir," before breaking into giggles again.

Visibly wrestling with his own grin, he reached for her collar, the neckcloth hanging over his wrist. He turned the collar up, the starched points—a little limp now after Willsly's hasty alterations—reaching her cheeks, the duke's fingers briefly brushing her jaw. Putting the neckcloth around her neck, he drew the ends over her shoulders and towards him so they were an even length.

"For this knot, we start so, with the ends even." He passed it around her throat several more times until the ends left to him were about a foot long. "Left—your left—goes over right, like so..."

His face was serious now, his eyes on the task. His long, strong fingers worked nimbly at the finicky procedure as he described it to her, but she found her attention wandering up to his jaw, a little stubbled now the hour was late, and his firm, straight mouth. His cheekbones had hard edges, but there was a softness to the short lashes guarding the dark, focused eyes. He looked up from the neckcloth, and she hastily looked anywhere else.

"And there, Harry, is the Coachman knot," said the duke, standing back. "Simple and perfectly serviceable. You wouldn't embarrass me looking so in public."

She returned his smile. "Thank you, Your Grace. Oh...but is that what I should call you? When we are in public?"

"If you were *my* nephew, and I happened to like you, I might let you call me Lucian. But as you're only the nephew of my friend...it still ought to be Your Grace, *Harry*." He said it sternly, but there was a gleam in his eye—one that made her suddenly aware of the fact that she had, until now, very frequently omitted the *Grace*.

She coloured. "Yes, Your Grace." But it was better, she told herself, far better than calling him *Lucian*. The thought filled her with an odd sort of fear, a chill that shivered down her spine.

He checked the time on his watch with a lift of his brow. "That late! Well past the hour such benighted youths ought to be asleep." His tone softened. "I expect you're greatly fatigued, Miss Littleton. If you can manage to sleep on this rolling tub, then I hope the morning finds you refreshed."

Having recently been recalled to her manners, she curtsied, albeit confusedly, having no skirts to hold. "Thank you, Your Grace. Good night."

"Good night. And Harry," he called after her as she reached the door. "No throwing boots at my man in the morning, do you hear?"

She flashed him a grin. "I promise, Your Grace. But only because I'm sadly lacking any boots to throw."

His laugh followed her from the room.

Five

It was almost afternoon when a knock came at Lucian's door and Hester—*Harry*—made himself known.

"Come in."

She walked in, smiling shyly. Blue-green daylight came through the small window, not bright, but different enough to the evening's lantern light to make him blink, as though he were seeing her in boy's clothes for the first time.

Her hair had dried into something almost fashionably rumpled, and her trousers—he glanced again—yes, her trousers were a different pair, tailored with greater precision over her slim hips. She was now also sporting a dark green satin waistcoat, which, he was fairly sure, Willsly had known to be one of his favourites. Alas. But it was sacrificed to a good cause.

"Getting there," he said. "However, that neckcloth is abominable."

"I know," she admitted, looking more impish than chastened. "But I found I'd rather forgotten everything you taught me last night. Your Grace," she appended hastily, bobbing a curtsy.

"None of that," he said, getting up from his desk.

"But you said I was to call you—"

"The curtsy, Harry. You need to bow."

"Oh!"

"Like so." He demonstrated, ignoring the fact he felt absurd. She made a terrible attempt.

"No. Like this."

She made another attempt, just as bad as the first. So again he demonstrated. And again she sketched a bow, until they were bobbing at each other with such rapidity they both burst out laughing.

"Good grief," he said. "At least it's Lisbon we're headed for and not Bond Street. Come here." He beckoned her over.

She came to him, biting her lip against a giggle and looking such an absolute ragamuffin with her necktie all askew and her grey eyes staring up at him that he found himself laughing again as he freed the fabric from her throat.

"Creased," he chided, "ruined. But I'll not foist the carcass of your depredations on the poor overworked galley staff. They've no time for extra starching and ironing. You'll have to make do." He retied it, ordering her to pay attention this time.

"Better," he approved, standing back and surveying his handiwork. "You ate breakfast?"

"Yes, Your Grace."

"Willsly brought you some shirts to alter?"

"Yes, Your Grace."

"Good. Then you have something to occupy you. Now I must work, but come to me after dinner and I'll give you another lesson in the art of gentlemanlike behaviour. How to divest yourself of your family's fortune over cards, perhaps. Or call a man out for a duel. Complain about the wine being corked while in your club. All very necessary skills, I assure you."

He made to turn away to his desk but found she had not quite returned his smile.

"What's the matter?" he asked.

"Nothing, Your Grace. Only..."

"Only...?"

She fidgeted with one of the buttons on her waistcoat. "Only that I wondered if you would mind very much if I brought my sewing into this room. I'd sit very quietly in a corner somewhere so that you wouldn't know I was here at all. The closet—erm, I mean, the room next door is very small and has no window, and I find it somewhat...somewhat confining. It being so small. And airless. And dark."

He looked at her with his brows raised. "Willsly's room? He's never complained."

"N-no... But perhaps...even though I'm only a governess...I'm not quite used to...to...servants quarters."

He laughed. "But, dear boy, I thought you had a fondness for small, enclosed spaces? The inside of a trunk, perhaps?"

She pulled a face but only for a moment, replacing it with a politely blank smile and a bow of her head that almost became a curtsy before she remembered just in time to stop herself.

"Yes. Of course. I won't intrude."

"Wait," he said, catching her arm as she turned away. "Don't go off in a huff. I really must work without interruption, you see. Otherwise I..." He trailed off with a sigh. "Oh, very well. Sit far from my desk. And make no sound. Understood?"

She brightened at once. "Thank you, Your Grace!"

He must be softer than he'd thought, he decided ruefully, looking down at his desk covered in state secrets and military intelligence with a civilian sitting barely four yards away. Impossible, though, for her to read them from that distance. And any time he glanced up and saw her in the corner of his eye, her head was bent to her work. Or, increasingly often, directing a longing look towards the window.

It was set in the wall above his bed, and he was sure that if there had been room, it was the place she would have set her chair. As it was, she was sitting in a somewhat shadowed corner, not far from the innocuous-looking trunk that had been the start of all their troubles.

"You may sit there if you wish," he said with a sigh, pausing to attend to his pen.

"Your Grace?"

"On the bed. Then you'll be able to look out of the window you so clearly covet."

He turned to look at her properly and found her wincing at being caught.

"And I was trying so hard not to annoy you," she lamented.

"Then try from over there." He pointed to the bed. "Where I don't have to endure the burden of guilt."

She smiled her thanks and hastily gathered her things, moving quickly to sit cross-legged on the centre of the bed. The pose seemed quite natural to her, and he wondered if she'd ever sat so while in skirts. But that was hardly a pressing question compared to the intentions of the French general that he was trying to decipher from the intercepted correspondence on his desk.

They each returned to their work, and other than the incessant creaking of the ship, the shouts and activities of the men on deck, the waves crashing against them, the wind in the rigging, and the ticking of a clock he kept intending to silence, it was quiet in the cabin but for the scratching of his pen and the faint rustle of the fabric on Miss Littleton's knee.

Until she said, "That's Old French, isn't it?"

He glanced up in surprise. "I beg your pardon?"

"*Escu* for shield instead of *écu*."

He went very still, hand subtly moving to cover the document before him.

"I'm sorry." She frowned at his reaction. "I didn't mean to interrupt. You were muttering aloud," she explained, when he continued to stare at her.

"Good Lord. Was I?" He blinked down at the documents on his desk, inwardly cursing his lapse of attention.

"Don't be embarrassed," she hastened to reassure him. "I often do so myself when translating. I presume that's what you're doing?"

He paused for a moment, then leant back in his chair, adopting a casual smile as though nothing on his desk was of any importance at all. "Do you do much translating, Harry?" he asked, turning the topic to her.

"I suppose I do," she admitted. "Languages are...rather an interest of mine."

"Is that so?"

"I got it from my parents, I suppose. They were both philologists, linguists—amateur ones."

"Go on."

He didn't even have to feign his interest. And Miss Littleton was happy to comply—he'd already learnt she liked to talk, not in an empty-headed way, but because she had one of those active, energetic brains. She would probably walk around in the same manner too, if they weren't confined to such small rooms.

"My father became increasingly dedicated to it, retiring from his work as a solicitor shortly after I was born. He had some treatises published—my mother co-authored them, but, of course, she wasn't listed as a contributor. Though if you read the dedication, you'll find a very affectionate reference to his good friend—that's my mother, you see."

"And they taught you? This is what you were referring to when you said they educated you and your brother?"

"Yes. Languages, obviously. But that lends itself to the study of geography and history—indeed, my mother's main interest was the study of how languages change over time. My father's was more to do with structure and semantics. But they both complemented each other."

"How many languages do you know?" he asked, recalling yesterday's conversation with new interest. "You mentioned French and Italian?"

She gave a small nod, seeming discomforted at being asked to sing her own praises. "Well...yes...those two. And Latin. Spanish. Portuguese. German. And some Flemish Dutch—it's always very interesting when there's a linguistic melting pot of sorts. Indeed, it's the regional dialects I've always found most fascinating. The subtle differences. And what can be interpreted about the people and their history by—" She stopped herself just as he found himself wishing he wasn't restricted by secrecy. Her language skills could have reduced his workload by half, or more.

"I apologise," she said abruptly.

"Whatever for?"

"It is...um...unladylike to go on so. Not to mention boring."

"Luckily you're no lady, Harry. And I'm seldom bored by intelligent conversation."

She returned his smile, then laughed. "Do you know, the most ironic thing of all is how often I wished I were a boy like Charles! Then I could have gone to university and studied it all in the way I wished. Made a career of it, even. But I suppose, in the end, lack of money would have stopped me just as much as my sex—as it did for poor Charles."

"Does he share your enthusiasm for languages?"

She nodded eagerly. "Yes. We were always fairly evenly matched."

"I'm sure his knowledge can only have helped him during his army career," he said kindly.

She nodded, though her face shadowed.

"I fear your knowledge, however, was of less help in your career as a governess?" he prompted, to distract her from her unhappy anxiety for her brother.

"Oh, French and some Italian is always welcomed by employers, though normally only to a basic conversational level. I've only had two positions so far, and I was fortunate that the first was to a very open-minded family who wished their daughters to have a broader education than most. The second was…less convivial…though that had more to do with… Well. Never mind. It was not unpleasant, altogether, and one of the perks of the governess life is that your evenings are often your own. You're not part of the family entertainments, you see, and so you're not normally required at your post, but the other servants also do not…quite see you as one of *them*, so…"

"You're left to the solitude of your bare and freezing attic chamber?"

She smiled. "Something like that, yes. But I didn't mind because it allowed me to get on with my—" She suddenly stopped, eyes wide, then looked quickly away.

"What?" he urged. "You can't leave me in such desperate curiosity as that. You wouldn't be so cruel," he coaxed, leaning forward in his chair and smiling.

She laughed despite herself. "I always find myself telling you much more than I intended!"

Of course she did. It was a facet of his character he'd deliberately cultivated—part of what made him so useful, and, as such, he preferred not to think about it, the manipulation of others being something he found debasing. Especially now he'd been doing it so long he barely realised he was doing it at all.

Indeed, in this instance, he couldn't seem to stop himself.

"But, alas," he said mournfully, "you haven't told me quite as much as I could wish."

When she still ventured nothing further, he leant forward

again, elbows on his knees, hands clasped, and with what he hoped was an engaging twinkle in his eye. "Is it terribly secret, Hester?"

The use of her real name drew her attention—another deliberate tactic. He excused himself with the knowledge it was nothing but genuine, friendly curiosity. And besides, he'd promised to be her protector, had he not? Any fool knew it was madness to proceed on a mission with incomplete intelligence. The fact he'd often previously done so was neither here nor there.

"A lover," he quizzed her, with a devilish smile.

"No! Nothing of the sort."

"Worse?" he asked in horrified tones.

She laughed. "No! Or not..." She frowned, conflicted by her own thoughts. "Not *worse*...but still...very far from approved of."

"Now you *must* tell me, because my imagination is conjuring up all sorts of unspeakable things."

Shaking her head, she gave a short laugh. "No... It is only that I... I have been writing a book."

"A book! Not, I take it, a lurid novel?"

"No. A very dull treatise on French dialects. But...you can see why it's something I ought not speak of. Being a woman. And a governess, with little to commend me but my character. If it were known, it would draw criticism I'm unlikely to have the resources to counter. The Parlings might shelter me, I suppose, as they have done between my last positions, but I'd be loath to bring the judgement of the world to their door. And I couldn't live on their charity forever."

"You mean to publish the book?"

She gave him a cautious look. "Under a pseudonym, yes. It would... It would actually be the second book I've published."

He looked at her in surprise. "You have already done so?"

"The first volume. This would be the second. The first sold well, and...you know so much already, I might as well confess the whole. I mean to earn myself a living, Your Grace. Enough to retire from being a governess. And to...perhaps...when Charles returns home, if he has some income of his own, to set up a home together. We will support each other, you see."

The look she gave him was defiant, but not aggressively so, her chin up, her eyes steady on his. It was pure determination.

He sat back again in his chair, regarding her for a moment. This smart little mouse was worthy of respect. "I see no reason why you could not."

"You approve?"

"I don't *disapprove*. I believe I said enough yesterday for you to understand that there's some flexibility in how I view the rules of society—of what is proper. And when necessity rubs up against propriety...I'm as likely as not to be found on necessity's side."

"You're a very unusual duke," she stated.

He laughed at that unexpected pronouncement, made so guilelessly. "No, Harry, the wonderful thing about being a duke is that one can be as unusual as one likes, and there are very few people who can do anything about it."

The King, he thought glumly. Or rather the Regent, currently—or, more accurately, those advisers and politicians who held the true power at this strange time. And perhaps, he allowed, always had. All of them, the Regent and his advisors, they were the ones who held the end of the chain of obligation by which he was tethered. With all his advantages over Miss Littleton, he wondered, out of the two of them, which was the more free?

Her eyes suddenly lit with an idea. "What if I stayed a boy? When I return to England, I could remain Harry Trunkton. I could study openly, publish openly—"

"And let the Parlings think Hester Littleton dead?"

"No…" she said, frowning, but by no means as deterred as he'd hoped. "They might know the secret. They wouldn't approve, I think, but they wouldn't expose me. I could visit my publisher's office myself, go to all the libraries, the society talks." Her eyes brightened all over again, and he felt very cruel for saying what he had to say next.

"Miss Littleton. No. Put it from your mind. It is impossible."

Six

THE DUKE WAS DIRECTING his implacable will towards her once more, but the dark certainty of his eyes couldn't take full effect. Not when her heart was suddenly full of the brightest vision she'd yet had in her life.

She saw herself walking unaccompanied down London streets. Visiting the library at the British Museum, turning her steps towards Fitzroy Square and entering the Philological Society as one of their own. She could give talks, present her findings, publish articles in *The European Magazine,* retire to the coffee shops for earnest debate and—

"Miss Littleton," the duke repeated, "Harry Trunkton will cease to exist the moment we reach England."

She met his eyes, then looked away with a murmured, "Of course," because it was clear he wasn't to be persuaded. It mattered not. She had the rest of her journey to work on her plans. The four or six weeks that had loomed so awfully before her now seemed like providence. What better way to test if it was practical? It was the perfect training, free from any eyes who might recognise and discover her. And with her new identity firmly in place when she returned to England—

A heavy sigh made her flight of fancy stutter, like a strong gust forcing a bird down to land. The duke's gaze was rueful.

"I'm beginning to fear I've done my job too well," he said in tones of heavy irony.

Her lips pressed together, a small, contrite smile. "Admittedly, the idea has fallen on very fertile ground."

He sighed again, shifting in his seat, his expression changing to one of open curiosity. "You must see, however, that you've no need to go to such lengths or to sacrifice so much. Your mother combined her philological passions with her womanly life, still received the blessing of husband and children while studying too."

"Because her husband permitted it. But my father was a man like no other. The very best, most tolerant, wise, and understanding of men. I'd never be so lucky as to find another like him."

"Why not?"

"What chance do I have of finding *any* worthy husband? I've no face nor fortune to recommend me."

The duke paused. "To be blunt: did your mother?"

"She was...different from me. A very genteel, very elegant, softly spoken lady. And no, not what society would've ever called a beauty, but still well featured. She had...*countenance*. And when she smiled, then, yes, I would've said she was beautiful."

The duke regarded her thoughtfully. "It's true enough that beauty can take many forms. But, young Harry," he added, smiling now, "surely the husband you require is one with his mind on higher things than the physical form. Yours would be a meeting of minds, would it not? You'd bond over verb declensions, he'd bring you bouquets of knotty Latin. I can see it perfectly. Heads bowed together under the rose bower, murmuring sweetly over Germanic syntax."

She laughed. "An enchanting picture, Your Grace."

"And one that would be permanently denied to poor Harry Trunkton."

"Both Mr Trunkton and my philological beau have the same flaw, Your Grace. They're entirely imaginary. Besides. This entire conversation is just as much nonsense. I've no wish to marry and never have."

"You've never had a *tendre* for any young gentleman? Mr Tom Parling, perhaps?" he suggested with a twinkle in his eye.

"Tom? No!" She was genuinely astonished by the suggestion. "He's as much a brother as Charles has ever been."

"An elder son at one of your governess positions? The cousin who began to visit his relations so frequently all of a sudden? The young curate with the unfortunate lisp?"

She laughed at this last suggestion, although the first had made her stomach flip. Somehow, he knew, because he leant in.

"An elder son," he mused, very pleased with himself. "I knew it. Tell me all."

"How is it I've barely known you a full day and you know more of my life than almost anyone?"

He smiled faintly, shrugging one shoulder. "I'm a good listener. Now, pray, sate my ears. I'm desperate to hear how you broke this unfortunate man's heart."

"I did no such thing!"

"But you didn't return the swain's affections?"

"Lord Hindley should have known better than to direct them towards a governess."

"A peer?" His eyebrows rose in surprise. "I congratulate you on your conquest." Then, more seriously, "I hope he did not annoy you, Miss Littleton?"

"No, no, nothing like that. Viscount Hindley was always impeccably well behaved." But the trace of concern lingering in the duke's expression made her feel the need to explain the whole. "He was the eldest son, as you guessed, his father having died some years previously, but he lived with his mother and younger sisters at their house—it was quite near to Manchester—and he was some eight years older than the eldest of his sisters, but he seemed content to live quietly at home rather than in town, unlike many young men of independent means—"

"I suspect the governess's allure," the duke murmured in the tone of one solving the murder in a mystery novel.

"Phoo! Nothing of the sort. He'd been living at home all his life. I think... I feel he was perhaps...not quite cut out for town."

"No dash?"

"Not an ounce. A very...quiet, humble sort of man. Of timid manners."

"Bookish?" suggested the duke. "He sounds perfect. Why am I not addressing the Lady Hindley, pray?"

"The *opposite* of bookish."

"Ah."

"He once," she said, managing to keep a straight face with some difficulty, "asked me if anyone had yet discovered where the sky went at night."

There was a moment's silence while the duke absorbed this. Then he burst out laughing, knuckles to his lips. "Oh no," he mourned, when he was able to speak. "Say not?"

"Yes. I'm afraid so. And also, during the course of a very confused conversation, it became unavoidably clear that he thought broccoli to be...baby trees."

"Good Lord," breathed the duke, awed. "And so you appeared to him as an intellectual giant—a positive goddess of genius. No wonder he fell under your spell."

"I fear it was something like that," she agreed with a frown, still troubled by the recollection of what had been an uncomfortable period of her existence.

"So why not marry him? He would worship you. Give over his library to you, bring you every book you requested like a faithful hound."

She gave him an incredulous look. "You could not think I

would marry such a...a..."

"Clodpole? Slowtop?"

"And besides, any match would be the greatest presumption on my behalf. As if I could accept a viscount! Pure folly. We would be shunned, his family injured, his sisters...! You must guess his mother saw the danger. I removed myself before she was forced into asking, and we parted amicably enough. She was good enough at least to see that I was the unwitting and unwilling recipient of his affections. I was lucky. Many a mother wouldn't have seen it in so charitable a light."

"This is why you were at Rowlands," he concluded.

"Yes. Waiting for another position. I'd applied to several and was any moment expecting a response."

"Now I see why the trunk looked so inviting," he teased.

She laughed. "Yes, I suppose I've made my desperate escape."

Her heart lifted. Perhaps she really had!

But he must have sensed the direction of her thoughts. "This is a temporary diversion in your life. *Not* the start of an entirely new route. Do not, Miss Littleton, torture yourself by repining on dreams which are impossible."

"It was rumoured there was a doctor who did it."

"I beg pardon?"

"No one knew the name, or wouldn't say, but in the academic circles my father corresponded with, there was rumour that a recent graduate from the Edinburgh Medical School was, in fact, a young woman who'd been living as a man for some time."

"And you predict a happy life for the lady, do you? With these rumours already swirling around them?"

"Well...I don't know...but it suggests it might be possible. Like with Lady Lamb's hair, there's a precedent."

"I seem to have convinced you of my tolerance too well. Everything we do on this journey is to *preserve* your reputation. I'm attempting to save Miss Hester Littleton, not do away with her entirely. Do you understand me? Put it from your mind, whatever daft scheme you're currently concocting in your deplorably overactive brain, for I will not permit it to come to pass. You will return to England with your reputation as unsullied as you left it, ready to take up your life just as you left it—and, yes, if you wish it, to marry and bear children—"

"I do not wish to marry! Why must you go on about it so!"

"One day you very likely will, and you'll return to England in a manner fit to do so."

"Because women must?" she said with a tinge of bitterness she couldn't quite suppress.

"Why is it such a poor fate? To have a companion for life, a friend to your soul, a support for all life's trials? To be loved, Miss Littleton, as you surely deserve. Protected. Even cherished."

"And this is why you offered for Jane, is it? *She* is to be the friend to your soul, your life's companion? This person, who you met once at a ball two years ago?"

She'd meant to say it with arch humour, the sort of sardonic comment he so often made. But it came out with the heat of anger—heat that bloomed over her cheeks as the duke sat back in his chair, the smile in his eyes cooling.

"I said it was *you* who required a husband with a mind on higher things. I make no claim to be such a man."

A hollow laugh escaped her. "No. Indeed."

"I cannot simply make any woman my duchess."

"And I suppose only the most beautiful woman in England will do."

She winced. Why was she arguing? And with him of all people?

"Yes, Harry." The dryness of his voice was scalding. "I'm glad you understand. I require a wife far above the common touch."

"She won't have you, you know, duke or no."

"I'm hardly going to force her. I shall simply find another."

He turned back to his work, flipped open his inkwell, and his pen once more began to scratch smoothly across the page, a clear end to their conversation.

She stared at him, still hot with irritation from the argument. She didn't *want* to stop arguing. She wanted to tell him he was a fool.

How could someone so...so intelligent, so witty, so...wise and warm...be so blockheaded? It made no sense. But what did she know of dukes? Maybe they all collected beautiful women the way they did other beautiful things, homes full of everything the most exquisite. What did she really know about him at all?

Her fingers had clutched creases into the shirt on her lap, and she attempted to smooth it out, returning to her needlework with the echo of their conversation a throbbing heartbeat in her ears. She hadn't only been goaded into unreasonable anger—it mattered nothing to her who he married, so long as it wasn't Jane—he'd also drawn all her secrets from her. And so swiftly! She cringed at the memory. Not even Charles or Jane knew as much as this duke, a veritable stranger.

Charles had known of her attempt to publish, but she hadn't received the publisher's reply until after he'd gone. Of Lord Hindley he knew nothing, the whole of it taking place long after he'd already sailed for the Peninsular. Jane knew the whole of *that,* but nothing at all of the book. Hester hadn't wanted to chance catching her in the scandal, if it ever came out. And yet the Duke of Cumbria—the Duke of Cumbria!—knew all!

She felt almost as exposed as last night, when the dampness of linen had betrayed her form. Although, true, she was self-aware enough to realise it hadn't taken much exertion on his behalf. It seemed she was as guilty of wishing to talk about herself as any other weak soul. But why did he ask at all? He couldn't care for the prattlings of a nothing governess.

She glanced at him, lifting her eyes from her needle without lifting her head, having no wish to be caught studying him. His dark head was bent to his work, the hard jaw set in concentration, the dark eyes intelligent and focused. His hand moved smoothly, writing in his swift, steady way. There were all sorts of documents on his desk. Letters of various paper types, some crisp, some worn. He had a small leather-bound book, the cover worn smooth, to which he often referred. A dictionary of sorts, perhaps. A language reference, if he truly was translating, as she suspected. But to what object?

Diplomacy was the vague reason he'd given for his journey to Lisbon. She hadn't known he was a diplomat, but the politics and actions of London's greatest names held little interest for her. Mr Parling sometimes grumbled over the news while reading his paper. Jane and her sisters enjoyed reading the *ton* gossip from town. But Cumbria's name had seldom been spoken—this duke, at least, the second. Of the first duke, his father, she knew rather more. He'd been Mr Parling's friend, albeit in their youth. He'd later gone on to a life of politics and become advisor to the King before the days of his illness. It was in gratitude to his service that the dukedom had been created, Mr Parling's old school friend Viscount Millbeck being raised to First Duke of Cumbria—and far beyond the Parlings' touch.

That was as much as she knew. Of *this* man, who sat writing nearby, she knew nothing.

"Your staring," he said, pen not pausing its work, "is as distracting as your conversation. If you hadn't given such a heartrending account of your quarters, I'd send you back there this instant."

She hastily dropped her eyes, blushing furiously, just as he looked up with a smile.

"I will go, Your Grace. I mustn't disturb your work."

She gathered her things and stood up from the bed, her legs

stiff enough from sitting in one position for so long that she failed to balance against the tilting of the floor and stumbled. The duke caught her arm, steadying her where he sat. He looked up at her.

"My work is of little consequence," he said, releasing her arm and pushing the letters aside as though to illustrate his point. "Innumerable invitations to balls and such."

"In Old French?"

"Some of my friends like to show off." He stood, which happened to bring him into very close proximity, and lightly touched her hair, twisting a lock in his fingers and rearranging it over her forehead—an action which happened to scatter her wits. "Better," he said. Then, "It's a great pity my secretary was too ill to accompany me on this journey."

"Sick?" she repeatedly stupidly.

"Yes. Ring that bell for tea, will you?"

She did so, then turned back to the room to find the duke in the act of tidying away the documents on his desk.

"My eyes grow tired after a few hours' work. Willsly assures me it's on account of my advanced age."

He said it smilingly, but she found her voice was quite serious. "Surely you cannot be very old, Your Grace?"

But instead of giving her his age, he laughed. Their brief argument might never have been. "I appreciate your faith, Harry. It's much more to my taste than Willsly's assurances, believe me. Ah, here we are." A man rapped on the door, opening it at the duke's command. "Tea for master Trunkton and myself, if you please."

"Yes, Your Grace."

"I suppose there are no maids on this ship," Hester said thoughtfully after the man departed. "All the servants on board a ship are male, are they not?"

"Yes." The duke moved his desk chair to a small table where

another chair was already positioned. He smiled at her. "It's unlucky to have a female aboard, you know."

"But this is not a naval ship?"

"No. My private yacht. *The Ondine.*"

"From undine? Paracelsus's elemental water beings?"

"I knew you would get the reference."

The praise in his voice warmed her, but she refused to be distracted by even such a tasty question of etymology. She was beginning to suspect *distraction* was the duke's sole intention.

She sat on the chair he offered her, suddenly suspicious of much. Like his rearranging of her hair. It might have been no more than a tool to distract her from the contents of his desk after she inadvertently stumbled too close. His instruction to ring the bell for tea was likely another distraction—something to make her turn her back as he tidied the documents away.

She'd already noticed he seldom answered a question with anything other than humour or deflection. He continuously changed the topic, often directing it back at her. And surely it didn't take hours to reply to invitations, not even the number received by a duke. He had two weeks ahead of him in which to do so, for goodness' sake.

Very well. If a game was afoot, she was surely equal to it. After all, she'd never been able to resist a puzzle.

"Do you use this ship often for diplomatic missions?"

"Oh, no. Nothing so boring. I'm a profligate dissolute, you know. It's a pleasure yacht. Let me tell you how much the dinner set cost, and you'll excuse me of anything so rational."

"Go on, then," she said, smiling. "Astonish me."

A knock at the door interrupted them. A man stepped in at the duke's command, but he wasn't bearing a tea tray.

"Message from the captain, Your Grace. Asks you to come up, if you please."

Seven

"Excuse me, Harry," Lucian said, "but I must answer the captain's summons. The tea will be along shortly. Enjoy it without me."

He left her without a bow, remembering, just in time, that she was not a woman, and followed the man along the passage to the stairs.

His light tone belied his unease. He met the captain twice a day for updates, and most evenings at dinner. The man would only request an audience outside those occasions for a matter of great importance.

But it wasn't, as he feared, his stowaway's true identity that had alarmed Captain Moore, but something almost as grave. A French ship.

"We spotted the lights in the night, and it's been managing to keep pace with us ever since, no matter how we try to outrun it."

Lucian lowered the captain's telescope from his eye and returned it to him. "They're determined, then." Too determined for his liking, almost as though they guessed the importance of the intelligence he carried. But they couldn't. Unless his cover was blown.

If the French ship gained on them, he would be forced to destroy his work rather than risk it being captured. If the French ship *caught* them, it was Harry he worried for. Her fate would be unpleasant if her sex was discovered.

"They may give up soon enough," said Captain Moore, "for they've managed to draw no closer."

"It'd be a fast ship that could outrun this one."

"Or a lucky one. You know how things go at sea, Your Grace."

"Are you worried, Moore?" he asked bluntly.

"I'm as wary as it's wise to be, Your Grace. For we can't slacken off for a moment, or they'll be upon us. And the men are tired of being always kept at it, but we must catch every bit of wind we can to keep a safe distance."

"Their crew must also be tiring. And likely to be in worse condition than ours. Pressed, most probably, and half-starved."

"Yes. Strange the things one hopes for."

Lucian returned the captain's crooked smile. "It always is in war." He nodded to the horizon. "I cannot like the look of those clouds, Captain." There was an angry grey bank filling the edge of the sky. "Will it hit us?"

"Wind's been erratic these last few hours and growing colder. Even if it misses, it'll be a choppy night."

Lucian frowned. "And we'll have to cut sail. But so will the French."

"Yes, Your Grace. If God's on our side, it'll do for the French. If He's not...it'll blow them right on top of us."

Lucian smiled. "Then I suppose we're about to find out whose side He's really on." He nodded to the man. "Keep me informed. And victual the men as they need to keep working—we cannot be captured."

The captain bowed and Lucian walked across the deck to lean on the railing. The air was bitter but refreshing after being down below for so many hours. The sea spray crashed, the water black. The power of the waves and the cutting prow of the ship, the smell of the sea and tarred ropes and the incessant noise of the rigging all tugged irresistibly at his spirit, no matter the concerns that weighed on him. In a day or two, perhaps Miss Littleton would be rehearsed enough to venture on deck. He suspected she'd enjoy it.

"No mangy frigate's going to beat *The Ondine*," said Willsly, appearing beside him.

"They don't need to—only bring their cannons in range and cripple us."

"Always said you should've got this tub fitted out with a gun deck."

"It might somewhat ruin the pretence of it being purely a pleasure yacht."

Willsly chuckled, the laughter seeming at one with the foaming water below—something wild and indefatigable about it. "What a dash you'd cut though, Your Grace. The pirate duke."

"Well, I *have* already abducted a maiden."

Willsly glanced up from the water, wind whipping through his hair. "For some reason as I can't rightly explain, that recalls me to an entirely different topic. How is young Master Trunkton? Still suffering with seasickness?"

"Terribly so," Lucian replied, his laugh constrained to the expression in his eyes, though their conversation was safe enough under the crashing sound of the waves. No one was nearby. "I'm afraid the affliction is still…abundantly apparent."

Willsly gave a slow nod. "It's a difficult thing to get over, I warrant. Might even take a lifetime. I suppose the young master isn't ready to venture about the ship?"

"Not yet. And perhaps not for some days. Which, strangely, recalls *me* to a different topic. I'll make my excuses to the captain and dine with Trunkton in my cabin tonight, if you could inform the galley staff."

"That so?" queried Willsly.

"I fear the boy needs some lessons in how to dine in company. As a true gentleman."

"Ah." Willsly nodded, looking pensively at the seething waters, thumb idly scratching a minor imperfection in the varnished rail.

"Spit it out, Willsly."

"Only as I wondered if Your Grace might not take a little advisory caution amiss." He gave a glance at Lucian's frowning countenance. "Being as I'm growing fond of the lad."

Lucian's frown turned stony. "Well?"

It was testament to Willsly's courage that he didn't flinch at this bluntly spoken syllable.

"*Well*, Your Grace, these young youths can be...ah...sensitive creatures. Easily ah, overawed by an older, experienced gentleman of such fine address as yourself, Your Grace."

"A compliment from your lips, Willsly? You astonish me."

Unabashed, Willsly grinned. "I'm as honest as a babe, Your Grace," he lied outrageously. "And speaking of which, or of stripling youths who've as little experience of the world as babes do—"

"Yes, yes." Lucian cut him off with a wave of his hand. "You're attempting to warn me that young Trunkton might be susceptible to my unintentional but obviously abundant charms. Believe me, he's not. He has himself informed me that he's immune to peers, clodpoles, and everything in between. And there's nothing in my manner to raise any hopes of...ah...*patronage*...on my part." He glanced around the deck despite the covering sound of the waves. "I treat Harry exactly as I would treat Harry."

"That's what I'm afraid of."

"Forgive my stupidity, Willsly, but I do not follow."

"What I'm saying is that you've been cloistered with the boy all day, chit-chatting"—Lucian narrowed his eyes at this description, but Willsly continued undeterred—"probably teasing the lad something vicious, laughing at him in that way you have, acting as if he really were nothing but a smart-mouthed schoolboy...and...well, if that ain't a recipe for making him infatuated with you, I can't think what is."

"You have a very strange notion of...young men," Lucian said.

Willsly met his look for a moment, but, apparently concluding his warning had been received as far as his employer would ever allow, he shrugged and smiled. "I hope so, Your Grace. And what would I know, anyway? Never had much time for...erm...such creatures myself."

As this was another outrageous lie, Lucian merely quirked a brow then resumed his study of the sea. The French ship was a speck, and not, he told himself, any larger than before. The clouds had thickened, the whole westerly horizon now dark and the sea already more lively. The wind tugged his hat until he was forced to take it from his head and hold it, the skirts of his greatcoat slapping his thighs.

"My dinner with Harry will be cancelled anyway, Willsly. They'll be damping the galley fires soon." He flashed the man a rueful smile before he left the deck. "Cold meat and stale bread. Tell me why I ever go to sea?"

Miss Littleton had finished her tea by the time he returned to his cabin. She was, once more, installed upon his bed, the same shirt in her hands. It was becoming evident her speed with the needle didn't match her speed of thought.

He nodded to her as he closed the door behind him and set his hat down, shrugging out of his greatcoat and laying it over the chair where she'd sat for tea. For a moment, he felt an unfamiliar hesitation, an uncertainty of manner. But Willsly's warning, he was sure, was unnecessary. He suspected the danger lay the other way. He might attempt to treat Miss Littleton as if she really were Harry, but he was far from forgetting she was a woman. The memory of the evidence he'd glimpsed last night wouldn't quite leave his mind, no matter how hard he tried to repress it. It had been there again during this morning's tete-a-tete, a lingering hunger flavouring his thoughts, causing his eyes to drop, more than once, down the slim lines of her body, or dwell momentarily on the slender hands, the bare feet, the lively intelligence in her grey eyes.

It would be a relief to reach Portugal. On his last visit to Lisbon some months before, he'd made the intimate acquaintance of a widowed condesa—a Portuguese countess. And though he'd left England believing himself a promised man, now that he realised he was still free, he was not impartial to the idea of renewing the condesa's acquaintance, if the opportunity arose. This faint, unwelcome hunger needed slaking before it became an irritation.

"Is everything all right with the ship?" asked Miss Littleton.

"Captain Moore wished to inform me of an approaching storm. We may be in for an uncomfortable night."

She looked apprehensive. "I've been congratulating myself on avoiding the curse of seasickness so far, but I confess the larger movements already occasionally make me dizzy."

"You'll survive it," he said, his manner calculated to be more bracing than sympathetic, Willsly's warning still in his mind.

He returned to his desk, and they worked at their respective tasks in silence for some time, until the roll and pitch of the boat made any efforts with his pen impossible. A sharp squall of rain rattled against the window with such ferocity it was loud even over the other sounds of sea and wind. Miss Littleton jumped, pricking her finger on her needle.

"Pinked, Harry?" said Lucian, beginning to pack away his writing tools. "I suggest you lay down that rapier blade and withdraw from the field."

She agreed, smiling faintly, anxiety written across her face as she stuffed her sewing things into the small box Willsly had supplied her with.

Willsly himself came into the room to hasten along the storm preparations, packing away everything that was loose. The bell rang, calling all hands to the deck. Lucian ignored the urge to join them, knowing a civilian would only be an impediment to the smooth running of the well-trained crew. Instead, he gripped Miss Littleton's elbow as the floor pitched sharply, and nodded towards the door.

"Retire, Harry. Sleep, if you can manage it."

"I...I think I'm too afraid to close my eyes."

She said it with a brave attempt at a smile, but her trembling tension came through the grip he had on her arm, and she flinched at every sudden movement of the boat. Lucian met Willsly's eyes and saw the unhappy resignation there. When the man spoke, only someone who knew him as well as Lucian would've been able to detect his reluctance.

"I'll check your room is all stowed away, young sir, if you'd prefer to stay here for a little while. Mayhap you'd feel braver with some company."

Her grey eyes had never looked wider as she turned them up to Lucian's face. "Is that...? May I, Your Grace?"

"Only if you promise no waterworks," he said ungallantly. "We've enough trouble with water outside the ship. I won't have you leaking any within it."

She managed a laugh, and he directed her back to the bed. "Sit there. It's attached to the floor and won't move."

He left with Willsly for his dressing room, sitting down to aid the removal of his boots and grimacing at Willsly's silent frown.

"Give me some charity, Will. There's nothing of romance about this. You see how terrified she is. If stark terror doesn't kill off Cupid's approach, then either one or both of us casting up our accounts will see the blasted bowman drop dead. And you know better than to think I'll take advantage of having her with me in my bed tonight. A genteel virgin? A virgin of any rank? What kind of a dog do you think I am?"

Willsly carefully stowed the Hessians in their case. "As I said before, Your Grace," he replied, his voice low. "I don't believe the lady's person to be in any danger from you. It's the state of her heart after a night spent clutching your shirt front that troubles me."

"I'll be repellent, never fear. Maybe I'll turn on my own waterworks and flinch and cower at every drop of the ship, spend the whole night gibbering into my pillow. Harry'll be quite safe."

"Hm," grunted Willsly, unimpressed. "And if I didn't believe you'd instead spend the night attempting to comfort her fears just as you're now attempting to comfort mine, maybe I'd be able to rest easy."

"Well, what would you have me do?" Lucian asked with a touch of exasperation. "Let the girl suffer alone in her hutch?"

"No. I'm not saying there's anything you could do different. Just that you ought to be warned of...the natural consequences, so as you can be on your guard."

"Willsly. I'm always on my guard. As well you know."

"Aye," the man replied, smiling. "But this isn't one of Boney's agents. It's a creature far more dangerous."

Eight

LUCIAN RETURNED TO HIS cabin, stripped of boots and coat, and found the fearsome creature sitting pale and miserable on his bed, arms hugging her knees to her chest and looking extremely thin and small.

He crossed the room, fighting the bucking floor, and braced a hand on the bed's headrest as he rearranged the pillows with his other.

He patted the cushioned area. "Sit back against here." She did so, and he sat on the bed next to her likewise, the foot nearest the side drawn up to brace himself against falling out—and to maintain some distance between them, a small nod to propriety, though he already knew the effort was likely doomed.

"A few hours," he said, "and it'll blow itself out."

"Is...is it a bad storm, as these things go?"

"No. I've lived through far worse. *The Ondine* can take it, never fear."

She nodded, looking straight ahead, legs stretched out and hands clamped between her knees. Willsly had extinguished all the lanterns, and though it was only late afternoon, it was now very dark in the cabin. What could be glimpsed of the sky as the ship bucked and reared showed solid black clouds that blocked out the whole sun.

"I'm sorry to be such a burden on you," she said.

They were close enough that he could hear her without too much trouble over the groaning of the ship, the pounding of the waves, and the screaming wind. Her head was only a few inches from his on the pillows they shared, their height difference meaning he was looking down on her newly shorn locks, the curve of her ear, the line of her cheek and jaw. He couldn't see her eyes.

"I could hardly work right now. The only thing to be done at a time like this is endure it."

She nodded again, but said, "I mean the whole trip. Every speck of trouble I've brought to your door."

"You've already said so once. Don't be tedious."

Her breath of laughter was a faint gasp. "Very well, Your Grace."

"Now, Harry," he changed the subject, "I sadly forgot to pack a supply of *Sporting Magazine* for your education, but we'll turn the time granted to us by this storm to good account. I propose to give you a solid grounding in the vulgar cant any young gentleman of quality ought to be fluent in." He braced one hand on the bed by his hip as the ship dropped alarmingly. "Forget ancient Greek. Your philologist's mind will find this fascinating."

She managed a small laugh, then gasped as the boat slammed down again, bumping them both together, her slender hip against his, their shoulders touching. He'd known it would be impossible to keep any kind of distance. Warmth came through those points of contact, regrettably pleasing.

"I...I'm afraid..." she began brokenly, pausing as the boat seemed almost to spin in a sickening manner. "I'm afraid I probably know more cant terms than you. I'd prefer to spend the time"—her voice halted as another wave hit—"listening to...to you telling me about yourself. You have"—another crash—"my whole life story...and I have none of yours."

He paused fractionally before saying, as lightly as the angry motion of the boat would allow, "There's nothing of interest to tell."

"You listened to mine. And that was nothing but the ramblings of a drab governess."

"Ah, but you'll allow—" He broke off as the boat slammed down once more, so hard his teeth clacked together and his stomach collided with his ribs. "You'll allow that the best stories are those peppered with tragedy and dire straits, hardships and injustice. My life"—the boat seemed to jump—"has been nothing but privilege since birth. There is"—he closed his eyes briefly as his stomach sought for balance—"no story to tell."

"You said to Willsly you were once poisoned!"

Had he? Oh. Yes. When he'd first discovered her in his trunk. He must've been more unsettled by her discovery than he realised to have been so indiscreet.

"By an appalling brandy."

"And that he was stabbed in the thigh!"

"Saving me from London footpads. Come to think of it"—he braced as the ship plunged—"I ought to give him a raise."

"And that he'd faced mortar shells!"

"Military demonstration gone wrong."

"I don't believe you!"

"You wound me, Harry!"

He was almost glad when the fury of the storm cut off her reply. As much as poisonings and stabbings might distract her from her fear, they were hardly topics he could pursue.

The boat crashed down again as though smote by a giant's hand, and they were tossed together on the bed, her side pushed hard up against his, his arm going instinctively around her shoulders. She fitted right inside its curve. *A safe harbour,* some stray corner of his mind thought, somehow floating around poetically in the middle of this horror, the way a furious wind whips the lightest sea spray from a thundering wave. *She fits, and she's warm...* He was glad of it and shouldn't be.

His other hand and his leg braced them from being thrown from the bed entirely. But the storm only grew in ferocity. Miss Littleton moaned and hid her face against his chest, her breath dampening the linen above the V of his waistcoat. Her fingers curled into the waistcoat's buttons, into the gaps between them, Willsly's prophecy made true.

She was trembling, and so he held her firmly, his arm tight around her shoulders, hand pressing her head against his chest as though, if he could only anchor that part of her, hold it there in a nest of warm breaths and heartbeats, all the rest might follow.

"How would Charles comfort you, if you were afraid?" he asked, bending his head to her ear to make himself heard over the screaming weather. Her hair caught against the stubble of his jaw.

"I...I was seldom afraid when Charles was there."

"And your other friends? Miss Parling—what would she do, if you had a nightmare?"

"I never did!" Even in her terror, she found her humour. "I was always the one comforting her!"

He smiled. "I can believe that. Tell me how you'd do it?"

"Well, I would hold her. And..." A great dip as though the ship were falling to the bottom of the world stole the breath from her words. When it landed, the crash rattled both their bones and she couldn't suppress her cry of fear. He tightened his grip, closing his eyes as though better to channel his courage to her.

"And...and..." she whispered, "and I would stroke her hair."

So he did that too, the hand that was already holding her head to his chest moving over the locks he himself had cut, his broad palm flattening them, smoothing them, the span of his fingers large enough that his fingertips were on the softness of her cheek. Again and again, stroking, soothing, while the storm around them raged, too violent now to permit for speech at all.

It was as much comfort to him as her, though he wouldn't examine that thought too closely. There was cowardice in it—fear of the storm—yes, he was afraid—but also of tomorrow, of a memory to come: soft hair under his palm and the curve of a warm body against his. It did no good knowing such things.

The dawn light was weak and grey by the time it eased. Miss Littleton slept, and Lucian still held her. That was how Willsly found them, stepping into the room at Lucian's quiet, "Come in," and taking in the scene without a word.

"Captain said to tell you there's no sight of the French. They've lost us or foundered in the storm. And we've taken minimal damage. He said to tell you it seems God's on our side after all." His eyes fell to the sleeping woman, Lucian's hand still on her hair. "If that be so...well. They do say He works in mysterious ways."

Nine

HESTER WOKE TO FIND it was as though the storm's nightmare had never been. The duke sat working at his desk, fully dressed once more, cleanly shaven, his coat and cravat as crisp as ever. She was still on his bed—though her circumstances were much improved by the absence of her sewing.

She sat up, her body stiff, her jaw and head aching. The duke looked up from his work, easily interpreting her wincing movement.

"You've been rigid with fright for hours, your body continuously braced against the motion."

She grimaced, rubbing her temple. "And my head shaken like a dice box."

He smiled. "An apt simile." Then he gestured towards her with the end of his pen. "And you look exactly as bad as you feel. Ring for Willsly and get some fresh clothes, if he has any to bring you. The ship might have survived the storm, but that neckcloth is a victim beyond hope."

His abuse had no effect other than to make her smile, and she didn't move straight away, but sat looking out of the window and marvelling at the sparkling water and fine blue sky. "It's hard to believe such a transformation is possible."

"Rich, coming from you, Harry, my boy."

She looked around with a laugh, but when her eyes met his,

she grew serious. "Thank you. For last night."

It ought to have been embarrassing, remembering how she'd trembled in his arms, her face pressed to his chest. And it was, a little. But as his dark gaze hooked hers and held it for a moment, she knew there was more to the heat stealing across her cheeks. One cheek in particular felt warm, heated by the creases of a linen shirt, firm skin and muscle, and the beating of a heart. If she let herself, she could still feel his pulse in her own blood.

His gaze moved past her and went to the window, to the clarity of bright sun and a new day. "Think nothing of it."

He went back to his work, and she nodded, though he wasn't watching, because it was good advice. *Think nothing of it.* He clearly didn't. She stood up from the bed—then whimpered, regretting the speed of the action.

The duke glanced over. "It'll wear off once you walk about."

"Do you think I can today?" She adjusted the twisted waistband of her trousers, tugging the rucked garment to lie straight along her thighs and retucking her shirt. From the duke's flat-lipped observance, it seemed the action displeased him. *His* clothes probably didn't dare to go crooked. "Having survived a storm on this vessel, I've a greater curiosity than ever to become acquainted with it."

He frowned in thought. "Maybe shrouded in one of my coats—and strictly in my company, so I'm there to check any ungentlemanlike thing you might say or do. In fact, I'd suggest you not speak at all. The problem is, once it's known you're up and about, the captain will want to be introduced to you. And I'm far from convinced you're ready to pass inspection."

"And I have no shoes," she said, wriggling the offending toes.

"Quite," he agreed, giving them a grim study.

"But I've been thinking... And what *I* think is that I removed my boots before climbing into the trunk, as the space was so tight, and they were—let me know if I'm saying this correctly—*damned* uncomfortable, Your Grace."

He met her grin with a lift of his brows. "Getting precocious are we, brat?"

Her smile broadened. "I'm quite up to snuff, Your Grace."

"You're an unlicked cub. A lubber and a looby."

She laughed with delight at this demonstration of his cant vocabulary, but her rejoinder that he must be a *beetle-headed chawbacon* to think so was, perhaps fortunately, prevented by the arrival of Willsly with breakfast.

"That'll keep warm a while," the duke said, nodding at the cloth-covered tray. "Willsly, take this scamp and fix his rig suitable for company. I can't eat looking at it."

"Yes, Your Grace."

With only a brief protesting glare at the entirely unrepentant duke, Hester followed Willsly into the antechamber and to the door of her little room, where he pointed out some folded clothes on the bed.

"Thank you," she said. "I hope *your* night wasn't too uncomfortable?" He seemed less cheerful than usual. But also...perhaps befriending the duke's servant was another way to uncover some of his mysteries.

The man smiled faintly. "Thank you, sir. I reckon none of us enjoyed it, but at least I was below decks, not above. The main thing is we survived it."

"Indeed! I'm afraid I was very cow-hearted and hardly believed we could. It feels a miracle to be walking and talking today as though nothing at all happened."

"We're all thankful for that to be the case."

"I'm trying to persuade His Grace to let me venture about. Do you think I'll succeed? There must be parts of the ship where I'd be unlikely to see anyone. But he's afraid the captain will want to meet me."

"Aye, well, he's the captain. Ship's his domain even if it's

His Grace who owns it. He wouldn't be worth his salt if he didn't want everything on board to be known and accounted for. Besides, you're a gentleman of quality. Young as you are, you'd probably be invited to dine with 'em if you was known to be up and out of your berth."

"So what's all this for," Hester said, gesturing to her butchered hair and men's clothing, "if I'm to be hidden away in these two rooms my entire journey?"

"Have patience, sir. You'd do well to abide by His Grace's caution. He's a clever man and knows what he's about. And it's all for your sake, don't forget." He looked at her ruminatively for a moment, then added, "Though I dare say it'd be good to get you out of His Grace's cabin as much as possible."

Aha. From Willsly's manner, there was more to that statement than met the eye. "To let him work?" she ventured. "His...his work is very important, I believe?"

"That's more than the likes of me can say." Willsly moved into the small space and shook out a shirt from the folded pile. "This is the third I've done. Reckon that'll have to do you for a while, sir, else His Grace will be running out. Pity half his clothes were left behind. Those servants of Parling's ought to be whipped."

"I would've thought packing was his valet's responsibility," she said, so sweetly Willsly laughed in appreciation.

"Ah, you've enough cheek to make a true lad, that's for sure. I'd already left for Portsmouth, I'll have you know. Had something important to attend to for His Grace. Life or death mission, it was."

"Oh?" Her heart squeezed, sure a clue was forthcoming.

He leant in. She held her breath. And Willsly said...

"Burgundy."

Had she misheard? "Burgundy?"

He grinned. "Mighty fond of the stuff, His Grace. Can't

travel without it."

Hmpf. Very well. She tried one more tactic, toying with the shirt he'd handed to her. "This tiny room... I know I'm an unwelcome distraction to His Grace, and I'll try to spend my days here and keep out of his way, but Willsly...how did you stand it? I feel I can hardly breathe in here."

"Well...I'm busy enough that I'd only be in here to sleep, and all I want for that is a bed and blanket. I've slept in far worse rooms—and often enough in no room at all."

"Outdoors, you mean?" She kept her attention on the shirt, apparently studying the stitching. "Were you a soldier before you became His Grace's valet?"

Even with her attention on the shirt, she felt the assessing look he gave her. Prying into the privacy of another person's servant was bad *ton*. Heat climbed her neck.

"A man born to the life I was is often many things before he falls on his feet—if he ever does." He stepped away. "There's warm water in the basin." He winked as he turned to leave. "If you want to shave, *sir.*"

When Hester returned to the duke's cabin for breakfast, she found him waiting for her at the small table where she'd drunk her tea the day before, all the furniture now restored to its usual places from its bad-weather storage. He got up before she could sit, and sighed, beckoning her to come to him, then quickly retying her neckcloth with an accusing look.

"I thought you were a quick study, Harry. If you can conjugate verbs, you can tie a simple knot."

Hester only smiled, made awkward by a guilty suspicion that she might have tied her neckcloth poorly in order to procure the very ministrations she was currently receiving from the duke's deft hands. But that was the sort of sneaky trick Georgina or Elizabeth Parling might attempt during one of their juvenile flirtations and definitely not the sort of thing Hester Littleton would ever do. So she decided not to think about it.

But her comfort wasn't much increased when they sat down however, for the duke immediately stood up again and altered her grip on her teacup, then put his hands on her shoulders and pushed them down and back until she was forced into a leaning, slouching posture.

"And even your arm on the back of the chair, thus." He demonstrated when he sat down again, putting a booted foot on his knee for good measure. "Men sit differently when no ladies are present. And remember, you might be a stripling of fifteen, but, like every deplorable youth of a similar age, you believe yourself to be at least ten years older. You strut about like you imagine a man about town would, adopt every vulgar mannerism you can, secretly wish your mother would let you wear a Belcher neckcloth, and cannot decide whether Brummell or Alvanley should be your god. I suggest neither."

He sipped his tea and watched her as she mirrored the swaggering seat he had demonstrated, elbow on the chair back, knees spread wide. Her attempt was met with a shake of his head. "In fact, on reflection, I've decided you're a young man of bookish, scholarly habits, timid, quiet, and often too shy to speak in company."

"But I don't wish to be such a man, dammit," exclaimed the dashing young Trunkton, chin held at an arrogant jut as she tried not to laugh.

The duke nodded to himself as though he hadn't heard her and repeated, "A very *quiet* young man, who seldom speaks unless spoken to, and even then only in monosyllables. Your flight from the country inside my trunk wasn't prompted, as

I initially believed, by prankish high spirits, but by a strong disinclination to return to school, where you're much despised by your peers. And rightly so, for you are a milksop."

She threw her head back and laughed.

"I'm actually serious for once, Harry. It would be an easier act to perform. And far quicker to perfect. You and Willsly, in your different ways, have persuaded me it would be good to move you to new quarters as soon as possible."

Hester sobered at that, sitting properly in her chair again and busying herself with the teapot. She was being too much of a nuisance, forever here in the duke's cabin. A night spent cowering in his arms had clearly given him a surfeit of her company.

"New quarters?" she asked.

"One of the guest rooms."

She looked up in surprise.

"No," he said, answering her unspoken question, "this isn't the only bedroom on board. You've been here until now because I could hardly transport an obvious woman through the ship, and I wished to keep you under the protection of my close supervision until I felt your secret would be safe. As far as the crew knew, you were terribly afflicted with seasickness and needed constant supervision—far easier for Willsly to look after you and render his services to me if we're in the same place. Plus, I'm obviously a considerate fellow and take the duty of care towards my friend's young nephew seriously. But you now look almost the part. You're learning to act the part. Willsly and I have done as good a job as we can of spreading the news of your assumed identity around the various strata of men aboard. And, with the dangers of the storm recently passed, your unexpected arrival is no longer the only topic of interest. If you're not yet safe, you're certainly much safer than you were."

"I see," she said, strangely hollow.

"And," continued the duke, "I'm now as certain as I'm ever

likely to be that you're not, in fact, a cleverly disguised French spy."

She stared at him in astonishment. "You thought that?"

"A faint suspicion crossed my mind that it might be the reason for your bizarre ingress into my life. But I think both your character and your backstory are beyond even French ingenuity. They have the illogic of truth about them."

"So that is why you asked me so many questions about my life! I knew you couldn't really find it interesting."

"Having an ulterior motive for one's questions doesn't at all preclude the possibility of finding the answers interesting."

He smiled, but the hollow feeling deepened, accompanied by the sting of mortification. Of *course* he hadn't really enjoyed her company. Of course.

But it would've been even more mortifying to let him know how she felt, so she forced an answering smile, though her insides felt bleak and silly indeed. "It would've been very ingenious of the French to insert me into the Parling's circle as a baby."

"Spies are normally bought, not born. Especially those who are traitors to their own country."

"And is it your diplomatic work that you fear might attract the interest of French intelligence?"

If her question came close to the truth that he seemed determined to hide from her, he didn't show it, but casually buttered a roll. "Yes."

"You really are a diplomat, then? I hadn't heard anything of it."

"Are you a close follower of international politics, Harry?"

"More so than I am of *ton* gossip. I've only infrequently heard your name mentioned in connection with either."

"As I've told you, my life is a very uninteresting one." He smiled before he took a bite of his roll. "Eat up, boy. Soon, I'll show you your new room."

The duke left her alone after breakfast, leaving his cabin to—presumably—arrange for her removal to her new quarters. Or perhaps he was going to speak to the captain. Or perhaps he was going to his secret laboratory to create a batch of invisible ink, or go on deck to send semaphore signals to hidden ships. In short, she still had no idea what his business was but was increasingly convinced it was both secret and quite possibly official in nature.

A spy? An agent of the Crown? Military intelligence? That great tactician, Viscount Wellington, was rumoured to have a whole army of spymasters in his command. Might the duke—rich enough and powerful enough to travel how and where he liked, and well connected enough to gain entrance to any door—might he be one?

It was deliciously exciting to think about. She'd always preferred to read mystery novels to romances—a preference her whole family had shared. Indeed, the four of them had even invented their own coded ciphers, spending the long winter evenings coming up with more and more fiendish ways to encrypt such valuable messages as: *Mama, Charles still owes me three pence for the licorice he bought last Wednesday.* He never had paid her.

But for all her excited imaginings, when the duke returned, the sole item in his possession was a very dull pair of thick, woollen stockings. He handed them to her with a bow.

"Compliments of one of the ship's boys. The crew heard of your shoeless plight, and a young urchin has sacrificed these to you. They are, I'm assured, knitted by his mother's own hands—and, importantly, as yet unworn."

She looked at them, stricken with guilt. "I can't take the poor child's stockings."

"He's thirteen if he's a day. And don't worry, I'm sure a suitable coin will make its way from your hands to his, courtesy of Willsly."

"But I—"

"Have no money with you, yes, I know. Do use your supposedly large intelligence—which I'm daily beginning to doubt the existence of. The coin will come from my purse, but Willsly will say it's yours. You might be a milksop, Harry, but I'm pleased to say you're at least conscious of your obligations."

She sat down and pulled on the stockings, scowling. They were itchy, and a little too big, and looked rather odd against the fine fabric of the duke's adjusted trouser hems. But they were warm, at least. She'd been only too aware of the cold breezes that came up between the floorboards whenever she stepped off the rug in the centre of the cabin's floor.

"Can we go now?" she asked, her curiosity at seeing more of the ship pushing out her chagrin at the duke's words.

He scanned her briefly from head to foot, then pulled the blanket from his bed and put it around her shoulders. She peeked up at him as she gathered the corners tight in her hands. There was the very chest she'd lain on all night. It was inches away and felt like miles.

"You're ill, remember," the duke said. "Feeble. Probably dazed. You're certainly not up to making small talk, or quite possibly eye contact."

He sighed at her mulish expression, like a man knowing he had made a bad bet, but led the way to the door. "Come along then, Harry."

They crossed the antechamber of his dressing room and he opened the door. She ducked past him, acutely aware of the shoulder that brushed his arm in the narrow space.

Think nothing of it.

The door led, disappointingly, to nothing but a narrow passageway, albeit one that was almost as finely decorated as his rooms. He turned left, and after several yards, the passageway ended in a flight of very steep wooden steps, almost a ladder. They climbed these and were in another short passage running at odds to the first, stern to bow, she thought, rather than across the ship. At either end was a panelled door.

"Dining room," he said, pointing what she guessed to be aft, towards the stern.

"Oh! Can I—"

He sighed again. "Yes."

He led the way and opened the door, stepping aside as Hester walked into the room.

She gasped. It was proof of how long she'd been on board, confined to the smaller rooms below, that the space seemed immense to her. It must've spanned the whole width of the ship. And though the walls were strangely sloping, just like all the others, and the ceiling quite low, it was as lavishly decorated as any room Hester had ever seen. There was plaster scrollwork, gilt panels and elaborate painted scenes. Chandeliers swayed from the gilded and painted ceiling beams. There was a dining table for twenty at least, but it had been pushed against the wall, and all but a few chairs were stacked in corners. A row of paned windows, much like those in the duke's cabin, spanned the far wall—the entire back of the ship.

"This must be a ballroom, too," she exclaimed.

"Yes, small as it is. Willsly and I currently use it for exercise—fencing, mostly. In fact, you have Willsly to thank. It was his idea that you might make use of this room in the mornings, if you require a change of scenery from your bedchamber. You're likely to be undisturbed."

"I would love to! But only the mornings, you say?"

"As I said, Willsly and I make use of it. We fence most afternoons. And from four o'clock it is being readied for dinner."

"Could I—"

"No. I am not teaching you to fence."

She huffed, annoyed by his easy ability to predict her thoughts as much as his refusal. Clearly able to read this too, he rolled his eyes. "We're preparing you to survive the next six weeks of your life, Harry, not to take London by storm as the next chief Corinthian."

She pulled a face but gave no other rejoinder. In truth, she was a little awed by the room. The more she saw of the ship, the more real she realised it to be. This was no common packet on which he'd booked a ticket. This was no naval vessel on which he was being given a ride. This was his very own yacht, designed and built at his behest, every plank and nail paid for by him. A floating pleasure barge to add to the houses and estates he owned.

Many men owned houses. Few owned as many as a duke. And even fewer owned private ships of this size and luxury. She'd sometimes seen the King's yacht, *The Royal George*, in harbour at Portsmouth, and marvelled at its beauty. She wondered how *The Ondine* would compare if seen from the shore. A duke's yacht. The man she talked so sportingly with, whom she was treating with increasing familiarity, whom she had lain against all night—that man was a duke. She needed to remember it.

Think nothing of it was good advice indeed. Think not of a firmly beating heart or his arm around her. Think not of his smile or the way his teasing set light to something inside. She was only a nuisance in his life, a messy little task to be tidied away in a room out of sight.

"This way," he said, gesturing back towards the door.

She tore her eyes from the expanse of windows and followed meekly.

"Yes, Your Grace."

Ten

OVER THE COURSE OF the next few days, Lucian frequently reminded himself it was a relief to have Miss Littleton stowed safely halfway down the ship.

If he ever found himself debating whether it was truly necessary—perhaps bored, perhaps arguing that mere friendship was no risk to either—then every night spent wakeful in his bed argued back. The slim pressure of her body against his had left an impression weighty as stone. He cursed in the dark, and in the daytime he worked, refusing to dwell on impossibilities.

He certainly had a lot to do, and for once, was grateful. The documents in his possession had been handed to him almost at the very moment he left England, collected by Willsly in Portsmouth from a London agent—easier to avoid them falling into the wrong hands if they were safely surrounded by miles of sea water.

They were, for the most part, fairly innocuous, being on first inspection nothing but letters sent from France, Spain, and Portugal to England. But they had all been flagged as being of interest by Bode or Willes in the shadowy depths of the secret office where most foreign mail was diverted, and the wheat, as it were, separated from the chaff.

These documents had been filtered further still, containing certain suspicious keywords or phrases suggesting they were not the innocent letters they pretended but coded communications. Lucian's job was to attempt to crack, or at least categorise, the code they were written in, create a summary report, and hand the whole lot to one of the chief codebreakers at Lisbon who would then finish whatever Lucian had left undone in his two weeks at sea and communicate whatever was of relevance to whomever in the army needed to know it.

That was the more covert of Lucian's tasks. He also carried messages and intelligence of British origin, both political and military. And, officially, he was going to Lisbon to woo and reassure their Portuguese allies and several of the influential Spanish nobles who had fled their home country when the French first turned upon it.

All of this was very important and had nothing at all to do with thoughts of bare white toes in rough woollen stockings or the deplorable state of a neckcloth—reveries which frequently crept into the long silences of his cabin. But really. It'd been a week and she still couldn't tie it.

He'd taken to doing it every morning. They still shared breakfast together—after all, he couldn't abandon her entirely. He needed to continue her gentleman's education. Check on her wellbeing. And constantly remind her to go nowhere but the dining room, her room, or his own.

"But when can I go on deck?" she asked again, on their seventh day at sea, spreading a liberal amount of jam on a toasted muffin.

"When you're ready to dine with the captain."

"And when will that be?"

"When I say so. And that will not be until long after you learn to stop pouting like a schoolgirl."

"I don't pout!"

"Like a fish. A very small fish."

She ate her muffin as angrily as anyone had ever done such a thing, the effect of her fury somewhat diminished by the blob of jam on her lip. He leant across the table and swiped it away with his thumb—then licked his thumb clean before he'd even thought what he was doing.

"At least you eat as disgustingly as a schoolboy," he said before either of them could properly register the moment.

"And you're as...as...arrogant and high handed as a..."

"Duke?"

"Yes! And that is not a compliment."

"No. More a matter of fact."

She finished her breakfast hardly speaking to him, then flounced off—very odd to see in trousers. Breakfast quite often ended thus. If he allowed himself to ruminate on the matter, as he inevitably did now, with the slam of a door still echoing in the air, it put him in mind of sunlight focused through a lens. Too much of something concentrated in one place. Smoke inevitably emerged.

He refused to sigh and finished his own breakfast with slow deliberation while Miss Littleton went to do whatever she did during the day. Read a book in the dining room, most-like. He'd produced a dusty chest of them from under his bed a few days ago, explaining he hardly ever got time to read on board.

"Too busy working," she'd commented, sceptically.

"Mostly too busy entertaining," he'd corrected her, lying.

She'd flipped through the volumes on offer, declining Dante on having, she explained, had the enjoyment of it permanently ruined by attempting to teach it to a very disinterested fourteen-year-old.

"Uninterested? You astonish me."

"I read it long before that age and adored it!"

"In the original Italian, I suspect?"

"Of course!"

In the end she selected a very dry-looking book of history

and an exceptionally lurid-looking novel he'd had some qualms about letting her read, until he reasoned to himself that it might as well form part of her gentleman's education. And so she spent her days in idle luxury in the sunny window of the dining room, and he spent his days slaving over French and Spanish, and they probably both would've wished the roles were reversed.

But one day, he was forced to seek her assistance. He had little choice. After all, he told himself, hesitating with a hand on the door of his cabin, he'd lost time to her at the start of the voyage. And the storm which had done for the French had also hastened their journey by at least a day, the sagacious captain running before the wind until the last moment to escape their pursuit. He would've rejoiced if he'd not hoped to be more ahead in his work by the time they landed.

So he went to seek her out, entering the dining room with a piece of paper in his hand like a note of admittance. Miss Littleton was ensconced on a nest of cushions in a beam of sunlight. The gilt around the room glittered, scattering lights on the floor which danced with the ship's movement. One of them played around her hair, lighting up the soft brown locks with a halo of gold. She gave him a curious look, putting her book down.

"No, don't get up," he said, gesturing her to remain where she was. "I'd sooner disturb a sleeping cat."

It really was a very cat-like look of narrow-eyed curiosity she gave the paper he passed her. He sat down on the floor beside her, staying silent as she scanned the words he'd copied out. Isolated from their source letter, they could reveal nothing to her.

"These are numbers," she said. "In French. But all of them slightly misspelt."

"Are there parts of France where they commonly write numbers like this? Could it be perhaps a regional or dialectical variation?"

"Not to my knowledge."

He nodded. "Thank you."

She gave him the paper back, and he folded it slowly. The answer was exactly what he wanted to hear and put the whole of the letter into a very interesting light. A good little spy would be racing back to his desk, brimful with excitement and determination. He wouldn't be tempted by the play on sunshine on his shoulder blades or the drowsy scent of the heat-soaked rug.

Miss Littleton looked at him, head tilted like a curious robin. Did that make him the worm?

"Why do you want to know? Is this another invitation from one of your friends?"

"Something like that. Teasing me with a riddle."

Her eyes lit up. "Is it a type of code? Numbers often are, you know."

The light came through the window like crystal. The waves lulled, languid as stretching cats. And part of him applauded her intelligence even as another part sighed in regret. Because... Time to go, before that curious robin pecked too deep.

"It seems to be all the rage now," he said carelessly as he stood and brushed some flecks of dust from his trousers. "Everything military is these days, from the braiding on a lady's riding habit to the tassels on my Hessians. Shockingly frivolous, if one thinks about it. Which I seldom do."

He smiled his farewell, but she didn't answer it, fixing him with a frowning look instead. "You don't have to tell me the secret of your work. I've no right to know it. But if I can ever help you, will you do me the favour of asking? It would go some way to relieving the guilt I feel for burdening you. And..." She smiled. "I think I'd enjoy it. Translation and language questions are exactly my favourite tasks—as you know."

He dismissed the suggestion from his mind, then immediately recalled it for a proper examination. *Could* he ask her for help, pressed for time as he was? Wellington was planning an imminent assault on Badajoz. There was a chance the information Lucian carried could turn the battle. And for tasks like this, where individual words or phrases were separated from their context...?

The only risk would be revealing the nature of his work to Miss Littleton, and one of his key virtues as an intelligence officer was how little he was suspected to be one. A frippery, idle diplomat? Yes. But the Duke of Cumbria a codebreaker? No.

It wouldn't be the first time he'd trusted an outsider. Occasionally, he'd had to put his life into the hands of virtual strangers. Making quick judgements of a person's character was one of the many talents his handler often greased his vanity with whenever Lucian showed an inclination to retire from his enforced obligations. And when time was of the essence, getting the job done was often far more important than getting it done quietly. Willsly, for all his skill and discernment, was an advocate of *that* particular philosophy.

He frowned down at Miss Littleton. From her expectant expression, some of the thoughts crossing his mind must have been readable on his face. The cat already had at least one paw out of the bag.

"You must be very bored," he said, needing more time to think.

"Hugely," she agreed.

"Are you not working on your book?"

"I've none of my research notes."

"That seems a poor excuse."

"You're distracting me again."

"Am I?" he asked, smiling away her suspicion. "From what? Oh. Your novel." He nudged it with his toe where it lay on the carpet by her knee. "Is it half as ghoulish as it looks?"

She gave him a narrow-eyed look but let herself be diverted.

"Worse. There's a sinister hunchback whom our heroine caught a glimpse of one dark, shadowy night and clean fainted dead away."

"Of course. A predilection for fainting is a prime requirement of the breed."

"But we, the reader, by a series of subtle clues involving a particularly distinctive pair of cuff buttons, have been given reason to believe the hunchback is none other than the handsome Lord Bravecourt."

"Who is, one might reasonably believe, very brave?"

"Indeed! And disguises himself as a hunchback to—"

"Terrify poor maidens? The man sounds like a cad."

"No." She gave the toe of his boot a remonstrative smack—a miniscule tap, but he felt it up his spine. "To bravely investigate the crime of his murdered wife."

"I take it back. My sympathies to the poor man—I presume he loved his wife?"

"Desperately."

"Well, of course. A tepid, watery love is never found in a novel."

"No," she agreed, laughing. "And mere affection doesn't exist."

"But why a hunchback?"

"There's a local fable of a hunchbacked ghost."

"Convenient."

"But," she said, looking up at him with a smile, "I believe both the hunchback and the lonely, tortured character of Lord Bravecourt are fundamentally written to the same purpose."

"Oh?"

"They both show our hero as distant, elusive, unknowable. A figure as shadowy as the dark night itself."

"You think Bravecourt is really the villain?"

"Is that what elusive, unknowable men are?" she countered, a gleam of victory in her eyes. "The villain?"

He grinned, evading the snare. "Oh, undoubtedly! Never trust a man who lurks in bushes."

"Or never answers a straight question."

"Straight questions are so vulgar, though, don't you think? A lover of language such as yourself, Harry," he said, grin broadening as he began to walk away, "knows the true beauty of words is making them a labyrinth. Make your conversation a palace," he called grandly from across the dining room, almost at the door. "Let your mind be baroque!" And with a flourishing salute, he quit the field, smiling in a way he hadn't in days.

Eleven

Hester was surprised when the duke walked into the dining room again the next day. Her heart skipped, just as it had last time, and her eyes went to his hands, eager for another puzzle—another clue—but instead of paper, he held what appeared to be a bottle of port.

"Tomorrow," he said, fetching some glasses from a side cupboard before sitting down on the floor beside her, where she was, once again, nestled comfortably in a pile of cushions, the novel on her knee, "you'll dine with myself, Captain Moore, and First Officer Irwin."

Her heart gave another thump, but in apprehension this time. "You think I'm ready?"

"We've little choice. You're known to be up and about, and you eat too well for your seasickness to be believed."

She would've protested—curse the man, she was no glutton!—but very vividly came the memory of a strong thumb brushing jam from her lip. So instead, she sought some relief for her feelings by scratching aggressively at the itch under her woollen stocking.

"Fleas?" suggested the duke, voice mournful, eyes twinkling.
"No!"
He laughed, and she once again wondered at her own choices. She'd spent most of a very dull and lonely week attempting

to *think nothing of it*. Occasionally, she reached a pinnacle of rationality in which she was sure, once returned to land and her normal life, sanity would return. Very sensibly, she'd invested some effort reassuring herself that every girl was supposed to have at least one infatuation—the younger Miss Parlings had already had a dozen apiece—and that although it'd taken her until three-and-twenty to have one at all, she was at last having one in grand style, her object being the most unreasonable and impossible of men.

A duke? How absurd.

A sarcastic, teasing, incorrigible duke? How fitting a punishment for her folly.

"I've taught you how to sit," he said, "and how to hold your knife and fork, now I'll teach you how to drink port. And"—he pulled a silver case from his inner coat pocket—"how to smoke."

She blinked at the cigar case.

"First Officer Irwin, being a bold-spirited young man, will certainly press you to try one. He's uncommonly fond of cigarillos. As are all of us," the duke added reflectively, "who've had much reason to visit Spain and its neighbour."

"I once tried snuff," she admitted. "I didn't care for it at all."

"You'll probably dislike smoking too, but you're a gentleman now, Harry, and that involves doing a great many things you don't like purely to impress your stupid friends and prove you're just as stupid as they are. I won't have you embarrassing me by coughing up a cat."

"No," she agreed, laughing—and, as always, tumbling far from her pinnacle of rationality. But...it was warm in the valleys of his humour. "I promise I won't."

He smiled, then pulled the stopper from the port. "I'm glad to hear it. But first, let us wet our whistles."

The measure he poured her was much smaller than his own.

She took the glass with some amusement.

"Ought I admit I've tried port before, Your Grace?"

"No, you ought not." He shook his head. "Port, beer, and snuff. Your brother and young Tom Parling have a lot to answer for."

"But it has—"

"Stood you in good stead?"

She laughed. "Yes. An excellent grounding they gave me."

"At least I have less on my conscience, finding you were corrupted long before you ever met me."

"I don't think," she said, grinning unavoidably, "that I've ever been a very proper sort of lady."

"It's the fault of that education of yours, I'm sure. Filling your brain with all sorts of ideas. Women's minds are not made for it, you know," he said sternly, breaking into a smile when she reached out a stockinged toe and kicked him lightly on the shin. "Come on, Harry, drink up."

"To what do we drink?"

"You wish to raise a toast? Youth," he suggested with a sigh, stretching out to lie on his side, propped on his elbow. "And folly."

Folly? Being here with her? No...that was wishful thinking, to believe he wrestled temptation. Probably she herself was the folly—her accidental arrival, this attempt to avoid detection. He was only laughing at her again.

She leant forward to touch her glass to his, then threw the whole lot back.

"Sip it, Harry! Good Lord. You'll be reeling in minutes."

"I drank to folly," she reminded him, holding out her glass for a refill. He obeyed dubiously. "And now," she said, "we'll drink to...to adventure, and new horizons, and...freedom."

Watching her, he made no move to lift his glass. "Hell of a toast, Harry."

"I'll only sip."

"No... What I mean...is that how you feel, stuck aboard this ship, confined to a few rooms, and unable to mix freely with anyone on board but myself or Willsly. You feel free?"

A strange pain stung her, like a scab catching, revealing something tender beneath. *Folly, folly,* to keep showing so much of herself to him. But what did it matter? An ocean surrounded them, sun on water, two strangers far from shore... She could fight all she liked for rationality and common sense, but here, with the duke, on board this Lisbon-bound boat, this was all a time that should never have been, created purely by mistake.

Under her skin, the port burnt hazily, and words formed, as he'd once said, with the illogic of truth.

"More free, yes, than I did as a woman in England."

"But how can that be?"

"I can move differently in these clothes, sit differently." As though to illustrate her point, she lay down, mirroring his position, so they were facing each other on their sides. Her fingers nestled into her cropped hair as she rested her head on her hand. The shortness no longer felt strange. "On that first night, when you cut my hair, you were wise enough, and kind enough, to free me from all but the most real and meaningful constraints of propriety. You may not have meant your words to assume such importance, but it was a lesson I'll never forget. Because as much as I've always tried to believe my academic pursuits and my...my unusual ways of thinking and feeling were not wrong, it's still difficult to truly believe it when the whole world insists a good woman is a creature very different to the one I've discovered myself to be." She met his eyes. "You freed me from a guilt I hadn't realised I was carrying."

There was a frown in his gaze, deep and dark with sympathy. He made a movement, as though to take her hand in comfort, and she tensed, heart surging. But he only set a finger to the carpet and briefly, absently traced a pattern.

"The world is greatly at fault if it ever made you feel you weren't good," he said. "And I've seen enough of the world to have seen wickedness and sin and weakness in all their forms. You haven't a trace of any."

"Common opinion doesn't agree with you, Your Grace. You know it well enough to joke about it."

"My comment on the dangers of education?"

"Yes."

"And do you believe any of it?"

"No."

"Well then."

She gave him a long look, dissatisfied with that glib response. "Are you always so certain of yourself, Your Grace? Have you never had reason to doubt?"

He looked from her to the ruby liquid in his glass, pausing before he answered.

"I've done things I would've preferred not to do. And I've often wished to do things I ought not." He ran his finger around the rim of his glass, smearing a drop of port which had clung to it. She listened hard to his every word—they were honest, rare as diamonds. "A great deal of my life has been spent chafing against an obligation which any true gentleman wouldn't wish to shirk, for it's undoubtedly one I'm bound by both duty and honour to perform. And yet, try as I might, I can seldom find anything but repugnance for it." He lifted his eyes and held out his glass to hers. "So yes, I often have reason to doubt myself. And I find I'd also be glad to drink to freedom, however selfish I am for wishing to gain it."

Twelve

Miss Littleton sipped her drink, watching him. Her smile seemed a deliberate attempt to ease the mood. Maybe the bitterness in his voice was unsettling. It unsettled *him*.

"Is this always how men talk after dinner? Isn't it politics and business and...farming...as I've always supposed?"

Lucian gave a soft laugh. "Oh, all of that, and horses and dogs and hunting. The best place for leather breeches, or an excellent wine one has discovered, or a recommendation for a skilled tailor who might be able to produce a coat just like Lord Who or Mr What was wearing the other day. And a great deal of gossip, of course."

"And women?" she suggested, smiling.

"Yes, but not, I fear, as often as women themselves would like to believe." He chuckled at her expression. "I know, I know, how unchivalrous, but many a man would rather talk for two hours about his horses than two minutes about his wife—*or* his mistress," he added, anticipating the mischievous way her smile was going.

"And you?" she asked, finishing her glass of port and holding it for another refill. "Do you discuss your—"

"Harry," he interjected, ignoring her glass. "I wouldn't talk about such things with you even if you'd been born Harry Trunkton. Men don't discuss such things with greenheaded boys, or even their own peers."

"I suspect greenheaded boys discuss such things a lot," she said incorrigibly, "if the conversation of greenheaded girls is anything to go by."

Lucian groaned and lay on his back, arm over his eyes. He heard Miss Littleton laugh, then the unmistakable sound of her refilling her glass.

"For you?" she asked.

"Oh, why not," he muttered, holding out his glass in her direction without lifting the arm from his eyes. "I may as well be hung for a sheep as a lamb."

It was clear he had no need to teach Miss Littleton how to drink port. Which meant he had no reason to be here at all, until he gratefully remembered the cigarillos, for the sun coming through the windows was warm, and the gentle rocking of the boat felt suddenly wonderfully relaxing.

"How's the novel?" he asked. "Are we any closer to discovering the murderer?"

"Not yet, but I think a clue is close to hand. The heroine, Angelica Thorogood—"

"Let me guess, she's an angelic and thoroughly good type of creature?"

"Yes! How did you know?" said Miss Littleton, laughing. "She is dining with her elderly chaperon—who I suspect will soon fall asleep—at Lord Bravecourt's castle."

"Of *course* he has a castle. Rather gothic, I suspect?"

"Rusted suits of armour and cobwebs at every corner. The housekeeper must be atrocious. But, far more exciting than mere decor: they have just *danced*."

He lifted his arm from his eyes and turned his head to catch the twinkle in her eyes. "And did she faint?"

"Not quite. But she did almost swoon at the feel of his manly arms around her."

"Goodness. A waltz. I'm not sure I should be letting you read this book, Harry."

"I've read Suetonius's biography of Tiberius." She chuckled. "I'm unlikely to be scandalised by a waltz."

Lucian, who had only the vaguest notion of that Roman Emperor's supposed depravities—learnt secondhand from the barely remembered gossip of his Oxford days—still knew enough to stare at her with horror before returning his arm to his eyes in despair.

"I see I've now scandalised *you*," she said with amusement—and absolutely no trace of apology.

He groaned and sat up, reaching for his cigar case. "How, Harry," he said, brandishing a cigarillo at her, "have you made *this* the more proper topic of conversation?"

"You brought them," she said innocently, refilling both their glasses.

He shook his head, tapping the cigarillo on the case before realising, it being daytime, that he had no candle or fire to light it from.

"One moment."

He swiftly left the room, fearing he must have drunk more port than he'd realised. The tipping of the floor felt far more insistent than usual. He collared the first man he saw and ordered a lit lantern, waiting impatiently, then returned with his prize to find Miss Littleton sipping her port and looking happily at the light sparkling on the window glass, novel forgotten at her knee, cushions scattered all around. The same sun that glinted on the windows splintered rubies all over the floor where it caught the bottle of port. It found the gold in the pale brown of her hair. She turned her head toward him, smiling, a cigarillo held in one hand.

"I am prepared and waiting, as you see."

If he'd ever seen a more inviting scene, he was temporarily

at a loss to recall it. He walked over as steadily as ship and legs allowed and resumed his seat on the floor at her side.

"I'll light it for you," he said, taking the cigarillo from her fingers. He opened the door of the lantern and touched the end to the small flame inside, then brought the cigarillo to his lips, drawing until the end glowed steadily. He handed it to her, nodding when she placed it between her own lips. "And do not—inhale," he cautioned too late, as she burst out coughing, her eyes watering.

She spluttered, laughing, and coughed some more. He grinned as he lit his own cigarillo and demonstrated, taking a sip of smoke and savouring it for a moment before releasing it smoothly from between his lips. "You sip the smoke, Harry, just like you sip the port."

"It's disgusting!" she protested, gamely giving it another go. She coughed again and reached for her drink, taking a large swallow before returning to her smoke. Lucian watched, caught halfway between dismay and admiration. In that moment, he felt perfectly sure Mr Trunkton wouldn't embarrass him.

"I'm getting the hang of it now," she said, blowing a small cloud from between her lips.

"You are," he acknowledged. Her eyes sparkled at him through the haze of smoke and he smiled languidly, giving in to the moment—it was his own creation, after all, and as such, he could hardly fight it—and stretched out once more on his side, smoking happily and feeling, for the first time in a while, that all of his cares were quite remote.

"It's still disgusting," she said. "I prefer the port."

"I can tell," he said, giving her almost empty glass a pointed look.

She let out another breath of smoke, fixing him with a look. "Describe your childhood." The eyebrow he raised didn't cow her. "If your life now contains some great secret," she continued, "your childhood surely didn't. I want to know about it."

"You can ask me a hundred times and it still won't make the answer any more exciting. Rather the opposite, in fact," he mused, "being more of an anti-climax."

"Don't change the subject again. And I don't care if you think it's boring. I want to know."

"Very well." He tapped the ash from his cigarillo and began. "I was born. I lived in a very large house on the edge of a lake—Thornley Castle. It's still my main residence. I had a series of nurses and nannies, then tutors and schooling. I went to Oxford. I came of age. I became Duke. Now I'm on a boat."

Miss Littleton gave him a scathing look. "Terrible. You're an awful man."

He grinned. "You're very cruel to my life story. I assure you, being born and everything that followed meant a great deal to me. I might even go so far as to say it means my very life."

She shook her head and lay down too, but on her back, looking up at the decorated ceiling. Lucian, propped on one elbow, had a very clear view of her face. And, with her attention on the ceiling, he was at leisure to study it, from the faint freckles to the flush of drink on her cheeks.

"I also lived near water," she began as he watched the shape of her lips. "In a small but very dear cottage with white roses around the door and hollyhocks swaying beyond the windows. There was a little lawn, and a small fence, and beyond that, a duck pond at no very great distance from the house so that we could watch it quite easily from both the sitting room and the study where my mother and father both worked. And we liked to watch it, because it may have been only a humble duck pond, but it was home to a beautiful pair of swans, who returned year after year and always managed to produce six or seven great, grey scruffy cygnets between them."

"Ah," he said, smiling gently, "these are the sorts of details you want, are they? Very well. I had a dog." She turned her head to look at him. "It was brown," he added diligently. "With four legs and a tail."

With her cigarillo clamped between her teeth, she reached out and gave his shoulder an indignant push. He caught her wrist in his hand, and she went quite still, staring up at him. And she stayed very still when he released her wrist in order to pluck the small cigar from her mouth.

His heartbeat seemed oddly loud, and hot with drink, and hazy with smoke. Miss Littleton's eyes looked much like that too—both warm and hazed. Her lips, pink and slightly open, seemed far too innocent to have ever been sullied by the dark column of his cigar. She would taste like he did, of smoke and port.

She took a sharp breath, still unmoving except for that sudden lifting of her chest. His eyes dropped from her mouth to the linen that hid her throat, the waistcoat that hid her form. He reached out and toyed with the end of her neckcloth, slowly, almost accidentally, beginning to tug it loose.

"Will you ever learn to tie these?" he murmured.

"I like the way you do it."

Her voice was a whisper, but it might have been a shout for the jolt it sent through him, the way it stopped the movement of his hand and made his eyes lift to hers. He thought there was a confession in it, one he both longed and dreaded to hear. And he knew full well he should not have brought them to a moment where such a confession might be made, even as he found himself without the strength of will to draw back from it. There were a million good reasons why he should not lie here looking down at this woman with his knuckles brushing her throat and her eyes locked on his. There were a million good reasons, and he would recall them all tomorrow when he wasn't drunk and Hester wasn't staring up at him with her eyes so wide and her body trembling with anticipation.

He let go the neckcloth, moved to touch her cheek—

A clattering from across the room made him jerk his hand away and hastily sit up, Miss Littleton sitting up too. Willsly had come into the room, his arms full of fencing equipment. One scabbarded foil had fallen at his feet—the source of the noise.

"Afternoon, Your Grace, Mr Trunkton," the expressionless Willsly said with a small bow for the former and a nod for the latter. He bent to pick up the foil and Lucian got to his feet, holding out his hand and hauling Miss Littleton up too.

"You did say three o'clock, Your Grace?" Willsly enquired.

"Yes." Lucian cleared his throat. "Yes. Yes, I did. Thank you for the...reminder."

Miss Littleton, very red in the face, said something about the port having made her sleepy and slipped from the room, giving a short nod to Willsly as she passed him.

The man came over, dumping his equipment unceremoniously on the floor and giving the port bottle, glasses, and smouldering cigarillos an assessing look.

"Another lesson," said Lucian. "To prepare Harry for dinner tomorrow. Or after dinner, to be more accurate."

"So I see. Seems like it must have been very instructive. Was maybe about to get more so."

"I'll not fence with you," began Lucian. "In either sense of the word." Hester would've enjoyed that word play, wouldn't have needed it spelled out. He smiled thinly. "For I'm far too drunk."

Then he took himself off for a long and punishingly cold walk about the deck, having a pressing need to clear his head.

Thirteen

HESTER WAS VERY NEARLY sick for the first time since coming aboard *The Ondine*. And it wasn't the rolling of the ship or even the port in her veins—both of which sent her stumbling into the walls a half dozen times as she made her way hastily from the dining room to her bed—but the sharp whip of humiliation lashing her guts.

She was very confused. Not about what she'd wanted to happen, for that she'd wanted the duke to kiss her, she was distressingly aware. It was the man himself that confused her.

Curled up in bed with a pillow over her screwed-up face, she kept seeing again his dark eyes looking down at her, and as sure as she'd been in the moment that she understood his look, now she couldn't be entirely certain it hadn't been something else. Something too complicated for her to even name. Puzzled and surprised and stormy and violent and sad and searching and hungry and—Oh! Well! What was the use of thinking of it? Maybe he'd just been drunk.

They'd both been drunk, and that was the start and the end of the whole matter and there was really nothing more to be said on it. Hadn't Charles and Tom, after some mischief or accident, excused the whole with a sheepish, *"Well, the problem was, we'd had a little too much to drink..."*? Men in their cups were stupid creatures. And so were women. And she was the most stupid of all, because she'd wanted a duke—*a duke!*—to kiss her, as dizzy and swooning for the want of it as Angelica Thorogood had been during her waltz! She despised herself. A viscount had asked for her hand and she had very properly denied him. A duke *looked* at her and...oh...she ought to be whipped. She would never try port again, would never be alone with him again, for the problem with the duke wasn't that he was so deeply attractive, but that he made her laugh.

She'd discovered, a week too late, her biggest weakness. Laughter. Laughter mixed with port. How silly it made her. She'd almost believed he *wanted* to kiss her. As if he ever could, when she was less a woman than she'd ever been, her appearance ridiculous in every aspect, from her hair to her woollen stockings. The Duke of Cumbria might seldom feature in society gossip, but that he was one of the biggest catches on the marriage mart was something no one could be ignorant of. And his minimum requirement for a wife was the incomparable, ethereal beauty of Jane Parling.

Hester had got this far in her self-denigration—by route of many circular, repetitive arguments and groaning recollections—and was just launching on an attack of self-reproach for being daft enough to mourn what the duke required in a wife when she had no wish to be his, or anyone's, when a knock came at the door. It was Willsly, bringing her dinner tray.

Very conscious of her bleary eyes, flustered face, and rumpled appearance, she sat meekly on the bed while he arranged her tray on the little table. She kept her eyes down, miserably expecting him to be brusque, offended, or disparaging. But it was worse, because he was sympathetic. The look he gave her as he finished arranging her dinner was soft and pitying.

That Willsly was a competent man, she'd known from the moment she met him. That he was an astute and thoughtful man, she'd known by the box of rags and hastily made girdle he'd placed under her bed soon after her discovery. He'd never said a word about it to her, and that it was his doing and not the duke's, she was entirely sure, for the knowledge and understanding of a woman's monthly needs were something only a man in household service was likely to know. She'd been desperately grateful to him ever since. But now there was gentle understanding in his rough face, older than its years, and it all felt too much, for she knew him now to be a truly *good* man. Pathetic tears stung her eyes.

She needed a confidante... Her heart was overfull... The effects of the port still lingered in her veins... "I've been very stupid," she admitted with a breathless gulp.

Willsly frowned in sympathy, the empty tray in his hands. "He has a way about him. It's not to be wondered at. None as knows him would blame you. And I did warn him."

She nodded. Swallowed. "I will do better. And get over it."

"You will," he reassured her. "And it'll be easier once we're all off this tub."

She nodded again, and Willsly left her to a dinner she barely touched.

It took a great deal of courage to arrive at the duke's cabin for breakfast the next morning and act as though nothing at all had changed.

But it was an attempt that soon proved futile, because it was clear from the duke's manner that something had very much changed. He ignored her neckcloth—and she'd tried very hard with it this morning, and as a result, it was abominably creased—and he didn't criticise her table manners, or posture, or the dearth of her conversation. He didn't abuse her at all.

Instead, he was very polite. It was horrible.

"I'll take you on deck when we're finished here, Harry," he said, "and show you around."

"Thank you, Your Grace."

"Dinner will be at five. You may present yourself to the room directly. Captain Moore and First Officer Irwin know about your lack of luggage, so do not trouble yourself over that. What you are wearing now will be adequate."

"Yes, Your Grace."

"And Irwin has offered to lend you his spare boots. They'll be closer to your size than any of mine, though will still be far too big, but you should wear them on the deck and must wear them when we arrive at Lisbon until we can find you a more appropriate pair."

She inclined her head, and no more conversation was had.

If she'd needed any additional help to souse the spark of her impossible infatuation, she would've found it the moment she emerged onto *The Ondine's* deck. They stood at the stern, the vastness of the vessel spread before them, the three mighty masts glorious under full sail, and two dozen or more men busy at their unending work. It was all his, the duke's, to command at will. They really were miles from England and speeding past the coast of Spain, and the Duke of Cumbria really was on a diplomatic mission in service to the King of England himself—for of that much, she was certain, however the duke attempted to evade her.

Below deck, looking out of the little windows, it had almost been possible to believe the sea was nothing but a framed picture, and the lavish rooms, small and strangely shaped as they were, were nothing but stage sets, like those she'd seen in pictures. But here, with the wind on her skin and the salt spray on her lips, in borrowed boots, borrowed stockings, borrowed clothes, and shorn hair, she knew for sure that the man at her side was really a duke, and she was really still Hester Littleton, governess, and no one at all.

The duke introduced her to the captain, who shook her hand briskly but kindly. "I hope you're feeling better, Mr Trunkton?"

"Yes, Captain Moore. Thank you."

"Still very pale, I see, but you've been below deck for a week. Get some sun on you, boy. Sit out here when you like. Do you like to whittle? We can find you a knife. Or one of the men could teach you some knots if you've a mind for that sort of thing."

"Thank you, Captain."

Seeming satisfied, the man nodded, exchanged some words with the duke, then excused himself to duties far more important than skinny schoolboys. The breeze that sped their passage made her shiver. The duke ordered her out of the cold and back to her room. And that was all she saw of him until dinner.

It was intimidating, but not quite so frightening as she'd feared, to walk into the dinner room. A fatalistic sort of curiosity as to what would unfold when she sat down with these three men as one of them leant her a strange kind of courage. And part of her hardly cared.

The others were there already, standing by the same window where Hester had so often sat, glasses in their hands. She very nearly curtsied when they all turned towards her but turned the flinching movement into an awkward bow.

First Officer Irwin, who was now introduced to her, smiled broadly, amusement in the blue eyes that so strikingly adorned his handsome face. As a young woman who'd more or less made her own independent way in the world, mostly bereft of protectors for many years, Hester had developed the ability to judge young men quickly and accurately. She knew Irwin's type. Smart, without any delicacy of intelligence. Physically strong and competent and proud of it. Arrogant and self-satisfied, but good-natured enough, so long as things went his way. He knew he was handsome and would use it like a weapon the moment he was free in port. Of young Harry Trunkton, she could tell he took little interest at all, except as a possible source of amusement on a dull and monotonous trip.

"Sick, eh?" he said amiably as they all took their seats. She suspected he was excited to be dining with the duke and trying not to show it, for it was a high honour for someone of his rank. "You have my sympathies, Trunkton. My first week at sea was miserable."

"If you have any sympathies, Irwin," said the duke, "spare them for the boy's parents, who know nothing other than the fact he has disappeared, and who, therefore, must be out of their minds with worry. If he hadn't been punished so thoroughly by sickness, I would've beaten him myself."

"True enough, Your Grace," said Irwin, clearly not daring to disagree.

The captain, who appeared to be a single-minded sort of man, then turned the conversation to their progress. It seemed they were only around three days from their destination. Hester listened, interested in the nautical terms of which she knew little. They were almost a language of their own.

They would sail into the mouth of the River Tagus and anchor there, the white buildings of Lisbon gleaming in the sun. She'd read of it. It was one of the oldest cities in the world. And, depressed as her spirits currently were, she couldn't be insensible to the excitement of visiting a foreign shore. Hester Littleton abroad! She'd suffer through much more than she'd yet done for such an adventure.

The duke's mention of her fictional parents had, of course, turned her thoughts to the Parlings. They truly must be beside themselves with worry, and the guilt, which she'd done her best to suppress as there was nothing at all she could do about it, crept steadily into her bones as the meal progressed. It suppressed her nervous appetite still further, until it was Jane's face that she saw before her more clearly than any of the current assembly. Jane, who would suffer the deepest, and Georgina and Elizabeth, who would weep hysterically and uselessly and make her burden worse.

Mr and Mrs Parling would worry a little for her, but more for the sake of their name and any notoriety that her disappearance might attach to it, especially as she'd been their guest at the time. They would keep her disappearance quiet at least. The Parlings would always hush any scandal that might hurt their fragile pride.

Talk around the table turned to Lisbon, to Portugal, to the state of things there. As befitted her age, she listened to her elders and betters in silence, her tightly wrought mind numbed by the murmur of voices, unspooling like a dropped cotton reel rolling out of sight beneath a table.

She stared, unfocused, at the silverware on the table, seeing the ship's destination looming there, in the candle-made shadows between the tureens and salvers. She saw a foreign port in the reflections of a wine glass... The journey was almost over.

From reaching Lisbon, it took little effort for her imagination to bring the ship back home to Portsmouth. Three more weeks perhaps, and then, what had seemed only yesterday morning to be a strange and endless dream, would all be over. She would return to her life, and the duke to his. It was likely she would never see him again.

The thought caused her to look up and straight at him for the first time that evening. It was unfortunate timing. The last course had been removed, and the port was being brought out. The captain himself served them, and the duke's dark eyes stayed on hers as the glass before her was filled. The scent of it made her feel strange. The whole moment did. The duke looked away, murmuring his thanks to the captain.

"Capital stuff this, Your Grace," he replied, sitting back down and taking an appreciative sip. "I know I say it every time, but it's well worth repeating."

Irwin added his ready assent, then took a case from his pocket, offering the contents around, a cigarillo clamped at a jaunty angle in the corner of his mouth. The duke's prediction seemed about to come true, for Irwin grinned as he held out the case to Hester. "Ever tried one, Trunkton?"

She was saved answering by Captain Moore, who frowned at the case. "None of that stinking smoke tonight, Irwin. If you agree, Your Grace? The boy's only just over being sick. I can't imagine the smell of these will help."

Indeed, her stomach was twisting, but not for the reason the captain assumed.

"You have a point, captain," agreed the duke. "Sorry, Irwin. I'll join you another night."

Gratified by this prospect, the young man put his case away with a ready smile. "I'd be honoured, Your Grace." Then, the two older men falling into some low murmur of businesslike conversation, Irwin leant towards Hester and began to quiz her on how she spent her days.

"I suspect you're dreadfully bored now you've run out of the entertainment of straining your guts. Beginning to regret your lark yet, eh?"

"Not yet. I'm excited to see Lisbon."

"I bet! Ever been abroad before?"

"No. Never."

"It's not the best of cities, especially now. Boney's lot sacked it something ruthless. But there's sport to be had if you're game." He gave Hester a doubtful look. "Are you game? And how old are you, by the way?"

"Fifteen, sir."

He whistled. "That all? I couldn't hazard a guess, somehow. Maybe I hadn't better show you round the town, then. I can't imagine His Grace would quite like it. What a place to cut your teeth, eh, though, Trunkton? Imagine returning to school with a Portuguese doxy on your card. That'd be a story to tell your friends." He laughed to himself at this before asking, suddenly curious, "Where *do* you go to school?"

"Ah, Harrow, sir," ventured Hester, feeling sure Irwin would've gone to one of the lesser schools. But...

"Then you must know John Gibson—he's about your age. Know his brother—Lord Kiethly now. My father was the rector on his estate, but we used to run together as boys. Little Jack too, not that he could ever keep up. He was a weedy scrap like you."

Hester was saved from answering by the scraping back of the duke's chair. He stood up and fixed her with a look. "Bed, my boy, before you pitch face down in your cup."

He accompanied her as far as the door, and her spirits received a small, albeit very unwise lift, because, bidding her adieu in a voice too low for the others to hear and with something like the normal gleam in his eye, he said, "No, you may not gadabout Lisbon with Irwin. And you will definitely *not* meet any Portuguese doxies."

But it was the last such gleam she saw for a while.

Fourteen

OF THE SEVERAL TIMES Lucian had arrived at Lisbon, he'd never been more glad to see it. They'd rounded the Rock of Lisbon—the *Cabo da Roca*—at dawn. *The Ondine*, now anchored within the sheltered harbour of the Tagus, shifted gently beneath his feet, the movement barely perceptible after so long at sea. All around was a crowd of masts and sails and small boats. The crescent of the city, buildings spreading for over a mile along the coast, rose on several hills, capped by *Castelo de São Jorge*—the Castle of Saint George. The day was fine, and the land beyond the city seemed far distant. As did the enemies and battles and starving armies on the march for mile after mile through all Portugal, all Spain, all France, and all the way across the continent to Russia—such was Napoleon's reach. Or his gall. But there was no sign of it here, if one discounted the naval ships and the scars on the city.

Lucian looked down at Miss Littleton beside him, who was currently looking very much like the boy Harry: wide-eyed with wonder, the disordered locks that tumbled across her brow tugged by the unsteady breeze, cheeks reddened by the hours she'd spent on deck over the last few days. The Portuguese shore wind held none of the heat of summer but felt warm after the open sea. The sun was shining and gulls wheeled in the air, their cries mingling with the faint shouts from the docks and the slapping of water and rigging and sails.

He hoped the city wouldn't disappoint her the way it did so many travellers. For, from the sea, the white buildings arranged on the artful hills looked like heaven, but up close it was a dirty, crowded place, and much ravaged in recent years, the war adding to the damage of the earthquake some decades before.

Miss Littleton didn't turn to meet his gaze, though his eyes lingered a moment on her face, enjoying watching her first sight of a foreign city more than he enjoyed the view itself. How easily he'd been tempted! He'd never suspected his honour was so weak. Perhaps it'd never faced such a test. But what good was his plan to disguise her as Harry if he ruined her himself?

No. Over-familiarity and too much port had led to danger, but the course had been swiftly corrected. He'd kept his distance, physical, and otherwise. Now Lisbon and work and the widowed condesa would ensure his hand stayed steady on the tiller. Distraction and fresh air and space would fix him, fill all the hollows inside. Crush the weak and wistful parts. And within three or four weeks, weather willing, they'd be back in England, and this unexpected wrinkle in his life would be smoothed and gone, leaving only a dent, not a scar.

He told himself all this and still he watched her face, not the shore.

The call came that the launch was ready, and they made their way down to it. Miss Littleton paused at the top of the ladder because, though the harbour was calm and the boats securely hitched, the little launch still seemed to go one way while the bulk of *The Ondine* went another. It was his own least favourite part of life at sea. But Irwin was in the launch and helped her down, and Lucian swiftly followed. The oars were taken up, and they were rowed to the dock.

"Watch your step," he advised as the gangway was set in place. He took a masculine grip on her elbow as she crossed to the pier.

"You've got sea legs now, and the stillness of the land will feel strange at first."

"I feel I'm still going up and down!"

"It'll wear off."

But he kept his grip on her arm, because within two steps she nearly stumbled, shaking her head. "How peculiar it feels."

Willsly, who'd gone ahead of them with their luggage and to prepare their apartments, was waiting for them with a carriage—lacquered, but dusty, and two skinny black horses hitched to it.

"Your rooms are all ready for you, Your Grace, and several letters and invitations already waiting."

Lucian nodded and nearly handed Miss Littleton up into the carriage, long habit taking over. But he turned the movement of his hand into a curt gesture, and she clambered in unaided.

"Have the driver let me down at *Palácio da Ega*," Lucian said to Willsly. "You take Harry on to our lodgings, settle him in, then show him the town. Find a tailor, for God's sake, and a cobbler. A hat. You know what he needs."

"Your Grace—"

"I've no need for a minder at this hour, Willsly. I'm only visiting Beresford's people. I must waste no time in seeing if a message has been left, and there's no one else who I can put in charge of the boy—you know why. Later, when the real business starts, of course you'll come with me. Keep an eye on what he purchases and intervene if you must—money is no object, but I fear the boy's *taste* is ruinous."

The man didn't smile at this and might have protested further at letting his master go about unguarded, but Lucian quelled him with a look and climbed into the carriage. It was built in the chariot style, the seats front facing, and a window before them. A perfect sightseeing vehicle, he thought wryly to himself as he sat down beside Miss Littleton, adjusting the folds of his greatcoat so they didn't smother her thigh, and removing his hat. She was looking raptly through the window at her side, nose almost pressed to the glass.

"Willsly will take you shopping later," he said as the carriage started into motion. "There are churches and sights enough to amuse any traveller. *Mosteiro dos Jerónimos, São Roque*, I suppose. The *Estrela Basilica* is pretty enough if you get that far. Willsly will keep you safe, but beware pickpockets and other rough sorts, and don't fall for the tales of beggars and urchins, for they are nearly all of them a con. Have you ever been to London?"

"No."

"Well, I suppose it wouldn't have done much to prepare you. Watch where you step. The streets can be filthy. Avoid alleyways. And remain within reaching distance of Willsly at all times."

"I suppose," she said hesitantly, "you'll be too busy to accompany us?"

"Yes."

She nodded and returned her eyes to the glass as they left the stone wharf.

"But," he added, unable to withhold the treat despite the mutters of common sense in the background of his mind, "it's likely I'll attend the opera or some other performance tonight—whichever invitation feels most interesting. If you can return from your shopping trip in one piece and with raiment fit to be seen in, you may come with me. For at least part of the evening."

She turned wide eyes on him. "Really? I may?"

He couldn't help his smile, however rueful it might've been around the corners. "I suspect attempting to keep you confined to quarters will only cause more mischief than it saves. You'll no doubt try to escape. Smuggle yourself out in the laundry basket, perhaps."

The smile she gave him surprised him, because it made him realise he hadn't seen it in days. And had sorely missed it.

"I would not!" she said, grey eyes gleaming with amusement while he fought the demented urge to touch that smile—trace it with a finger and capture it in his palm, the way one instinctively reaches for a feather falling softly from the sky. "But I would dearly love to see the opera."

"Portuguese opera," Lucian mused. "As Irwin might say, it's a fine way to cut your teeth. The dancers make our English ones look like nuns. But it won't shock you, I know, for *you* have read Suetonius's biography of Tiberius."

She laughed. "Did I admit that to you? That port must've been more effective than I thought."

"Yes. It goes down a little too easily."

The awkward pause that followed was a clamouring bell—definitely a call to change the subject, and quickly, before memories of Miss Littleton lying in the sea-filtered sun, pulse hammering under his slowly exploring hand, crowded into the too small confines of the carriage. Or any more than it was already there, in the shadow of her every movement, her every breath. He couldn't forget it, no matter how hard he tried.

He directed her attention to the sights they passed until the carriage stopped at *de Ega*.

Lucian found the military secretary at home, the hours of business being somewhat different to those of England, and, after being pressed into sharing a glass of wine, was given the correspondence he was there for. After that, he enquired if any of the officers of the 95th were in town and was directed to a lieutenant recovering from a shot that had pierced jaw and throat.

He could speak, albeit painfully, and, though he was surprised at being visited by a Lord Millbeck—Lucian had introduced himself with one of his minor titles—showed himself to be as sensible as expected of an officer of the greens, collecting himself almost instantly.

"Charles Littleton?" the lieutenant repeated, propped up with pillows in his bed.

"Out of Hythe barracks, arrived in Lisbon early in 1810 with the First Battalion, I believe."

"A private, you say?"

"I believe so. But a gentleman's son, Hampshire born. He's likely to have stood out from the common sort, and may, I hope, have swiftly achieved notice, having language skills that would've made him of use."

"I'm in the First, but I'm afraid I don't recall him." He paused, gathering the energy to speak again. "He wasn't in my company, or, I think, any of my brother officers'." He levelled pain-pinched green eyes on Lucian. His face was very thin. "It may be that he...was lost early on, before he...came to anyone's notice."

Lucian nodded in acknowledgement of this. "There's no record of his death in the lists." He'd checked before paying this call. "But I believe they're quite out of date."

"Yes," agreed the lieutenant quietly. "We've been scattered for a year, and this winter campaign..." He shook his head, then winced, hand going to the worn-looking bandage around his throat.

"I'll let you rest," Lucian said, standing from the wooden chair. The room was bright but shabby. The lieutenant's green coat, hanging from the wardrobe door as though he wished always to have it ready at hand, was ragged and weather-bleached, the buttons tarnished to black. "You're comfortable here?" Lucian asked, pausing at the door and looking back at the man.

"You have everything you need?"

"A mattress and four walls. It's paradise. So tell me why I long for a bivouac under dripping pines?"

Lucian returned the man's smile. "Because you're a soldier, Lieutenant, and I salute you for it."

"Give me swift passage to Badajoz and a cocked hat in my rifle sights, and I'll be well and happy enough."

Lucian smiled again and left the man to his recovery, pausing only to find the mistress of the house and pay the man's board for a month. It would be at least that long before he was fit to rejoin his regiment, and Lucian had never yet met a soldier who'd received his wages on time, or ever in sufficient quantity for his needs.

It was then time to make his rendezvous, and he risked the wrath of Willsly by not attempting to find him and avail himself of his assistance. He didn't know which part of Lisbon he and Miss Littleton would be in by now, and the time of the meeting that'd been among the correspondence received from Beresford was imminent. His contact must have been watching his arrival and clearly wished to make haste.

A curtained doorway in the back of the appointed coffee house led to a small private parlour, with one other door through which he presumed his contact would arrive and leave equally unseen via the backways. Lucian waited, as conscious of the documents in his pocket as if they were a live shell—conscious of one, in particular.

There were some letters and orders from England. And he also had his usual report, which was based on the *petits chiffres*—the common, simple French ciphers—in the intercepted correspondence he'd decoded on board and supplemented with the implicit intelligence it was his talent to analyse.

In the bundle passed to him at Portsmouth, there'd been a great many inconsequential letters among the ones containing explicit military secrets. Snippets and gossip from letters to relatives complaining of inconsequential things—that the mayor of some village had been turned out of his summer residence by French troops seeking billets, that a family in such-and-such a village had lost its donkeys, that a crop had been trampled underfoot in the Talavera, that forty sacks of flour had been plundered from such-and-such a bakery. All of it mundane and meaning little at all in isolation, for such acts happened every day in a country at war. But it was Lucian's task to piece it all together with the more obvious intelligence he decrypted and build a fuller picture of troop sizes and movements and locations. He would pass this report on now.

But, important as his report might be, it wasn't that which made him sit so tensely, awaiting his contact's arrival with increasing impatience. It was a series of misspelt French numbers. They'd been in the most inconsequential document of all—a laundry inventory and a lengthy complaint from a housekeeper to her sister. But why misspell the numbers if not to draw attention to them? It was a clumsy attempt at hiding a message, but Lucian was entirely sure that the numbers themselves were part of that most elegant of all devices: the Great Paris Cipher, Bonaparte's unbreakable code.

Or supposedly unbreakable. Wellington's chief codebreaker was already attempting it. He only needed some clues, a small key to turn the lock, and the whole cipher would break apart, and every single French dispatch the Guides and Spanish guerrillas intercepted would be readable to British eyes, Bonaparte's plans laid bare.

It could be the pivot that turned the entire war. And the clue that was needed might be found in these numbers, clumsily used. But the French mustn't suspect their unbreakable code might be broken...

Devil take it, where was the man? Lucian checked his watch.

It was twenty minutes past the hour they were meant to meet. Hardly late at all if this had been a fashionable, social engagement, but given the circumstances, it was enough to make him deeply uneasy. Ten more minutes went by, before Lucian, the back of his neck prickling and his chest heavy with foreboding, stood up, sauntered casually back through the cafe, and paused in the doorway, checking the street under the guise of pausing to look at his watch, before leaving for his lodgings—sticking always to the most populated streets.

His unease was hardly abated by finding Willsly and Miss Littleton hadn't returned. Presumably they were still shopping, or exploring, but he couldn't like their absence. He sent a messenger to accept the most important of his dinner invitations and got dressed, muttering to himself about his valet's desertion and knowing his irritation was both unjust and caused more by fear than by the fingerprints he left on his own boots, or his damned, cursed necktie.

After several hours spent in the house of an exiled Spanish noble, being his charming best and attempting to ignore his gnawing anxiety—the first more successful than the latter—he returned, heart lifting at the sound of voices in the sitting room.

He was smiling even before he entered the room to find Willsly in the process of moving a pile of boxes from his arms to the sofa, with Miss Littleton talking non-stop. The contrast between his valet's sour face and Miss Littleton's beaming joy made him laugh out loud.

"I see you enjoyed your shopping trip, Harry."

"Oh yes!" she said, hurrying halfway down the room towards him before checking her impetuous advance and coming to an uncertain stop.

"Shopping!" huffed Willsly, hastily putting out a hand to prevent one of the boxes from sliding off its precarious tower. "It's me that's had to do all the shopping, Your Grace. And spend the better half of my time tearing young master here away from every ragamuffin street urchin or fruit-selling crone he got stuck talking to."

Lucian's attention returned to Miss Littleton's glowing countenance, revising his initial assumption that her happiness was due to that most feminine of enjoyments: the exchange of money for goods.

"I thought I told you not to get snared by beggars and peddlers."

"I wasn't! I was *talking* to them! You have no idea how exciting it is to hear a language one has mostly learnt from books being spoken all around you. And the different accents! The pronunciations I had never even imagined! And the dialects I've heard! The new words, and shortenings, and interesting phrases. Oh, the vocabulary! And all the common turns of phrase—the slang and the cant. I thought I knew Portuguese. I was wrong."

"Good Lord," murmured Lucian as it became unavoidably clear his protégé had been gleefully indulging in the coarsest street talk imaginable.

"Just as talking to the sailors onboard ship made me realise I barely knew English at all," continued Miss Littleton, unaware of his deepening consternation. "I think I must make a dictionary. These phrases must be preserved. There is so much...much *vigour* and life to them. They are so inventive."

"You conversed with the sailors," he repeated slowly.

"Why, yes! What else was there to do for the remainder of our journey? I grew tired of that novel," she said, and quickly turned away to busy herself in an examination of her parcels.

Lucian met Willsly's defensive look.

"I tried to stop her, Your Grace. And we got almost all you could wish for."

"Yes," added Miss Littleton, looking up from her trophies.

"Obviously, there was no time to get anything made completely new, but one tailor happened to have a coat already made and did the little adjustment necessary while we waited in the shop."

"And quizzed the shop boy on all manner of vulgar terms?"

She smiled. "Not quite. Only on those related to clothing. Fashions change so quickly that language must change quickly to keep up. It's odd that even with everything, there are still many trends coming from Paris that are popular here."

"I'm sure it's fascinating."

"And I can return Irwin's boots. And…and your neckcloths, Your Grace. I have a supply of my own."

Lucian merely nodded, refusing to dwell on Miss Littleton's use of his neckcloths, or the strange reluctance he felt at the thought of her relinquishing them. Instead, he looked at Willsly, having much he needed to tell the man. "Attend me in my room, Willsly. I'll change for the opera. You must change too, Miss Littleton. We leave in an hour."

Fifteen

THE BUILDING THEIR APARTMENTS were in was as close to a palace as Hester was ever likely to enter. In fact, the duke had informed her on the drive from the dock that the building had indeed belonged to Portuguese royals before they fled the French invasion for Brazil.

The rooms were grander and more finely ornamented than any she'd seen, even making Viscount Hindley's house seem dull and dowdy in comparison. The walls were painted with elaborate scenes, the stairway had pierced stone balustrades, the floors were tiled in dizzying Moorish patterns, the ceilings were panelled or elaborately plastered, with more glorious pictures painted upon them, circled by gilded wreaths. Perhaps it was overdone to English tastes, but Hester was happy to marvel in it knowing she didn't have to live there.

She had a dressing room as well as a bedroom, and got changed into the unfamiliar clothes slowly, pulling on the white silk stockings and black knee breeches, and wondering how she'd feel if she were instead pulling on a new gown. It would be different, she thought. There wouldn't be the fear of having got it wrong, or of being discovered, but a dress would also do nothing but highlight all her deficiencies of form. In an evening dress, one always felt that one was *trying* to be beautiful because the dresses themselves were beautiful, and Hester herself could only ever feel like a disappointment.

But in the black and white of a man's evening wear, she felt disguised in every way. It wouldn't draw the duke's admiration—she'd never had any hope of that—but it might draw his amusement. His attention. It made him give attention to *her*, Hester, the voice who answered him back, the person behind the underwhelming appearance. And, try as she might, there was still a part of her very much addicted to the duke's attention.

A knock came at her door as she was buttoning her snug-fitting waistcoat—a sober grey silk. Willsly had strictly forbidden the red and gold striped affair she'd first set her heart upon.

"Yes?" she called.

"May I come in?"

Her hands and her heart both stopped at the duke's voice.

"Yes," she replied, an effort required to keep her voice natural.

He came into the room, and she learnt that when he'd dressed for dinner on *The Ondine*, he might as well have been dressed for a casual day's riding. She blushed at the set of his shoulders in his exquisitely cut coat, dropping her eyes to the closely tailored breeches which were no better, for they enclosed the muscles there just as tightly. Quickly, she returned her attention to the buttons on her waistcoat.

He came further into the room, then paused, taking a neckcloth from the pile Willsly had left on her dressing table.

"I'm here to offer my services," he said, smiling, though there was a degree of restraint in the stiff corners of his mouth.

She made a brief gesture at her throat. "It is already done."

His mouth quirked, that kindling light in his eye. "Debatable, Harry. Unless perhaps you mean *done for*."

She couldn't help the colour of her cheeks, but she refused to laugh. "I'm getting better at it."

There was a pause. The duke stood, running the strand of the neckcloth through his fingers. Hester pretended all her attention was on her final waistcoat button, but in reality it was on him, on this seesawing moment that rocked beneath her feet as surely as *The Ondine* had ever done.

She could say no more, and he'd leave with a gracious smile and a gentle admonishment to hurry up. And he'd never offer again.

I like the way you do it...

Something lurched inside her with the dread feel of death. Why was he here, making this offer? He knew what she'd admitted on that foolish afternoon, coaxed into truth by drink and sun and the keener warmth of him lying so close.

She suspected suddenly that he himself didn't know why he'd come. Probably he'd dressed it up in his mind as a joke, as he so often did. Thought perhaps it would be amusing to see how she fared with these evening clothes.

Or perhaps his visit to her dressing room was in the manner of an apology.

Or goodbye.

One last time.

I like the way you do it...

She walked towards him, shaking fingers undoing the waistcoat buttons she'd just done up, pulling the neckcloth from a too-hot neck. If she was capable of any thoughts over the beating of her heart, she didn't know what they were, just fragments, spinning and twisted, as useless as a tattered cobweb. The black silk that encased the duke's chest was before her eyes. She could look no further up.

"Very well," she said, dropping the crumpled cloth of her own attempt from stiff, damp fingers. She trembled, though her voice was steady. Animals in a trap were like this, their courage made of anger and fear. "If I don't meet your standards."

Her chin lifted, resolute. She met his eyes. They were very dark, and they felt like...like sorrow. Her courage faltered.

The duke wanted to say something, it was clear in his look, in the tension with which he held the new neckcloth between his hands. But he winced, some internal voice drowning out the others, and the moment crumbled, destroyed by a bland smile.

"Society's standards, Harry, my boy," he said breezily, as though nothing meant anything at all. "Not mine. We're all dogs wagged by the same tail."

He tugged up her collar, brusque and businesslike, the starched points of it reaching her cheeks. The scratch of them was better than tears. She focused on that, on the lines of his own snowy linen.

His fingers exerted their skill. They brushed the skin of her throat once, her jaw twice, a fleeting, glancing, accidental graze of his knuckle that sent a shudder down her spine though she stood as stiff and still as a soldier on inspection. Then he folded her collar down and stepped away.

One last time... There. It was done. She'd survived it. She would go on surviving it.

I like the way...

"Will I do?" she asked.

"See for yourself." He gestured towards a full-length mirror, and as she went to stand before it, he came up behind her with her coat, helping her into it, then placed her hat on her head. He adjusted the angle slightly before stepping back. Their eyes met in the glass. A slender, pale youth, and the tall, dark duke.

"Harry," he said, "I almost believe it myself."

A different coach took them to the opera, older in style but grander, with deeply padded velvet seats and four little pennant flags on the roof corners, each bearing the duke's crest. How odd, Hester thought, that he was obliged to bring those flags with him when he journeyed far from home. What strange, extensive luggage dukes had. No wonder he needed such a large boat.

He was sitting opposite her in the carriage, its interior lighted by a lantern either side. Spotting her twist of a smile, he raised a brow in enquiry.

"I'm thinking about Portuguese opera dancers," she said, purely to provoke him.

"Spoken like a true gentleman. But you needn't get too deeply into character, Harry."

"I enjoyed going about the town today. No one stared at me. Several old matrons smiled at me in a very motherly way, as though they wanted to take me home and feed me. And though the shopkeepers weren't always very respectful on account of my supposed age, they still treated me like a sensible person, able to make my own decisions."

"Ah, but if only they'd known the truth! That you're not a sensible person at all."

She would've kicked him—or nudged his shin with her toe—but he wouldn't forgive her for sullying the perfection of his stockings, so she contented herself with a glare. He chuckled, then looked away, tugging the fingers of his gloves straight.

"I'm glad you enjoyed your excursion, Harry," he said in the very proper voice she was beginning to hate. "You'll have plenty more time for sightseeing tomorrow too. But I insist you take Willsly with you."

"And you?"

"I'll be busy, much as I was today, charming our Spanish friends so that more young Spanish men are sent into this endless war to join the ranks of the British and Portuguese dead." He seemed to recall Charles's existence at the same time it was brought painfully to her mind, his eyes flashing to hers, chagrined. "I'm sorry. But I hate this war. Two steps forward and two back, and for what?"

She didn't speak for a moment. There was both everything to say about the war and nothing, and her heart was too full for either. Where was Charles now? Above the ground, or under it?

"If only it would end," she said, voicing the simplest of her thoughts. "I wish to God there was a way to end it and bring them all home."

The duke's eyes met hers for a moment, a spark in them as though he had an answer to her helpless plea. But maybe the spark was nothing but his agreement, for he nodded heavily and simply said, "Yes."

She was glad for the distraction when they arrived at the opera: the bright candlelight and the bustling silks and bobbing feathers and perfumed air, the women's laughter and men's deep voices. And the expectant hush before the curtain rose.

The music itself was beautiful. She enjoyed hearing a language sung. It added another dimension to spoken words, a way of stretching them and making them into art. Turning to the duke, she would've attempted to share something of this feeling with him, but his attention was caught, not by the action on the stage, but by someone in a box on the opposite side. A woman, her hand lifted in subtle greeting. Hester's eyes fixed themselves back on the stage, but it became harder to enjoy the music.

At the interval, the woman entered their box, accompanied by an elderly man, introduced as a relative, who soon obediently sat in a corner and began to fall asleep.

The woman was of the duke's age, but very beautiful, clearly a native to the country, with dark hair and soft, dark eyes bordered by full lashes. Her dress and manner proclaimed her to be a lady of high quality, and the duke introduced her as his friend, the Condesa d'Edla. The nature of their friendship would have been obvious even to someone who was not, as Hester had suddenly discovered herself to be, possessed of a deeply jealous nature.

Hester and the duke had risen at their visitors' entrance, and as they all moved to sit back down, the condesa took Hester's seat beside the duke. She stood stupidly for a moment, ignored by everyone. Then, sulky and wishing to be no part of it, she took a seat at the very back of the box, across from the dozing elderly uncle, where she could scarcely see anything of the stage. She was only punishing herself. There was nothing now to distract her from the condesa, who spent the remainder of the interval talking very charmingly to the duke in Portuguese that she seemed to suppose young Mr Trunkton couldn't understand.

"How surprised I was, dear duke, when I saw you sitting here accompanied not by some new beauty, but a mere schoolboy! And relieved too, it must flatter you to hear. I ought not admit the haste in which I sent round my card when your ship was spied in the harbour. I will pretend I was in no rush. Let us say I waited a whole hour."

The duke—as far as Hester could see from her seat in the shadowed depths of the box behind them—smiled slightly. "Two hours at least, Maria. It took you that long to choose which perfume to grace it with."

"You are terrible! And no. That was no struggle at all. I remember which one you like best."

The duke made no reply.

"But who is this boy, really?" the condesa asked. "You said not a relative?"

"The relative of a good friend. It's almost the same. Indeed, I like many of my friends more than my relatives."

"But for you to play nursemaid, Lucian! It is not like you."

"You know me that well, do you?"

"Of course I do. But even if I did not, what independent man wants to play at families?"

"If you think marriage and fatherhood make the thing more likely, I hate to disappoint your faith in my sex."

The condesa laughed.

"But is this some new fashion now, for the English youth?" she asked in a bantering tone. "The war has ended your Grand Tours. Is this how you now show your young men the world? On the coattails of its diplomats?"

"Something like that. I believe the boy has always had a wish to see the world. And I can say for certain that this trip has been the very making of him. Harry has been quite brought to life by it."

"And you? You are suffering it nobly!"

"I find it has been less gruelling than I supposed."

Pathetic that those words felt like praise to Hester. Her heart glowed at them, and she despised herself for it. Then, as though the cruel and ancient gods ghosting the exotic night air wished to prove exactly why such a response was unwise, the condesa leant in and said in a low, meaningful voice, "But he does not occupy your evenings, dear duke? Your nights are your own to do with as you wish."

Hester stood up and left the box.

She didn't quite know where to go. The corridor outside was mostly empty, just a few people making their way back to their seats. She headed for the exit, thinking perhaps she could find the carriage and wait inside it. She would plead a headache to the duke when he arrived at the end of the show. If he did.

A porter down in the marble entrance foyer looked askance at Hester when she asked the best way to locate her carriage in the streets outside, not much mollified by either Hester's perfect Portuguese or her explanation that she'd accidentally left a necessary item behind. But an askance look was a great improvement on the scandal she would've occasioned making the same request wearing a dress. Hester Littleton wouldn't be allowed to walk alone from the opera and stroll down the dark street, but Harry Trunkton could. Her alter-ego was almost becoming a friend, a sort of imaginary big brother, ready to get her out of scrapes.

The streets all around the theatre were clogged with waiting carriages, both lacquer and horses gleaming with satin sleekness in the lanterned dark. But the duke's wasn't hard to spot thanks to the pennant flags fluttering from its corners. There was a breeze coming from the sea, carrying the salt tang with it, sharper in the night air than she'd noticed during the day.

A street boy stood at their horses' heads, the driver probably gone to some taverna or cafe to wait, but he was looking the other way and didn't notice her. She opened the door quietly, in no mood for explanations, and climbed inside, wishing she had a light for the lanterns. It was very dark.

There would be a tinder box somewhere, she supposed, and she began to feel around the door for a compartment—then screamed, for out of the darkness a hand grabbed her wrist and a strange voice, weak and panting, gasped, "The duke, where is the duke? I must speak with him!"

Sixteen

Given Lucian had been watching Miss Littleton from the corner of his eye—all his replies to the condesa being made in an effort to make her smile—he saw the exact moment his efforts to depress the condesa failed and Miss Littleton quitted the box. Cursing inwardly, he murmured to his companion, "My young captive has escaped my watch. Forgive me for abandoning you, Maria, but the boy has a knack for finding trouble. And given the way he was talking about opera dancers on the way here, I can only fear the worst."

The condesa laughed but was clearly annoyed and protested the need for him to follow the boy. "He's not a child, dear duke, and will never become a man if he is not allowed to graze his knees."

But Lucian only smiled, bowed, and left.

Outside, the corridor was empty. He walked briskly towards the stairs down and caught sight of a slim, black-clad shoulder rounding the curve of the flight below. He followed but hung back at the foot of the stairs while Miss Littleton spoke to the porter, not relishing the scene that would undoubtedly occur if he were to waylay her here in public. She asked for directions to the waiting carriages, then swiftly left the building. Lucian followed her into the dark street, extremely unimpressed by this demonstration of impetuous stupidity. She might be safer as

Mr Trunkton than a lone woman but young gentlemen were hardly impervious. They were the favourite prey of cutpurses and footpads.

He kept her in sight along the cramped street. She stopped at his carriage and climbed in. There was a scream. He was at the door before he knew it, wrenching it open.

In the faint lantern light coming from across the street, he saw Miss Littleton with a hand to her chest, frightened eyes fixed on a shadowy figure that sagged on the backwards facing seat of the carriage. A hand was clamped around her wrist, pale in the dark. He freed her from it, already smelling the blood, feeling the weakness of the stranger's hand now in his, hearing the faint, struggling breaths.

A call came from the horse's heads—some boy, paid to hold them while the driver went to drink away his wait. The horses shifted nervously, jolting the carriage.

"No," replied Lucian in Portuguese, "stay with the horses. It's only my friend who tripped in the dark. He's quite all right."

He found the tinderbox and lit the carriage lanterns. A man, tanned but still ghastly pale, with blood foaming from the corner of his slack mouth, half lay, half sat on the carriage seat.

"Sit," Lucian commanded Miss Littleton, a hand on her shoulder to direct her to the seat opposite. She looked close to fainting.

"What message have you?" Lucian asked the injured man quickly. From the look and sound of him, he was almost dead. A lung punctured and much blood lost. There would be no saving him. But that this was his contact, he was sure.

"R-Raven...?" the man whispered.

"Yes."

"T-they stole...stole the papers. But..."

He almost lapsed into unconsciousness. Lucian took his hands and roughly chafed them. "Speak, man!"

"My notes...f-find them... L-look... Swan! If you know Swan... It's...all...all connected. Beware..."

The man went still. He would move no more. Lucian looked up and found Miss Littleton very pale and trembling, staring at the dead man. The floor of the coach was puddled with blood. If he could have hurried her away from the horrible scene, he would have. But it was not an option.

"Do you have courage?" he asked her, gently but firmly.

She dragged her eyes away from the corpse and looked at him, her expression lost.

"Do you have courage?" he repeated more firmly.

"Y-yes."

"Then remember it. And use it. Do not scream, please, or succumb to vapours. I can have no attention drawn to us. Do you understand?"

"Yes."

"I must search this man's clothing. Look away if you wish."

She did at first, as he took off the man's coat and felt through the pockets, pressing the lining between his fingers for anything that might be paper. But then, "I'll search it," she said, "if you attend to the rest."

"It's soaked in blood."

"I know."

He handed it to her, doubtful he should, but she took it and methodically continued the search. Lucian returned to the man, searching his trousers, the folds of his neckcloth, the ring on his finger. He took off his boots and searched those too, but it was Miss Littleton who let out a gasp, drawing out a tiny roll of paper from deep in the lining of the coat's hem. She handed it to Lucian, then they both jumped at a tap on the door.

"Willsly!" Lucian said. "Where the devil have you been?"

The man stood in the doorway and nodded down at the body. "Met this gentleman's friends, I reckon. They wanted to serve me the same trick."

Miss Littleton gasped, and Lucian spied the blood leaking down Willsly's arm and dripping from his fingers. His knuckles were grazed and bloody and there was a swelling bruise above one eye.

"Can you drive?"

Willsly nodded.

"Then we'll leave our coachman to his beer."

At the address he directed Willsly to, they quitted the carriage, leaving its occupant and its cleaning to people well used to dealing with such things. The three of them then climbed into a new carriage, and Lucian bound up the knife cut on Willsly's arm.

"This," he told Willsly, passing him the note Miss Littleton had found, "I believe to be the location of my contact's hiding spot. There may be journals and papers we ought to retrieve."

Willsly nodded. "I'll get them."

"No. You'll take Harry home. And then rest."

"Your Grace, much as it pains me to say it, in my current state you'll be the better fighter, and if Harry needs guarding..."

Lucian frowned at the man.

"I can search a room, Your Grace, but if it comes to a fight...my sword arm is weak now. And besides..." He glanced at the corner of the carriage, where Miss Littleton sat very still and quiet at Lucian's side. "I reckon your company is going to be more use to him now than mine."

Lucian turned his head. Miss Littleton lifted her grey eyes to his for a brief moment before looking away and fretting with the cuffs of her coat. There were bloodstains on her fingers.

"I'm quite all right," she insisted.

"You might be," Lucian said, "but I could do with a brandy." He met Willsly's eyes, silently conceding the point.

They'd intervened in a street brawl, Lucian explained to the startled housekeeper who opened the door to them. "And may we please have hot water sent up? We're both in need of a wash."

He assisted Miss Littleton up the stairs, his grip on her elbow changing to an arm around her waist as her steps slowed and tremors began to rattle through her.

"Nearly there," he coaxed.

When they got to their apartment, he helped her to a sofa, where she sat heavily, head dropping to her hands. Her shoulders shook, but she angrily breathed back her tears and insisted again, "I am quite all right."

He knelt on the floor before her and put his hands around her wrists but made no attempt to draw her hands from her face. He understood her wish to hide behind them.

"You are not all right," he said, with her pulse vibrating under the caress of his fingertips. How fragile skin was. "And it is quite all right not to be. Don't attempt to be more than human. It's better to cry now and feel the horror of it and wake up tomorrow knowing it's behind you. You'd wash a wound, would you not, before covering it up with bandages? Wash this with your tears. It'll heal the better for it."

"I am not...I am not *weak*."

"I know you're not."

"But you and Willsly...you're not affected at all!"

"We are, in our own way. And I've seen such things, and a dozen worse, very many times in my life. Don't wish to be numb to horrors, Hester. Such insensibility is against the grace of human nature."

She looked up, the use of her name reaching her in the way

he'd guessed it would.

"If I was really Harry, really a man, would you say the same?"

"Yes."

Her eyes were a little red and very bright with the sheen of unspent tears—and entirely open to him in a way that made his throat ache. Had anyone ever looked at him the way she did now? It was looking into a person's soul, something unfathomably deep, like the well in some fairy story, the water a sweet elixir, beautiful, pure, enchanting. But they were fraught with danger, the wells in those stories, because the fair folk always wanted a great price in return for one taste. Your life. Your soul.

She took a breath, shaky with suppressed tears, and looked down at his hands encircling her wrists. "Who was that man?"

Lucian stood up, taking her bloodstained hand in his and guiding her to her dressing room. The maid knocked at the main door as they reached it and he called for her to come in, waiting until the jug of hot water had been set on Miss Littleton's table and the maid gone again.

"Let's clean up, and then we'll talk."

He left for his own room, washing his hands and wrists and face, even though no blood marred the latter. But the smell of it was in his nostrils, as was the smell of the dying man's fear. His own fear. He swapped his evening clothes for buckskins and a riding coat, unsure what the night would demand of him but certain it wouldn't be sleep.

When he returned to the sitting room, he found Miss Littleton there, standing at the window, her expression very troubled. Like him, she'd changed out of her evening wear, but wore loose trousers and an untucked shirt, an ornately brocaded banyan over it, a riot of red and orange and purple silks and tasselled fastenings.

"I knew it," he said. "Fop to the core."

She managed a smile. "Men's clothes are very plain. I couldn't resist the chance for colour."

"Your dresses—if I correctly recall the one you wore at dinner that evening and the one in which you arrived on my ship—were both of the drabbest hue *and* the dowdiest cut."

"Yes, but then I was dressing as a governess. Now I'm dressing as myself."

He smiled at that and went to the sideboard. "Will you drink brandy? Don't tell me. Charles and Tom have already tried you with it?"

"Yes," she said. "And yes, to both questions."

"Of course," he murmured, pouring them both a glass.

He handed hers to her and they seated themselves—Miss Littleton on the sofa and him on the chair that stood at a close angle to it. She fixed him with a look and he felt strangely nervous. He wasn't usually the one being interrogated.

What would she think of him? He suspected the truth could only create distance between them, make her see him with suspicion—at best. Revulsion at worst. His life was one of dishonesty, the larger part of it lived in the shadows like the lifeless bulk of an iceberg.

He stared into his brandy, hand tight on the glass. He didn't want her to be repulsed. And he ought to. Oh, it would be so much wiser if she threw up a dam and stopped this gravitational flow, the pull that felt inevitable as floodwater.

"Will you give me full answers?" she said. "And not be evasive this time?"

His smile was as brittle as the glass in his hand. Still studying the amber liquid, he swirled it to catch the candlelight. "Will it surprise you very much to learn I'm a spy?"

"No. I think I'd guessed as much."

"I'm not the true sort of spy. I don't go among the enemy, pretending to be one of them and gaining their secrets that way. But I find secrets by other means—by remembering everything that's said to me in unguarded moments or otherwise, by piecing together scraps of information as though they are pieces of a puzzle and thereby making a prediction of what the whole image might be. Most of this information is found in letters. Our government intercepts all foreign mail, and some internal mail when it's sent to or by persons of interest."

Her expression was interested, thoughtful, but not scandalised. "I think we all assume such things go on. That's what you were doing, then, on board the ship? Translating French correspondence and seeing if it held anything of importance?"

"Yes. And from several other countries too."

"And that man?"

"My contact—military intelligence, I think. I was to hand my report to him—all my findings and my assessment of what it might mean—and he would see that it got to whoever most needed it. Wellington, most-like. I'm only one of his many intelligence gathering tools. In return, he would give me a report to bring home."

"And your diplomatic work, that is a cover?"

"It's real enough. And a cover also. I have a fast ship and the funds to use it and can move independently of the army or government—quickly and without the need for a long chain of command. The letters I was working on had only just been intercepted. I was the fastest courier for them."

"But not just a courier."

"No. By analysing them en route, I save the intelligence officers here even more time."

"You're a codebreaker too."

He gave a small nod.

She sipped her drink, the glass held very stoutly in her hand, her slim fingers wrapped around it. Because of him, they'd been dipped in blood.

"Why tell me all this now?" she asked.

"Because you've seen more than I can realistically hide. And I feel your curiosity would be a hindrance, possibly a danger. And because, Hester, I trust that you're on the same side I am. More than loyalty to my King or my country's global aspirations, my wish is to end this war in the swiftest, least bloody way possible."

"Yes," she agreed. "That is something I would give my own life for."

He smiled grimly. "I trust it'll not come to that."

Finally summoning the courage, he looked up and met her eyes. They were shuttered now, and troubled, the raw soul retreated back to its private chamber. But the eyes, the face... They were still utterly familiar. And dear.

"Hester..."

"Am I still to call you Your Grace?"

He knew what she meant by that. A pretence had been dropped between them. If he was to call her Hester, then he ought to be Lucian. A shiver ran down his spine.

It wasn't new to him, this urge for life and skin and touch after stepping into the shadow of death, but this was more than that clumsy rebounding instinct. This want...this need...felt like life or death itself.

A knock at the door snapped the humming thread between them. It was immediately followed by the entrance of Willsly, dirtied, bloodied, coat torn, but his eyes flashing and his step firm even as his hand—which held out a leather satchel to Lucian—shook badly, blood and grime worked into the skin and under his nails.

"You found it?" Lucian asked, standing up and pushing Willsly to sit in his place. He opened the satchel and found it stuffed with papers. There was a leather notebook nestled among them.

"Aye. Though I fair tore the place apart looking for it. That cove was wicked canny."

Lucian scanned his dishevelled form. "Need a doctor, Willsly?"

"No."

"Have this then." He passed him his brandy and began to rifle through the pages. Miss Littleton fussed around Willsly until the man gave in and let her examine his injured arm.

Lucian frowned at the notebook, Willsly watching him.

"Is it what you wanted?"

"It might be. But it's encrypted. And I don't immediately recognise the cipher." He glanced up from the book. "Willsly, before he died, he mentioned Swan."

A very grim look came into the man's eyes. "Devil take it. Then it's worse than we feared."

"What?" asked Miss Littleton, looking up from her gory task. She was bathing Willsly's arm with her own brandy and a clean corner of bandage. "What is it?"

"The fact my contact was murdered, and almost Willsly too, suggests we've been found out by the French. Or..." He paused, reluctant to state the matter aloud. "Or that there's a traitor on our side. And has been for a long time, if Swan was caught up in it."

Her eyes widened. "A traitor?"

"If it's the French, they're very keen on stopping me making this communication. Which suggests they know the importance of what I've found." Willsly sat forward at this, for Lucian hadn't told even him of his progress with the Paris Cipher. "But as only British eyes had seen the documents I'm travelling with..."

"Either they told the French, or they themselves have reason to stop the communication being made?" Miss Littleton said.

"Exactly."

"But Swan..." said Willsly. "How does that bear on any of this, given it was near ten years ago?"

"Perhaps he made the same discovery."

"But who *is* Swan?" asked Miss Littleton.

"My predecessor, of sorts. A British agent who worked in a similar capacity to me—translating, decrypting, analysing. I never knew or met them. Only knew their code name: Swan. They died around eight or nine years ago—supposedly an accident, but given the nature of their work, there was some suspicion at the time."

"And the same hand that killed Swan might be behind tonight?" she asked. "But then...that means you're in danger too!"

"Yes," agreed Lucian, studying the notebook once more. "Clean yourself up, Willsly, if Harry has finished tying that bandage. Get some rest. Sleep in my room; I want you close at hand."

"Yes, Your Grace."

He got stiffly to his feet.

"The men who attacked you—" Lucian began.

"Portuguese thugs," Willsly said. "Hired to it. And I made sure it was the last job they ever did."

Lucian met his eye, an answering grimness in his. "Good. And Willsly...I'm mightily glad you returned to us."

The man gave a crooked smile. "Well, I had to. You'd be lost without me, Your Grace."

Lucian returned his smile. "That I would. Now go and rest."

He nodded and left the room. Miss Littleton stared after him. "Will he be all right?"

"I'll make sure of it." He smiled at her and held out the notebook. "May I hope that a cipher based on what appears to be Portuguese digraphs is of interest to you?"

Seventeen

It didn't take long for them to both realise Hester's codebreaking abilities were on par with her translation skills. She was deeply grateful for all those long winter evenings playing at ciphers with her family.

"That is really what you did for amusement?" the duke asked.

"It was the countryside, and we had little money for any entertainments other than what we could devise ourselves."

They were sitting on the floor, papers strewn over the low table between them. Many were covered in neat lines and grids in her handwriting as she sought to break the dead spy's code.

"Well," he said, after a sip of the coffee he'd ordered to their room. "I suppose it—"

"Served me in good stead?"

They shared a laugh. "You took the words from my mouth."

"If only this were that easy," she said with a sigh, picking up the notepad once more. "You know, this script of his devising almost reminds me of one of my father's own. But here..." She flicked right to the back of the book. "This one is very different."

She held it out to the duke and he took it from her, brow creasing as he scanned the broken lines of numbers. He shifted position, excitement gripping him. "Good Lord, he was attempting to break it himself."

"His own code?"

"No! The *grand chiffre*—the Great Paris Cipher. It's what Bonaparte and his generals use for all their most important messages. We've been trying to crack it for years; it's said to be unbreakable. However..." He paused, looking at her for a moment, then, some decision being made, he reached into his coat pocket and drew out a folded paper. "This could be the very key we need."

She frowned down at the document he passed to her. "A laundry list? A letter of complaints? Oh...but the numbers! These are the ones you asked me about. They're all written wrong. To draw attention to them? Because not all of them are wrong... I wonder if there's a pattern here?" She studied it for a moment. "Yes! I think so. See, here it's correct, and here it's wrong, but there are two different ways they have written it wrong. Sometimes a simple vowel substitution, but sometimes the number is phrased wrong... And if the numbers in the letter relate somehow to the numbers in the list..."

The duke was watching her, intent, as she took up her pen and quickly began to write a list of numbers.

"You see?" he said. "If it is written *en clair*—in context—as I hope, given how clumsily the rest of it has been hidden...someone has used it very poorly. It might just be the breakthrough we need."

She nodded, still writing. It was exhilarating, this work—with him—an energy flowed between them that seemed only a natural extension of all the currents and eddies already there. Glancing up, she found his dark eyes intent upon her, appreciative and encouraging, but it wasn't only his admiration that sent a warm spark to thud down low and join all the banked embers deep inside. He was honest now—about this, at least. He'd given her the truth of his work, and with it, a screen had been taken from his gaze, as a shutter is drawn from a lantern.

The dark look burnt deeper.

But no time to think of that. She pulled her mind back to puzzles and logic and the scratch of pen and paper.

When a knock came at the door, the duke answered it cautiously. The hour was very late, the servants in bed. Hester glanced up, watching him exchange some passworded greeting, then open the door and converse quickly with their visitor without them entering the room. They left, and he locked the door and sat down again.

"A message to say another person will visit us—our contact's replacement. I asked for them to come at dawn because by then we may well have something even better to give them than I first thought, if we can crack any of this—the *grand chiffre* or this notebook and whatever it might say about Swan." Lucian frowned at the notebook. "The man who this belonged to was no ordinary contact. I believe he was Wren—my counterpart here."

"This French code ought to be our focus," said Hester. "It's what might bring the war to a quicker close, if it gives our army the advantage."

The duke nodded. "That's my thinking too. And a night spent attempting to solve it won't delay our hunt for the traitor much."

"You trust this new messenger?"

"They had the correct codes. It's impossible to trust anyone at the moment."

"Then we ought to take this to Lord Wellington ourselves."

The duke looked at her. "It's a very long and dangerous road across the Peninsular. Word has it that he's on his way to Badajoz, if he's not there already. And that will be a hard-fought battle. I'd not take you with me."

She almost protested, but there was no time to waste on such a discussion, so she got back to work.

Gradually, they began to get somewhere, teasing out meaning from the strings of numbers—working out the numbers for some of the most common words. She had a breakthrough about some tenses and what they signified for the meanings of the subsequent words, and the duke identified a block of false dummy code, the excising of which made their whole task far quicker.

By dawn, much of the task was done. "A few more hours and we would've had it all, Harry," the duke said ruefully, putting down his pen and easing an aching hand. "But Wellington's codebreakers will make short work of the rest."

"Even with this, they'll be able to understand the majority of any dispatches they intercept. It's only the more unusual words we don't have enough material to decode."

He looked at her across the table, eyes as tired as hers felt, but there was a deep warmth that made her forget her fatigue for a moment. Her heart, the daft thing, lifted and gave itself a squeeze.

"You," the duke said, "are one of the most intelligent women—most intelligent *people*; let us not limit you to a class of only half the world—I've ever had the fortune to meet. And your work here tonight might help bring a swifter conclusion to this war than anyone yet dreams of."

She was sure she looked extremely stupid at that moment and not intelligent at all. Blushing, she began to arrange the papers more neatly on their table. "We ought to make copies of this. And it wasn't me, it was you and that unfortunate man who lost his life to it."

"We'd made some chicken scratches. You took the lead tonight, Harry. *Hester*. I merely did all I could to keep up."

She was extremely glad when a knock came at the door. Lucian stood. "That will be my contact. I'll ask him to wait half an hour while we make copies—actually, he can help us. We should *all* make a copy."

He opened the door and a dashing young officer dressed in the red coat and black trousers of the light dragoons stepped into the room, a black plumed hat under one arm. He wasn't tall, and rather slight in build, but athletic and energetic in his stance. His hair was light brown, and his eyes—bright with intelligence—were grey.

Hester scrambled to her feet, near swaying. "Charles!"

Her brother blinked, staring at her, mouth hanging open for a moment. "Who—? No! What the devil! Who *are* you? You can't be!"

But she'd already thrown herself at him, her arms around his neck as she hugged him so hard he staggered. "Charlie, oh Charlie!"

"But it can't be!" He tried to set her back from him, grinning, frowning, amazed. "No! Hessie! How on earth...? What the devil? How can you be here and dressed like *that!*"

"It is me! It really is! Oh, Charles!"

He hugged her back so tightly she couldn't breathe.

Hester broke free, taking Charles's hand and dragging him to the duke, who was standing, watching the proceedings with his usual amusement.

"Your Grace, this is—"

"Your brother Charles, yes, so I see." He made a bow and held out his hand. "Mr Littleton—or, no, I correct myself, Lieutenant Littleton, judging by those stripes."

He shook the duke's hand. "Yes, sir. Or—" He glanced at Hester. "Your Grace? As my sister called you."

"The Duke of Cumbria," the duke replied. "Very pleased to meet you."

"So *you* are he... But..." And he stared once more at Hester. "Devil take me, Hessie. I've no idea what *you* are doing here. And in all that get up. And your hair!"

"A long story," the duke said. "And I must go and check on my servant who took a nasty wound in the course of his duty last night, so I'll leave the telling to Miss Littleton's more than adequate words."

He bowed, tactfully giving them their privacy, and Hester drew Charles down to sit beside her on the sofa. He stared at her, dazed, then started to laugh. "Lord, Hessie, what kind of a scrape have you got yourself into now? But, wait! First you must, you *must* tell me, is Jane...?"

"She is well! Completely well, Charles. Other than missing you desperately, of course."

Her brother's eyes shadowed with guilt. "If I could return to her..."

"I know, and you will. But to even know you are alive and well will be the greatest comfort imaginable to her. We've had no word! We did not know. And I thought you in the 95th, how are you a dragoon?"

"A long story too. But you didn't get my letters? I sent three at least!"

"Not one!"

"All intercepted? All sunk? And here I was wondering why no one wrote to me."

"We did. Many times."

"But you wouldn't have had the right direction. No wonder they didn't reach me." He pressed Hester's hand, searching her face. "By God, it's good to see you, Hester. Even if I scarcely recognise you. No, I'd know that face anywhere! But tell me, please, how did any of this come to pass?"

"Well, it was the duke, I suppose. He came to visit us to make Jane an offer—"

Charles stood up, hand going instinctively to where she guessed a sword normally hung at his side. "He did, did he?" He took an angry stride about the room. "The Duke of Cumbria!

Yes, Parling's old friend, I know. And I suppose they nagged her something vicious to take him, with me gone just as they wanted, and presumed dead—also just as they wanted, no doubt!"

Almost all of this was correct, but given the last thing she needed was for her hot-headed brother to call out the duke, she protested, "No! No! Not at all, Charles. As soon as I explained to the duke how things stood between you and Jane, he withdrew his offer."

"As if she would ever have accepted! Not my Jane!"

"No, of course not," Hester agreed promptly.

"But this doesn't explain how you came to be here." He cast a scowling glance at the door through which the duke had exited. "What hand had he to play in that? And I find you here, rigged out so peculiarly, alone with him at night and unchaperoned? Good Lord, Hester, just what has happened?"

"Charles, come," she coaxed, taking hold of his hand and drawing him back down to his seat beside her. "It's all my own doing. You see, I...I didn't quite manage to explain about Jane until *after* we'd left the country..."

Charles listened to her incredible story agog, alternately horrified and laughing until he could not breathe. "Lord, *Hessie*. Only you!"

"I know. But, you see, it's quite all right. My identity is safe. No one knows I'm here at all. And I'll be able to return to England with my reputation perfectly intact. As you know, the Parlings won't breathe a word of my disappearance to any of our acquaintances. At most, they might seek the assistance of a runner, but only in secret."

"Oh, yes," agreed Charles sourly. "We know how well their hopes for Jane rest on her good reputation, given her lack of fortune. And they'd *still* want to marry her off to a duke, even *if* they believed he'd kidnapped and ruined you. Parling never got over his old school friend Wellbeck being raised so far above him. Having Jane a duchess would do much to satisfy him, I'm sure."

The substance of what he'd said about her kidnap and ruin appeared to catch up with him, momentarily pushing Jane from his mind. He looked at Hester. "Sister, how can a brother ask this...but...you are well? He has...not injured you?"

"The duke has not touched me, Charles. As I've been trying to explain, this whole charade is to preserve my reputation."

"But there's a difference between the *appearance* of one's reputation and the *reality* of it." He ruminated on this for a moment until his grey eyes flashed with anger. "The truth is still the same, Hess. You've been alone in his company for weeks. By God. There's only one woman he should be thinking about marrying, and that's you! If he had any sense of honour, he would've done it already."

Hester looked up, heart skipping at finding the duke in the doorway. She didn't know how long he'd been there, but there was little hope he'd not heard her brother's angry declaration. It had been spoken loud enough to be heard even through a closed door. Yet the duke gave no sign. He merely smiled at her and closed the door quietly behind him.

"Willsly is asleep, Harry. And there's no sign of fever. I'm sure he'll be perfectly fine. He's recovered easily from far worse." Finding Charles staring intently at him, he explained, "Willsly is the servant of whom I spoke. He received a bad cut to the arm today."

"That's not the name I'm concerned with," answered Charles. He stood up from the sofa, then looked rather foolish because the duke pressed a glass of brandy into his hand and sat down himself, gesturing for the younger man to do the same.

"It's *Harry*, I suppose, that you don't like?"

"I don't like any of it, sir, Your Grace, to be blunt," said Charles, sitting down again. "You can dress my sister in boy's clothes and give her a boy's name, but it doesn't change the fact that she is not a boy."

"I'm aware."

"And so what do you mean to do about it?"

Hester winced, blushing, and wished she could treat Charles as she used to when he got on his high horse—namely, smother him with a cushion. But the young lieutenant in his smart uniform, with his skin tanned and weather-hardened, his eyes hardened too by things she could only guess at, and his lithe body honed to nothing but energy and muscle, was a very different man to the boy she remembered.

"I mean to do exactly as I've always planned. Return your sister to the Parlings' care as unsmirched as she left it. And no," he said, lightly holding up his hand to cut off Charles's retort, "I do not mean to marry her. I cannot make her a duchess. And, most importantly"—there was a faint gleam to his eyes, despite the firmness of his voice—"I have it on her own authority that your sister doesn't wish to marry at all."

"Tosh," spat Charles.

"But he's right," started Hester, though her insides were trembling as though from a hard slap. "I did say that."

"When things have got to this stage," Charles addressed the duke, "it matters not what the lady wants."

"In that we must disagree, for to me, her wishes will always take precedence over society's irrational dictates."

This must be how a boxer felt in one of the matches Charles and Tom had been wont to so avidly describe to her. The duke's first declaration had been a heavy blow from the left, this latest came from the other side entirely and left her dazed.

"Littleton," said the duke while Charles ground his jaw. "Two things you must know. First, your sister is perfectly safe with me. Second, I'll not deviate from my course. So can we pretend all the arguments you wish to unleash at me are said and done? They'll make no difference, and we have other things to discuss tonight."

"Charles," Hester added quietly. "Please, it really is quite all right. You don't need to fret over me. I promise you."

He looked at her briefly, still very angry. In a low voice, but one he surely knew the duke could hear, he said, "Of *your* honour, I have no doubt, Hessie. But that he can sit there and so calmly deny the duty of his own, I find hard to stomach. I could not call myself a man if I were in his shoes."

"The wonderful thing about my shoes, Lieutenant," said the duke. "Is that they're so very accommodating, flexible, you see. But may we move on? Your uniform, it has the look of the dragoons but you're not really one of them, I believe?"

"No. I serve Scovell. I'm in the Army Guides."

The duke nodded, as though this exactly confirmed what he thought. Hester was less satisfied by this answer, and, seeing her confusion, Charles explained.

"They're Wellington's intelligence corps. Major Scovell, my commanding officer, is his chief codebreaker and head of the corps. When my captain in the 95th discovered my aptitude for languages and maps on our passage to Lisbon, he decided to recommend my transfer. The exchange of regiment was made the day I landed."

"So that's why I could find no record of you," mused the duke.

"We're a little secretive by nature," admitted Charles. "We don't quite exist, you see."

"I suspect you've seen a fair bit of Portugal by now?" asked the duke, and Hester, who had experienced the tactic herself, recognised his friendly fishing approach to conversation.

"I'd say! I think I've ridden the whole Peninsula three times over."

"Know it like a local, eh?"

"Parts of it. We often keep to the back routes and wilder paths. Less chance of being spotted by the French."

"You've certainly got pluck, Littleton. I can't say I'd fancy riding alone to scout out enemy lines."

"And often through them! I admit sneaking through a French camp gets the blood going, but I'd choose it over marching into a line of French artillery. I think, God willing, we each of us end up pulling the plough we can best bear."

Hester, her blood chilled by this conversation and the very real dangers her brother faced daily, was glad when they moved back to the discussion of the documents on the table. Charles was fully aware of the importance of what they'd discovered, his hand almost shaking with excitement as they each began to make a copy of the decryption key. That done, he stood up, all haste to get gone.

"You ride to Wellington?" the duke asked.

"Yes. He'll be at Badajoz."

"A hundred and fifty miles or so."

Charles smiled. "I have a good horse. Arab, goes forever." He grinned. "Won him off a Portuguese captain. The man was blue devilled, all right."

"Charles—" began Hester, and stopped, her heart breaking. She hated the tears in her eyes. She hated saying goodbye. She hated the danger he rode into and how her cowardly heart wanted to beg him not to go.

He came to her, and kissed her forehead, hugging her tight. "Seeing you, Hess, it's set me up for months. I'll remember this. And this hair!" He tweaked a stray lock. "You'll go to Jane the moment you get home and tell her...tell her I..."

"Yes. Yes, I will, Charles. I'll tell her."

He swallowed, nodded, bowed to the duke, and left the room.

Eighteen

"Your brother will be quite all right," said Lucian.

Hester was staring, miserable with anxiety, at the door which had just closed behind him. Lucian picked up his brandy and gave it a meditative swirl. "After all, he has right on his side." He glanced over at her. "Go to bed, Harry. Get an hour or two of rest. We'll sail for England today, as soon as tide and winds allow."

She went without protest, as silent and lonely as a ghost. It was what she wanted, he knew, to be alone for a moment and not have to be brave.

The moment she left the room, Lucian followed Charles. He found the young man in the stable behind the house, just having mounted his horse.

The young lieutenant looked down at Lucian, his black hat now low over his brow, the black plume a shadow against the weak dawn sky. He frowned, his feelings clearly mixed, and was the first to speak.

"I would've asked for a word alone with you, Your Grace, if it would've made any difference. But as you've made clear that it will not, I'm at a loss as to what you can possibly have to say to me."

He looked very much like his sister and clearly shared her lack of reverence for Lucian's lofty station. As a specimen of youthful masculinity, he was hot-headed and stiff-necked, but Lucian preferred him to the spineless Irwin, who agreed obsequiously with everything he said.

"Having formed a pretty good estimate of your character in the last hour," Lucian began mildly, "I'm sure everything I have to say is something you don't wish to hear, and one at least you'd sooner strike me for than have me mention to your face. But let's not be boring; we'll start there, with the subject of Miss Jane Parling."

Charles stiffened.

"I left England having offered her my hand in marriage. I'll retract the offer when I return, unless the lady wishes to hold me to it." He cut the indignant Charles off before he could speak. "*Which* I am sure she will not. But you'll agree, it must be the lady's choice."

Hester's brother uttered an oath she would've been delighted to record in her vulgar dictionary. Lucian hid his ill-timed amusement. He supposed it was a serious matter, to Charles, at least, and that he ought to dignify it by not laughing. In truth, he'd long ceased to have any wish to marry Miss Parling. The proposition was rather like a wet pair of shoes: bearable at the time when the rain gradually soaked them, but unpleasant indeed to put on again once they'd been taken off.

"Don't fly into a rage," he advised Charles. "Save that energy for the ride."

"Very well, sir," said Charles, head flung back. "What else do you have to say to me? You said there were several things."

"This next, you'll hate just as much, but I'm compelled to say it. Littleton, it's in my power to arrange for your transfer to the intelligence office in London, where your talents are much in demand. And where, I need not say, you'll be out of harm's way. And free to marry Miss Parling too, which I suppose might be something you value even more than your life. You can sail today, on my ship, in your sister's company."

The young man went very pale, very still. When he spoke, his voice was a ragged whisper. "What manner of devil are you, to tempt me with this? And at such a time?"

"A brute, I know. The worst of men. But someone else can carry the message."

"I cannot leave my duty!"

"Yes. And it's unkind indeed of me to tease you with such forbidden fruit. If I have any kindness in me, it's for the one who would mourn you more than you know if the worst were to befall you."

"Jane—"

"I am speaking of your sister," Lucian interrupted him. "It is for her sake that I make this offer."

The lieutenant fidgeted with his reins, his agitation communicating itself to his horse—a high bred chestnut with defined Arab lines—which side-stepped, pulling at the bit. But Charles was an able horseman, soothing the creature with a hand on its neck, soothing himself, too, the duke divined.

"The rest of what I have to say is this," said Lucian, speaking to give the young man more time to gather his thoughts. "Don't put haste before caution. As important as the message you carry is, it's useless if it does not arrive and worse than useless if it falls into enemy hands. They cannot know the code has been cracked." Charles's focus was on his horse's mane, a strand of chestnut twirled around a tightly gloved hand. "And lastly," added the duke, "if you do arrive at Badajoz before it's taken, from everything I know of the earlier siege at Ciudad Rodrigo, the French garrison won't retire at the first breach. It'll be a hellish job. I won't advise you to keep out of it, for you won't listen, but keep your wits about you and don't sacrifice yourself for nothing other than heroism's sake."

"I thank you, sir," said Charles quietly. "But I know my job and how to do it."

"Yes, I'm interfering. It's a bad ducal habit of mine, but it's kindly meant." He inclined his head and would've made to leave, but Charles spoke again.

"I've no wish to die, Your Grace. You've seen Jane. My heaven waits here for me on Earth and I won't quit this sphere before I reach it."

"Then for her sake, as well as your sister's, may God be with you."

Charles didn't return Lucian's bow but held his eye. Slowly, stiffly, he said, "I'm not insensible to the efforts you've gone to on my sister's behalf. It was her impetuosity and recklessness that brought her into your orbit, and I'm sorry for the burden you've had. And while I do thank you for the care you've taken of her and am at a loss how to repay you for such an unusual service, to my mind, you've left the task incomplete. None of us here have asked for the trials laid on our shoulders and yet all of us who are gentlemen will do our duty by them." He didn't once look away but held Lucian's eye as he inexorably continued. "You refuse to take her as wife and give her the inviolable protection of your station, and why? Only because you think she is not equal to being your duchess. Well, *Your Grace*, my sister is equal to anything. If you think she's not good enough, then I'll not press the matter, for you don't deserve her, and I'd not have her made miserable by being bound forever to one who'll only resent her. Let this war be over and myself returned to England, and I'll take care of her myself. All I ask, as my current duties render it impossible for me to do so, is that you get her home safely, Duke. I will thank you for that. But I cannot love you for it. Hester thinks you're her saviour, but all this hiding of her identity is as much for your sake as hers, is it not? To prevent yourself becoming trapped into marriage with her."

Lucian inclined his head. "It is."

"Then I hope you'll be the only one to regret it. Though I fear all the damage will be on the other side. But you are a fool."

With that, the lieutenant turned his horse and was away.

Lucian found a servant and had a message sent to Captain Moore. Then he went back upstairs and hastily wrote some letters—some of very great importance to Beresford's people, and some to all the dignified persons whose invitations he would not be able to gratify, having been *called back to England by a family emergency, with most regretful apologies etc., etc.*

These, he left on the tray to be delivered later that morning. The first letters, and a copy of the decryption key, he delivered personally to an official he trusted. As always, he was pleased to return to his lodgings unmurdered by an unknown enemy.

With their notes tidied securely away and anything unnecessary burnt to stop it falling into the wrong hands, he went to his room and began to pack, very quietly, so as not to wake Willsly.

This task soon failed because every coat that wouldn't perfectly fold and every item that wouldn't fit into the place it normally fitted soon drove him to a murderous rage that would've had him sending the shaving box in his hands crashing against the wall and waking poor Willsly if he'd not swiftly quitted the bedroom and gone to lean his head against the cold glass of the sitting room window. He stood there for some time, watching Lisbon come to life under the morning sun.

The problem with being a duke… The problem with being this particular kind of duke, with a title inherited from a father shackled by it, was that he found himself shackled twice over, being subject to the same obligations his father was as well as to the memory of the man himself.

"You're more free than I am, Charles," he told the city, though the gallant lieutenant would already be several leagues distant. "You'll get to marry your Jane." *God be with you. With you and your blistering scold!*

He turned to find Willsly standing blearily on the threshold, blinking and rubbing his face.

"Alive?" Lucian greeted him, packing his feelings away with more success than he'd packed his clothing.

"Seems that way, Your Grace."

"You'll soon wish you weren't. We must be ready to sail by nightfall. We've a very busy day ahead of us."

"Aye," agreed Willsly. "Starting with me repacking those trunks you massacred."

Lucian chuckled. "As you please, Willsly. But go and see how Moore and the ship fare first. I want to know when he expects we can depart."

Willsly nodded and went to the door.

"And Willsly..."

"Yes, Your Grace?"

"First get some breakfast for yourself. And when you do come to the trunks...I beg you to please make sure there are no women hiding inside them."

The man grinned and left the room. Lucian moved from the window with a sigh, needing to shave and change, but a sound from Miss Littleton's room made him pause halfway to his.

He knew even before he reached her door that the sound was of someone in a restless sleep. Not quite the cries of a nightmare, but fretful mutterings. An unhappy voice, a cut-off whimper that was almost a sob.

There was no point standing here with his hand on the door handle debating with himself; it was obvious he would go into her room. It was obvious that he could no more walk away from the sounds of her distress than that her brother could leave his soldier's duty to flee for England.

He closed the door softly behind him and went to her bed, hoping to soothe her somehow without waking her. But her eyes opened the moment he reached her bedside, and she reached out, took his hand, and pulled him down beside her.

She was still dreaming, he thought. Not really awake as she burrowed, crying slightly, into his side and his arms came around her. They lay like that for a while, her head on his chest as it had been the night of the storm.

"He'll be all right," he said quietly, stroking her hair, hoping his voice might penetrate the wretched dream. "Charles will be all right."

She relaxed eventually, falling, he thought, into a deeper sleep. His arms tightened around her thin shoulders, and he pressed his face against her hair, overcome by his own sort of wretchedness and needing, just for one moment, to let his own weakness show.

She was asleep; there was no witness to see the Duke of Cumbria crumble and prove that he was nothing but a man as stupid and weak as all the rest. A man who didn't always know the right thing to do and sometimes wanted what he couldn't have. Wanted it desperately.

He held her tightly. She was so slight in his arms. But, somehow, she also seemed his one point of safety.

"Hester," he whispered against her hair, needing to name it. This moment, this feeling.

She moved, lifting her face. She might never have been asleep; perhaps she knew it all—his weakness, his fears, his wants, had known them since they met. It should've dismayed him, but he found himself smiling as her red-rimmed eyes looked up and focused on his.

"I'm sorry you didn't have a better experience of Lisbon."

She moved so they lay side by side, looking at each other, heads upon the same pillow. Her grey eyes were very close.

"I saw my brother," she said. "That was worth all the unpleasantness."

"You'll have to come back one day, when the war is over, and take a proper look at the place. Travel all around the country. See it properly. Spain, too."

She gave him a small smile. "I'm unlikely to ever travel, Your Grace."

"Nonsense. The income from your vulgar dictionary will set you up for life."

She smiled again but sadly.

"I know we have a long journey ahead of us," she said, "and much important work to be done decrypting that notebook, attempting to find the traitor, solving the mystery of Swan...but I feel somehow that our adventure is over. I must...I must start remembering how to be Miss Littleton again."

Lucian stroked a lock of hair back from her brow. "You've been her the whole time."

Her eyes held his. "Will you kiss me?"

When he froze and made no reply, she said, "As a goodbye. Or in celebration for what we've found out. Or to distract me from my anxiety. Or because you pity me. I don't care why, but it's what I want. Before reality begins again."

He smoothed that stray lock of hair back into place, keeping his hand very slow and steady as though a drumming pulse wasn't defeating all the sense in his body. "There are a hundred better reasons than those to kiss you. And a hundred more why I cannot."

"Are any of those good reasons?"

"Hester..."

"I like it when you say my name."

He paused again, his heart racing, his eyes dropping unavoidably to her lips. He watched them smile.

"I'm being terribly forward, aren't I? I told you I was never a very proper sort of woman."

"You have never been kissed before," he said quietly, a statement, not a question, his eyes still on those faintly smiling lips as his finger came up to lightly trace them. Her breath stilled beneath his touch.

"No," she said, barely a whisper. "I have not." He met her eyes again and her voice firmed. "You told my brother the only thing you cared about was what I wanted, not what society wanted for me. This is what I want. You. Lucian."

His name on her lips sent a shiver down his spine, a tremor that joined the heat swelling there, tightening him until he ached. But it could only be a kiss, just a kiss…a girl's first kiss, a press of lips… No, no. It should not even be that.

"Hester…"

She touched his jaw, a gentle but determined exploration, her fingertips scraping over his stubble, over his ear, into his hair. His eyes shut as the touch of her fingers sent his desire spiralling.

"Please, Lucian. I know I have no right, I know I'm a no one and you can never marry me, but—"

His finger on her lips stopped her saying more. "Hester." He scolded her with her own name, angry, though she only spoke the truth. But it was a lie when she said it. It was a lie because she didn't *know* the truth. She thought the problem was her. But it was him.

"You're not no one." His voice was low and strange, a soul's whisper. "You're the only one."

But…?

It was there in her eyes, in the pause between them. His body wasn't listening though. He was hard and heavy with want. It was exhausting holding back, denying and denying and denying… His finger was still pressed against her lips from where he had shushed her, and now it traced along them, uncovering a sigh, a warm breath that clung to his skin, skated along his palm, and escaped all the way down to the thin skin of his wrist where his pulse beat madly.

Skin was so fragile... They might die today, tomorrow, bleed out in a dark carriage, just another spy lost to the game...

"Every girl should have a kiss." Hester's whisper held back a desperate laugh, a wretched sob. "At least once in her life."

Once? It would be his undoing; it would be the breach that cracked the dam.

He took his hand from her lips and cupped her cheek; he bent his head...he kissed her.

"Hester."

He breathed her name as his mouth lifted from hers. She was so sweet, the press of her lips so soft and giving that one small kiss had to become two, and this time his mouth lingered, and the hand she'd slipped into his hair held him there.

She exhaled shakily, her eyes closed, a tremor going through her. He felt it in his own body, lying close against her. He pressed, gently, softly, and she sank pliantly onto her back. Now his thigh moved across hers, and he braced himself over her on one elbow. His other hand traced her cheek as he held himself there, determined to go no further, no matter his aching need.

"Lucian..." she breathed, and he'd forgotten already that he was supposed to stay still. His head sunk down to meet that breath; his mouth grazed over hers, tasting his name on her lips. At the touch of his tongue, she opened to him, letting him feel the warm inner lip, the dampness of it against his. He traced it slowly with his tongue and she gasped, letting him slide his tongue inside to meet hers.

So much for a press of lips.

God damn, he should stop. But the answer to every question seemed to be right there, in the soft welcome of her mouth.

She moaned and an answering noise came low from his throat, heat sweeping his thoughts, his arousal hard against her thigh, shockingly sensitive with want. Her legs were bare beneath the silk of the banyan; he could slide his hand up her calf, her knee, her thigh... His hips shifted against her, and, Lord, it would've been hard enough to stop, but she met the movement with her own, drawing a grunt from him.

Oh, curse him... What rogue was he? All his care and promises for naught?

"Hester, no..." His voice was hoarse as he drew her hand from his neck and pressed it shakily to his lips—a shield of sorts between them. "We must stop. I've already done more than I ought."

She stared up at him, pupils very dark, breathing hard. But she didn't protest. She must feel it too, the precipice on which they stood and how easy it would be to get swept over. For her, he suspected the sensation of it was new, and that the force of it frightened her a little. She nodded slightly and tried to smile, and he almost kissed her all over again for that.

"Yes," she said as he moved away from her and sat up. "I...I understand."

He still had her hand in his. Was loath to let it go. He pressed it to his cheek, to his lips, knowing all the things he ought to say. *It was wrong. It could not happen again.* But the words got stuck in his chest. They were a lie.

It wasn't wrong... It was the first right thing in his life...

But that it *could not happen?* Damn and damnation. He could weep. For that was no lie at all.

"You should start to pack," he said, getting up from the bed and tearing his soul. "We'll leave as soon as we're able."

Nineteen

A SPRIGHTLY BREEZE ALLOWED them to leave Lisbon harbour before nightfall. Captain Moore let the breeze take them westward, both to avoid the Portuguese coast and in the hope of finding fairer winds for their northward journey, but he was inclined to be pessimistic. Hester left him shaking his head in conversation with Lucian and went below to her bedroom. She took dinner alone there, exhausted by all that had happened now the bustle of their hasty departure was over.

In the morning, she broke with her routine of the outward journey and opted to breakfast alone too. She was in her accustomed place in the dining room, sitting on some cushions in the morning sunlight that came through the row of windows, when Lucian found her. It was the first time they'd been alone together since it had happened, and his guarded smile told her he knew she was avoiding him and why, and he would not mention it.

Your secret is safe with me, his smile seemed to say. Except it wasn't. None of her was safe from him, and she knew his own secret too. She knew lots of things now that she couldn't forget, like the taste of him and the pressure of his body half covering hers. It was why wishes ought never be granted. Everyone knew it was unwise.

Time and time again, she'd taken herself to task for repining over nothing more than a kiss. Kisses were nothing! Jane, she knew, had kissed Charles on more than one occasion. She'd sighingly told Hester all about it, no matter how Hester tried to avoid listening. Georgina Parling had once kissed some young friend of Tom's who'd been visiting. And Elizabeth, a girl to worry anyone who loved her, had kissed three. Of course Tom knew nothing of this. But it all proved that kisses meant nothing. She'd been the oddity, to have never stolen one or had one stolen, but she wasn't the sort of girl men ever sought to get alone in shrubberies.

And this wasn't that sort of kiss, her rational brain protested. It wasn't a hasty peck of lips to be giggled over afterwards—to be giggled about even as it happened. It was the razor-sharp edge of a very great confession, it was the rattling pebble that preceded a rockfall, it was the beginning of the fall itself... No. Too late for that. She'd already fallen, long before she lay there and begged for a kiss.

But the shame wouldn't come. How could it, when he'd clearly felt the same? She wasn't enemy enough to her sex to take the sin of desire upon her own shoulders. Men felt it, were unapologetic about it, were even, if the ribald stories she'd read were true, somewhat proud of it—found their own animal instincts amusing and even egged them on. There was a whole industry of prostitutes in service to it. So, no, she wouldn't blame herself and acquit him when they'd been equals in want, if nothing else.

If that was all it'd been, she would've forgotten it sooner. But the confession hadn't just been in the kiss. It was the duke coming to her room, lying beside her, holding her in his arms while his own breath shook and he breathed her name against her hair as though it was the last gasp of a drowning man. And that same confession, it had been in the kiss too, interwoven through it all, stitched into the touch and the taste and the heat of it until there was no separating them.

That was what had passed between them. It was *that* the duke had said they must stop and now, with every look and word, promised her he would forget.

He sat down beside her without saying anything, and she turned the page of the book on her knee so stiffly it tore a little near the top.

"I find it's worse," she said, "to have been teased with joy and had it removed. It's far worse to have hope than have none."

The duke looked at her, hearing the betraying agitation in her tone. She forced it from her.

"I'm speaking of Charles," she said. "I cannot stop thinking about him, out there, alone. Now that I've seen him... Now that I know he lives...and...and what he faces... It was easier when I'd heard nothing of him and almost stopped hoping."

The Ondine moved sluggishly, the rocking of the ship hardly greater than it had been in harbour. They'd be becalmed on this sea for weeks. No news would reach them. On those back roads and wild passes, he might never even be found.

"Your brother is experienced, clever, energetic, and courageous. Let us trust him to come through safely."

"A hundred and fifty miles!"

"Harry..."

Something deep inside her cringed away from the name.

"I know, I know." She closed the book with a snap. "I will put it from my mind."

"Don't ask the impossible of yourself. But have faith in your brother." He smiled wryly. "A man with Miss Parling waiting for him will not quit easily."

She gave a hollow laugh. "Like Helen of Troy, I suppose. If a face can launch a thousand ships, maybe it can bring one man home." She sighed. "I hardly know what to tell Jane. She'll be happy in the extreme to know Charles lives and is well, but that we had to leave him behind, and facing such a mission..."

"I'd dwell on his lieutenant's uniform," the duke suggested. "And how dashing he looked. It might prove fairly distracting."

Hester gave him a flat look, managing to avoid looking at his mouth. Memories of it crept continuously into mind. She shook her head, smiling as a new idea occurred to her. "But of course, they can get married now! A lieutenant might not be as grand as a—"

"Duke?"

"But surely Mr Parling will give his permission?"

"He will. Because I'm going to order him to. Indeed, I think the man must be a nodcock not to have done so already. Anyone could see that with a little assistance Charles is a man who'll achieve much in life. It is pure snobbery that has kept them apart."

Hester raised an eyebrow and muttered, "Imagine!" But if the duke heard this critique on his own choices in a like situation, he chose to ignore it.

"If your brother remains in the army, he'll not be a lieutenant for long. He already has Major Scovell's eye, and likely that means Wellington's too. And if he leaves the army, I already have a position in mind for him in London."

She opened her mouth to thank him, but the duke added, in his usual laconic way, "Of course, I'll need to have a few words with the lady myself beforehand. And her father. How embarrassing it'll be to admit I've changed my mind."

"You needn't fear offending Jane. She'll be very glad."

He gave her a mock bow. "My ego thanks you."

"What will you do now, though?" she asked, pretending the question didn't make her heart thump painfully. "You had a motive for proposing to Jane."

He picked up a cushion and put it behind his back as he leant against the panelled wall. "The Regent has a list. A half dozen ladies whose fathers' gratitude at gaining a duke for a son and a duchess for a daughter would greatly benefit himself."

She stared at him. "I can hardly believe Jane was one of them!"

"No. She was my own choice. Beautiful enough, you see, to make Prinny sympathetic to my wishes. It's hardly a secret he has a weakness for women. Her face would probably have brought his leniency for my act of rebellion. Such beauty is useful, you know—the soft power of diplomacy. And she was far more palatable to my mind than the other women I'm supposed to choose from. It wasn't much of a choice, but it still would've been my *own* choice, which is all I had grown to care about. They already own my life. I wanted this one decision to be mine."

"So you are...are being sold off!" she said, horrified.

"The dukedom of Cumbria has only ever been a tool of the Crown. The King created it for my father to bind his counsel to him—bind his loyalty, because my father's political wisdom was a crutch he came to rely on as his health worsened. I inherited the title, and with it, the chains."

"But you are still a duke. You cannot be *forced*."

He smiled bleakly. "Can't I? Have you ever said no to the King...or the man who holds the King's powers?"

"But what do they threaten you with?"

He shifted his seat, moving the cushion to a more comfortable spot. "Oh, it is nothing so vulgar as all that. They don't need to *speak* their threats. I would merely...lose favour. Life, in a hundred subtle ways, would start to turn against me. Business ventures would fail, investments would flounder, court cases would be brought against my ownership of certain tracts of land, invented relations would appear out of nowhere to contest my claims, bastards I've never sired would be thrown at my door, scandal would dog my steps, and, in my line of work, it would be very easy to invent some crimes against me. Perhaps it was me who had that man killed in Lisbon. Perhaps I killed Swan. Perhaps I've been leaking evidence to the French for years. It could all be easily done."

"And this is the Crown we are fighting for? This is who Charles is risking his life for this very moment!"

"No," the duke said gently. "We do that for our country. We do it so foreign soldiers do not alight at our shores and rape and pillage every village the way they did in Portugal and Spain."

He met her eyes, his own soft and sympathetic, as her chest rose and fell with the passion of her indignation. *Now you see,* his expression said. *Now you see why I cannot marry you.*

Why he would never kiss her again.

Yes, she saw him as he really was, a bound prince, shadows all around him. And she, with her plain face...she didn't have the power to break the curse.

She turned her head away to hide the sting of tears and let out a long, shaky breath.

"Here," said the duke, pulling a familiar notebook from his pocket. "Shall we see if we can make any progress on this? Perhaps if we can find Swan's real murderer, I'll be free of that charge at least."

Twenty

"I'm certain this cipher doesn't translate to either Portuguese or English," Miss Littleton said sometime later, papers in her neat hand and his own slanted stroke strewn all around them. Surely this was a new torture technique some of his less savoury acquaintances would be delighted to learn the trick of. Working next to the woman you craved, watching untouchable lips frown in thought, your heart cracking a little further with every creak of the ship's timbers. "And the methods used remind me of my parents' techniques. If only I had their notes here."

"Do you have them? At the Parlings'?" asked Lucian, shifting his position on the floor. Miss Littleton might be happy working here, but he was beginning to wish for a chair. Four-and-thirty and too old to sit on the floor; old enough to know he should never have kissed her.

She knew everything now. Knew the stark chains that bound him. They clinked, awkward, in the silences between them. Shameful, to be revealed as a duke with no real power. He might as well be *The Ondine*, blown at the world's whim. Mayhap he'd be dashed against the rocks and left broken and sinking.

Perhaps he already was.

"Yes. A whole box full," she said. "The house was cleared after they died. The Parlings wished to let it straight away. But I saved all their journals and papers."

"And they really taught you all this? Codebreaking as well as languages and everything else?"

"As I said, it was something of a parlour game to us. And there's not much difference, you know, between breaking a code and deciphering an old, unknown language. My mother had an interest in those. Well, in cuneiform scripts, in particular."

Lucian smiled to himself at learning more of this rather remarkable family. "Of course she did. She'd read Grotefend, I suppose?"

Miss Littleton looked up in surprise. "You know of him? Yes! She corresponded with him frequently on his work deciphering the Niebuhr inscriptions." She gave her own fond smile. "We may've been a very modest family living quietly in a modest cottage in the Hampshire countryside, but you wouldn't believe the visitors we had. Great minds from all over Europe came to speak to my parents, and they were forever in correspondence with experts and amateurs. One of my earliest duties was to read such letters to them over breakfast, because they couldn't even wait that long to get started on the day's work."

"What a heavenly picture of intellectual life. And all the time the roses were scenting the air around the doorway and the hollyhocks swaying beyond the windows," said Lucian, remembering her dreamy description of her childhood home, "and the swans were paddling in the duck pond…"

He trailed off, meeting her eyes, the same idea occurring to them both.

"No…" she breathed.

Lucian sat forward, aching bones forgotten. "You said the swans in the duck pond were visible from the study window where they worked?"

"Yes…"

"Two expert linguists, who just so happened to enjoy codebreaking and ciphers, in frequent correspondence and with many visitors?"

"Yes... But..."

"And who died in the same year that Swan died—eight years ago, you said. Miss Littleton, how did your parents die?"

She looked at him, her grey eyes very serious but resisting, denying. "It was...it was a very brief illness of the stomach. Something they ate." She looked at him again. "Something they *ate*," she repeated. "*Poisoned...?* No... I can't believe it... My parents murdered..."

He moved closer to her, taking her cold hand in his, fighting an urge both gallant and entirely opposite to pull her into his lap. She stared at nothing, too many thoughts all occurring to her at once.

"But they *can't* have been spies," she broke out, "or intelligence officers, or anything of the sort like you are. They never went anywhere! Never even to London!"

"Swan was a codebreaker. But where it is a part of my duties, it's not my main one. There are others much better at it than me. My main utility is my ability to travel at speed, on this ship, or over land, and with little care for cost—and also my title, which allows me access to many homes and offices a lesser peer might be denied. We're recruited and used in whichever way we're best suited for. Swan was a codebreaker," he repeated. "And your parents' house, so near to Portsmouth and the mail packets and any other boats and visitors..." He swore under his breath. "And my father, a friend of the Parlings! He once used to visit them often. Your parents dined with the family, did they not?"

"Yes. They were close friends, despite the Parlings' later snobbery."

"So my father would have met your parents. The value of their language skills would've been immediately obvious to him." He met her wide-eyed stare. "It was he who recruited them, or recommended it, at least. I'm sure of it."

She shook her head, but he could see the idea was beginning to be believed. It fitted the facts too well to be easily denied.

"Your father was a spy too?" she asked.

"No. But he made use of their intelligence. He had an ability to analyse it all and interpret it and make likely predictions. It was one of many things that made him so useful to the King. And it's what he taught me to do too. Though I've no taste for the politics of either court or government. I keep to the road as much as possible to avoid it."

"So he raised you to this life."

"I believe it seemed clear to him I'd be allowed no other. It was the price we paid for our family's advancement."

"And now we're all caught up in it." The look she gave him was clear and steady. "I'm in danger too, now, aren't I? In continuing my parents' work, I've made myself vulnerable to the same fate."

He squeezed the hand he still held. "No one knows that Hester Littleton was with me in Lisbon. And Harry Trunkton is a mere boy. I believe you're as safe as you could possibly be—but it means..." He paused. "I'd wanted to make your contribution known to the Regent. To ask for some reward, some recognition to come your way, but..."

She shook her head again. "I don't want it."

"We'll find the traitor. Then we'll all be far safer."

Her smile was grim determination. "Then we should get back to work."

They worked until dinner and took that meal in Lucian's cabin, neither willing to break from the task which had taken on such feverish importance. They ate in a very uncivilised manner, still reading or writing and paying the barest attention necessary to what lay upon their plates. Until, looking up from his work, Lucian focused on Miss Littleton across the table from him, a hand pinching her forehead as she squinted at her work, the end of her pen between her teeth, and found himself chuckling.

"What is it?" she asked, looking up.

"I was wondering if this was exactly how your parents carried on." He gestured to the books among their dishes, the notepad he held in his left hand with his fork in his right.

She laughed, smiling at the scene as she sat back in her chair and took it in. "Yes. Exactly so. But worse. My father's sleeves were forever spotted with ink, but I cannot believe yours ever would be."

He pulled a face. "Absolutely not."

The laughter in her eyes met his and got tangled up. Like two carriage wheels locking on a crowded street. No. That was hardly poetical, was it? Held none of the warmth in her gaze. Nor the heat.

A man looking at a woman, alone in a darkening chamber, all the notebooks and work and fears dropping out of sight, as though a curtain came down and left only the two of them here, alone…

A man with his heartbeat suddenly thudding everywhere: in his throat, in his wrists, in his thighs. He remembered their kiss. Found it amazing he'd had the strength to pull back. Ridiculous things, men, in moments like this, all animal heat and brutish longing, and as sensitive everywhere as a raw-shucked clam.

Still not poetical, Lucian.

But he shouldn't be wanting to be poetical; his pulse shouldn't be hammering away at his good intentions. It never got any easier. He never managed to want her less. He looked down at his plate. Felt the pen thin and hard between his fingers, and gripped it.

"And my mother," Hester said, the bluster of embarrassed confusion in her voice; he'd not managed to hide the heat in his gaze, "was known to sketch runes on the tablecloth, much to our housekeeper's despair. And once, when my aunt came to visit and scolded her for her unladylike preoccupations, she spent all the evenings of her visit embroidering cuneiform script on our pillowcases rather than our initials."

Lucian smiled, relaxing his hold on the pen. "I'm beginning to see that you never had much chance of being a proper lady at all."

"No." She laughed. "None at all."

Again, he stayed smiling at her a moment longer than he ought, then dragged his eyes back to the notebook. It was no good. His eyes were tired and grainy; his thoughts would no longer focus. At least not on anything other than the woman sitting across from him. He set the notebook down with a sigh.

Miss Littleton had returned to her former preoccupied pose, now tapping the pen against her mouth as she muttered to herself.

"You'll get ink on your face, never mind your cuffs," he chided her.

She glanced up at him from under her lashes and merely smiled.

He stood up, stretched, wandered about, and found Willsly in his dressing room blacking his boots despite his firm instruction to rest.

"But it takes my mind off the pain, Your Grace," protested Willsly with a sacrificing, seraphic smile that didn't at all remove Lucian's suspicions the man was playing chaperon.

"Go and find an off-duty seaman to fleece at dice," said Lucian, unmoved. "Or get acquainted with the French brandy you smuggled aboard. And remove the dinner tray. We finished a half hour ago."

"Feeling a little tense, Your Grace?" enquired Willsly innocently, getting to his feet. "Pity I couldn't fence with you this afternoon. But another few days should see me fit enough."

"Another few days will see you overboard."

Willsly grinned. He was the sort of man who liked vicious horses and wild weather. Lucian's current mood had aspects of both.

"Maybe so, Your Grace. And I always do find that a good dunking in cold water is a suitable cure for many a thing that ails you. If I might venture to suggest you try it?"

Lucian narrowed his eyes. "You may not."

Willsly held his ground. "It'd be a sight less permanent than the…ah…other approach. And a sight less damaging to all parties."

"Go and do your job, Willsly."

He paused significantly. "But I am, Your Grace."

"The tray, Willsly. I'm in no need of your advice."

The man's bow was more of a shrug, but he went into the cabin and reappeared with the tray, giving his master no more counsel than a very speaking glance before shutting the door to the passage firmly behind him.

Lucian returned to his cabin and found Miss Littleton had returned to her favoured position upon his bed, though there was nothing but the endless dusk of the ocean sky to be seen beyond the window.

"It might be German," she said, not looking up from her notes. Lucian sat at his desk.

"German?"

"The language encoded by this cipher. Do you know anything of Wren?"

"No. But I believe he was English."

She shrugged, scratching through a set of glyphs. "Even so."

"Even so," he repeated, eyes lifting from the movement of

her pen to the mouth frowning over it, the delicate chin, that disreputable patch of freckles. Grey eyes met his.

"Are you tired, Lucian?"

His heart hitched at her use of his name. "No."

"You're looking at this bed with longing."

He got to his feet and abruptly paced the length of his cabin, where he then occupied himself trimming the wick of a light that did not need trimming.

"But it's probably a good thing if you retire to bed, Harry," he said, turning back to the room, without quite looking at her. "We've, none of us, had much sleep lately."

"Does it help? Calling me Harry?"

The boat seemed to drop beneath his feet, though the sea was still unnaturally calm. *This is a role reversal,* a detached, observing voice said at the back of his mind. *She sits serenely upon the bed, calmly picking at your secrets, unravelling you...*

"No. It doesn't help."

A full and pounding silence was her answer. Then the slow, meticulous movement of putting her notes away, leaning over to set the whole lot down on the floor by the bed.

She lay down.

"You might not be tired, Lucian, but I am. Tired of pretending."

He stared at her, a slim figure on the white sheets.

"Pretending? You know everything now. You know why I can't marry you."

"I'm not asking you to."

"No? Just to ruin you? Then what has this whole charade been for?"

She turned on her side, a loose, languid movement, entirely the opposite of the oak-hard knots inside him. With her head cupped on one hand, she stretched out her other arm, turning the palm this way and that in a casual examination.

"I find...I'm not really here. No one knows where Hester Littleton is. No one knows what she is doing. I find..." The hand drew back, clenched into a fist on the sheet by her chest. Now her body was taut as rope. "I find I'm going mad, Lucian. Denying this, acting as though it's nothing at all, when it...it's everything."

Forced-back tears choked the end of that sentence, and Lucian started forward on instinct, sitting down carefully on the edge of the bed.

"I'm sorry," she said, face hidden in the crook of her arm. "I tried to be strong. I tried..."

He stroked the hair he'd cut what seemed so long ago. It was already growing longer. A few weeks more, and she'd be returned to drab dresses and schoolrooms. Harry would be no more.

His hand tightened convulsively, buried in the soft locks, catching them between his fingers. A tug on the scalp, nothing that would've hurt her, but enough that she turned her head, lashes wet as she looked up at him. He loosened his fingers to accommodate the moment, let the strands run through his fingers like water.

She brought her own hand up and held his there, palm splayed, cupping her face.

"I've tried too," he said. "Hester...I don't know what to do."

And there, there was an admission he'd never made to anyone, hardly even to himself. Lucian Grey, second Duke of Cumbria, did not know what to do.

He looked to Hester for advice.

"All I want," he said, his voice cracked and raw, "is not to hurt you."

"We both know that's not possible."

He closed his eyes as the pain of that broke over him. He felt her shift beneath his hand. Softly, she pressed a kiss to the base of his thumb. Sparks scattered, burning up his spine, even as the impossibility of it all felt like death.

"You once told me to forget about propriety—the stupid, non-essential parts. So don't be stupid now, Lucian, with this talk of ruining me. Is that really what you think? I'm ruined by this?"

"No."

His eyes snapped open as she moved to lie on her back again, still holding his hand, and now, maddeningly, freeing the button at his cuff.

"So if it doesn't injure me in your eyes, and if it doesn't injure me in my own..." She spoke as she worked on his sleeve, her voice conversational even as she folded the white fabric back to bare his wrist. "And if the world knows nothing of it... Or is it God you fear? Does God not care about your Portuguese condesa? Maria? Or any of the other women you've undoubtedly had."

"It's not God, Hester, it's myself."

His muscles were locked, rigid, but deep inside, he trembled. *This is how it feels to fall... Honour crumbling, nothing but dry pebbles, beginning to slide...*

"You can't marry me," she said, running a thumb over the tender veins in his wrist. "And...well...I'll marry no one else now. But I know the loneliness of the life that awaits me and how flat and small everything will appear after this adventure we've shared. And something in me revolts against going quietly back into that cage. Don't you see, don't you understand?" She pressed a kiss to his pulse, and Lucian, throbbing, let his eyes sink shut—let himself drown, just for a moment, in the warm swell of want.

"I can't have you," she said, a hitch of emotion breaking the calm bravado of her voice, "except for now, before our journey ends. And it is...it is *insulting* when you look and talk as though this feeling between us isn't real and as though we aren't running out of time."

"Hester..."

"If you don't want to hurt me, at least admit you feel this too. One more truth, Lucian, before we both go back into our boxes."

Twenty-One

THERE WAS SOMETHING PLEADING in the duke's eyes. But then he bowed his head with an exhale and turned over the hand she held so that her palm was clasped within his.

"I've tried so hard to preserve your reputation. I *promised*."

When he looked back at her, the familiar implacable will was in place but edged with something sharper.

"Do you really want the truth, Hester? The truth is that I love you. I've loved you by slow degrees. If you love words, you should know that yours are a magic spell. Every one is a brushstroke, revealing a perfect form." He squeezed her hand. "You."

Her racing heart swooned to a stop before racing off once more as his gaze slowly tracked down to her lips, then back up.

"The truth is that I admire, no, *worship* your mind. The truth is that I adore every moment of your company. The truth...the truth is, that if it wouldn't prolong the war, I'd wish the wind never blew again and we could stay here forever. I've little I want to return to. Not without you."

He spoke the words as though they were weapons he thought might hurt her. They did. Joy this big was painful. She was surprised she could speak.

"It might be weeks yet."

"But it will come."

"Everything ends. One way or another."

"Death?" There was a great deal of bitterness to the arch of his brow. "It's long been my only hope for escape."

That confession seemed to embarrass him. This must all be very strange to him, admitting so much. He was looking out of the window beyond her, mouth flat, eyes stormy.

"Lucian..." She called him back to her, half smiling though she was hot all over, trembling.

His dark eyes hooked hers. "The truth, Hester, is that I desire you to distraction."

Heat flamed low in her belly.

"Do you...do you really?"

It was a dream, this moment; they were enclosed in a giant's heart, the very air hot and pulsing.

He stilled, hand tensing around hers. Then he breathed a soft laugh.

"Yes, Hester."

"Kiss me again?"

His gaze tightened. "That's not really what you're asking."

Her thigh muscles clenched, restless, as though they could still the swirling heat low in her stomach. Now it was her turn to shy from the truth.

"Will you kiss me?" It was a whisper. A plea.

Ruin me...please.

"Madness," but he was talking to himself. "It's all been madness since you climbed out of that damned trunk."

But he hadn't moved, hadn't let go of her hand. His eyes roamed once more to her lips, then down, skating the length of her body and right to that point where all the heat was gathered.

Her thighs pressed together again, that ache insistent, and he knew, his chest rising on a deep breath, his hand hot around her fingers.

"Kiss you?"

She gave a small, sharp nod, and then he was leaning down, warm and close, and he...pressed a kiss to her forehead.

"Lucian, that is not what I—"

"Shhh."

There was a smile in his voice, damn the man. A smile in the curve of his lips as he brushed them across her cheekbone and then—*oh*—to her mouth.

She sighed, a breath of ecstasy, and his mouth came back to catch it, to return it to her with a touch even sweeter and fuller.

"Hester..." Her name was a low caress, his breath warm on her cheek as he brushed his lips against her. "Do you think I have the strength to pull back again?"

"I don't want you to."

His exhale was a tormented ghost. But he shifted his position, the bed dipping as lay down beside her. They lay facing each other, his face close to hers on the pillow, as it had been in Lisbon. His finger traced over her cheek, light as silk, but leaving a trail that shivered down her spine. His dark gaze held hers with fierce focus.

"I love you. And I'll ruin you. I told you once that I'd always been able to return to society a gentleman, no matter what I'd had to do. But I won't be after this."

"I love you," she said simply. Because it *was* simple. "And I want this. You think too much."

A smile cracked his gravity, slowly growing broader as he gazed at her. "So it seems you really *don't* want a man with his mind on higher things."

She grinned back. "Not right now, Lucian, no."

His gaze tightened at the use of his name. It seemed to do something to him. Good to know.

His hand brushed over her cheek again, but this time it slipped into her hair. He watched it, as though the simple gesture entranced him, the sight of his fingers disappearing among the strands. Her heartbeat kicked up another notch, everything inside her humming as the laughter fell away from his eyes and the intensity returned. He moved, so that she was on her back, then he met her eyes once more before he kissed her again.

Her third kiss…and it was just as thrilling as the first. Intoxicating and strange and alien and wonderful. He knew exactly how to do it; it didn't matter that she did not. His lips were warm and sure, then came the wicked feeling of his tongue: a taste of her lips, and then sliding delicately inside to touch against hers. Strange, how blissful it felt to be invaded like this, the taste of Lucian in her mouth, the heat of his breath on her skin, the pressure and weight of him over her. All of it only made her want more, her body turning loose and melting and open.

"You have no idea how much I want you," he breathed, his forehead against hers. His knuckles skimmed over her cheekbone. "Know it," he said, brushing her lips again, "know it always—another truth—that whatever happens, I wanted you every day I was with you, I want you now, will always want you…"

She tilted her mouth to his because that was easier than talking. He groaned as she opened to him, his tongue once more finding hers.

She kissed him back, let him taste her as deeply as he wished, no games or evasions now. She was so hot everywhere, far too hot, pulse racing, her heaving chest confined by the neckcloth wound around it.

And still he kissed her, even as he shrugged out of his coat, fitting the action into necessary pauses for breath. He lifted her to sit up, a hand under her shoulders, and helped her out of her own coat, helped her clumsy fingers undo her waistcoat buttons and pull it from her.

There was a pause then. He met her eyes, asking, checking, before he slowly slid the knot of her neck cloth from her throat.

She was already pulling her shirt free at her waist, and his hands came to settle over hers, stilling them for a moment.

"It's what I want," she said, and he gave a minute nod before, together, they lifted her shirt free and over her head.

A shiver went through her, as much from his eyes on her bare skin as from the touch of the air. He ran a finger along her collarbone, drawing a delicious shiver, then down to the white cloth that hid her breasts. "This is my neckcloth."

"I always wear yours."

Something like pain crossed his face. She felt it too. A surge of everything still unspoken, that might never be spoken because it was only doomed. Then his hand ran down to her stomach, his other came to join it, and together they encircled her waist as she knelt on the bed before him.

She shivered again, but differently this time, the way an animal does when confronted with a much larger beast. She was very small, his hands very large.

Had she really had the courage to bring him to this point? The Duke of Cumbria, serving kings, that far-too-clever codebreaker, that implacable, unknowable man; somehow she teased him and begged him for kisses... But the breath he let out was unsteady; he was as shaken as her.

As though he must do it before he lost courage, his hands went to the fall of her trousers and undid the buttons with practised ease. She lay back on the bed, and he drew the garment from her, underclothes too.

He sucked in a breath, one hand tracing lightly up her thigh. He was barely touching her but her skin was singing, almost unbearably sensitive. Her heart thudded as he trailed a finger over the hair between her thighs and his eyes lifted to hers. He nodded to the fabric that bound her.

"Will you take that off for me?"

Lifting herself to her elbows, her hands went shakily to the knot at her spine. Once, twice, the cloth unwound. She dropped it to the floor.

The air against her was almost more than she could stand. He drank her in, eyes roaming, in no hurry, though she could have cried out with anticipation, with needing—she *needed, oh God...please...*

"Perfect," he praised her, his voice low, not taking his eyes from her for a moment as he undressed himself.

It was her turn to look as he pulled his shirt over his head, revealing the muscles of his stomach and chest, the dark scattering of hair. No hiding anymore, no secrets... His shoulders were strong, his arms corded with slender muscle.

"I don't have to explain things?" he said, a smile in the corner of his mouth as he unbuttoned the fall of his trousers. "Not knowing your reading habits."

She smiled back, though her heart was racing, and her eyes kept dropping to what he was revealing. "The classics are very educational. I won't faint."

His smile broadened, a little wicked. "Words to bolster any man."

But when he came back to the bed, he lay with no part of him touching her.

"We don't have to. You asked for a kiss."

"Lucian. I want to." A little wickedness crept into her own smile. "And you once told me the only thing that mattered was what the lady wanted."

She felt the rumble of his laugh as he leant down to kiss her throat, her collarbone. "It's true. In all parts of life, it's true. But especially this one."

With his mouth light against hers once more, he moved closer, his hot body brushing against her skin, all the muscle and the strength of him laid bare. And the silken hardness of him against her hip.

His hand ran down her back, pulling her more firmly against him. It was strange, and it was glorious, the strength of a man's body against hers, his chest against her breasts, the hot, silken weight of him now against her stomach, but most of all, it felt right to be like this with him. She wasn't shy or doubting. It felt as natural as anything had ever done, an inevitable extension of all the things that flowed between them, all the words and looks and smiles that had drawn them closer, stitch by stitch, until she hardly knew where she ended and he began.

His thigh moved further over hers, and she wondered if this was it, the moment of the act all humanity gave such importance. She felt ready, crazed with a need for more, for him—an instinct she knew from her own explorations and that his first kiss had brought blazing to life. But still he lay beside her, not over her, and he kissed her very gently as his hand slowly stroked down her chest and cupped her breast.

The sensation made her gasp, his hand so warm and large, her sensitive bud pressed into the heat of his palm. He looked down, watching his hand on her breast, then met her eyes, the darkness in his molten. "Do you like this?"

"Y-yes."

"Tell me what you like. What you don't like. But don't worry, we'll go slowly."

"I told you I'm not an innocent!"

"There's a great difference between reading of something and experiencing it."

She could think of no better reply than to run her hand down his chest, learning the feel of his muscles beneath her fingers, and down further, while he tensed, eyes dark on hers, until she found the hard heat of him and wrapped her hand around it. He breathed an unintelligible curse and sank his head against her shoulder as she explored the thick ridge of him.

He groaned, but his hand stilled hers. "I've wanted you too

long to stand much of that."

She smiled her triumph and he kissed the grin from her face. "Imp," he scolded, mouth moving to her throat as his hand returned to her breast. His thumb found her peak and brushed over it, making her whimper, and he looked down at her with his own smug smile, repeating the action. "Do you like *that*, Hester?"

"Yes," she gasped, surprised at how intense it felt.

"And this?"

Now he moved his mouth to her breast. His tongue flicked her instead and she panted, shocked all over again. Every bit of heat and throbbing tension she'd felt before suddenly grew tenfold.

"And this?" he said, which was all the warning he gave before his lips closed around her and he sucked, making her moan. He moved his head to her other breast and repeated the treatment, and she momentarily lost awareness of her surroundings.

"Lucian..."

"The sound of you moaning my name, God, Hester..."

His released her from the torture, watching her face as his hand came to rest on her thigh. Her heart kicked, thumping painfully as he ran his fingers up, pushing her thigh gently to the side. She didn't need urging but opened her legs, the expectation of his touch agony. She needed him there, *please, please...*

He groaned as his fingers brushed against her. She trembled, thighs tight, stomach tight, as his fingers swirled and slid where she was warm and slick. Then one slid slowly in, thicker and surer than her own fingers ever were. She moaned at the sensation, reaching for his shoulders, his neck, pulling his mouth down to kiss her.

"You're clenching around me," he murmured against her lips, as he slowly tested her with his finger. "So tight... But I fit you. It doesn't hurt?"

"No... No. It's...good."

He added another finger.

"Ohh..." she breathed, hips shifting of their own accord.

A satisfied gleam in his eyes. "You like this?"

"And you like to hear me say so." It was an effort to talk. His hand didn't stop moving.

"If it's true."

"It is. I like it. I...I like it very much."

He praised her with a kiss, then his head went to her breast, his thumb swept over her down below as his fingers slid slow and sure within her. The sensation was all too much.

"Lucian... Lucian..."

"That's it, my love, go on..."

Love was the word she heard. *Love*...as she surrendered to pleasure and heartbreak both.

Twenty-Two

LUCIAN WATCHED HESTER'S FACE as the pleasure broke over her, easing her gently through it before slowly taking his fingers away. She opened her eyes, breathing hard, and looked up at him. It was more than he could do at that moment to speak, so he kissed her instead, hoping he didn't betray how shaken he was. Because as keen as the arousal that had been stirred by the sight of her body was the protective urge that'd accompanied it.

He hadn't expected it, hadn't felt it before, not like this: this need to hold her, not just for pleasure, but to shield her, so unbearably precious was she. To hold, and to possess, and to make her his in every way a man could, or even as a beast did, and stand snarling between her and the world.

Well. There was a nice puzzle for his puzzle-honed mind. How to dedicate your life to protecting and having a woman you could never be with.

Hester ran her hands into the hair at the back of his neck, bringing his thoughts back to a preferable present. She pulled him to her mouth then stroked down his neck and along his shoulders as they kissed. Smiling against his lips, her hand moved down between them to take him in her grip. He let out a breath, eyes sinking shut. She stroked over the sensitive tip and he hissed.

"Will you tell me what *you* like?" she said, hesitantly letting go.

Devil take him, for he what he said was, "We've done enough," even as he took her hand and guided it back, closing his fingers around hers. "We have"—his breath caught—"done more than we should."

"But far from all." She smiled up at him as she stroked him. He let go her hand, but she didn't stop. And he should make her stop.

"Suetonius," he said, struggling to speak. "Dangers of education—"

"What's this? Lucian Grey, incoherent?"

He cursed and stilled her hand.

"You're still a virgin, Hester. We've done"—she gave him an experimental squeeze—"devil take it—enough."

"It won't ever be enough," she said, voice incongruously serious given the position she had him in. "Not between us."

"And if I get you with child?"

"You know how not to."

She released him—mercy and torment in one—and threaded her fingers through his hand, shifting until he was on his back and she was half lying over him.

"You've shown me a foreign city and travel," she said, "and adventure and danger and death and intrigue, and I refuse to go back into the little box that's deemed appropriate for women, the small scrap of the world men leave us, denied as we are from politics and business and commerce and sport and even art and science and philosophy..." Trust Hester to be talking like an orator even as his hands irresistibly slid up her legs to cup her bottom and settle her firmly atop him. "Won't you open up this corner of experience to me? It's my only chance. With you, I feel safe. There's no other man in the world I'd trust to do this and not despise me, or hurt me, or afterwards attempt to control me with the secret of it."

His grip on her hips tensed at the thought of any of that. Her chest was against his, hearts beating as one, as she looked down, earnest, entreating. How good it felt, her skin against his, no barriers between them. He felt drunk from it.

"When we get back to England," he made himself say, "I will walk away. We will have done this, and I will have to walk away, and you'll despise me—as you should."

She paused, finger tracing down his chest, her mouth twisted with a frown. "I'll only despise you if you think me too weak and stupid to know my own mind."

Too many arguments crowded his thoughts, most of them old and tired. She kept looking at him, then raised herself onto her knees, one either side of his hips. Still looking at him, she gripped the base of his straining shaft and guided it to her entrance.

"Hester..."

She had lowered herself until he was touching the wetness of her. But she paused when he said her name, his every muscle locked tight.

"If there's a way to marry you, I'll do it."

That startled her. But all she said was, "I know," then she lowered herself.

He let out a low breath as her warmth and wetness started to envelope his tip, hugging it tight. Oh God...white-hot pleasure burned all the thoughts clean from his mind, the dazzling blindness of lightning's aftermath. Still she pressed down, taking him deeper. She made a small noise, pausing, and her eyes met his, her confidence starting to turn to doubt, and embarrassment, and something vulnerable that pierced him far deeper than any duty placed on his shoulders by King and country.

His darling...breaking herself upon him... How could he take this? How could any man be worthy of this?

"Does it hurt?"

She didn't want to say it, but she nodded.

"Come here." He slid his hands up her arms, from wrists to shoulders, and pulled her down so that he could kiss her, the two of them still tentatively joined, him aching and rock hard, just cupped in her hesitant wetness.

He kissed her slowly, deeply, pulling back to murmur, "We don't have to."

"But I want to."

Her voice was tight with frustration and embarrassment. And he knew her well enough to know she meant it and didn't want to have to beg.

"I'll only despise you if you think me too weak and stupid to know my own mind."

"Then let me help you, my love," he whispered, kissing her again. He cupped her breasts as he did so, rubbing over the sensitive peaks, again and again, until she was panting. Then he reached one hand between them and started to circle the delicate bud just above where they joined.

"Oh...that feels..." She moaned faintly and he felt her open to him. Instinctively, seeking more, she started again to sink down upon him, and he slid deeper, and deeper, until, with a whimper from Hester, he was buried to the hilt.

He closed his eyes tight, fighting for control. But she took him... *God*, she took him so well, clasping his whole length in pure pleasure.

His breath was ragged. "You're all right?"

Her eyes met his as they had done once before, wide open and exposed, revealing her down to her soul. But there was heat swirling with the rawness of her emotion, and an impish smile crept into the corner of her mouth. "You look like the one in pain."

He had to laugh—and how strange that felt, held deep inside her. "Not pain, I promise you."

His hips shifted, his stomach muscles rigid with the effort of holding still. She gave a surprised breath at the slight movement, and he held her hips, slowly beginning to rock her forwards, backwards, only the slightest motion up and down while she grew accustomed to his size.

She was awkward at first, but she made a noise of pleasure, then another, finding her rhythm, and he nearly lost himself far too soon. *Lucian Grey, incoherent,* he mocked himself in her voice, *Lucian Grey, spilling like a schoolboy.*

It didn't help much. And now he was looking up at her body, at the small breasts with their reddened tips, the curve of her ribs, the thatch of damp hair where he disappeared inside her. That really didn't help either.

He gritted his teeth, struggling, but unable to help watching himself move into her as though this was his first time too. It might as well have been; he wanted only this, only her.

He let his head sink back, exulting in the feel of her working him, but soon enough his hand was tight on her thigh, guiding her to a stop.

"We have to move if...if I'm to control when and where I..."

Thank God for her quick understanding. Her eyes widened, her cheeks flushed, but she moved off him and lay down. And then, perhaps with more haste than he was proud of, he was over her, gently finding his way back inside. Joining them again. *God, forever...*

He moved slowly, a hand under her hips, tilting her further open.

"All right?" he breathed.

She nodded, gave a whimper of embarrassed pleasure, and buried her face against his shoulder.

He closed his own eyes, letting touch and feeling override his other senses. His body urged speed, but he went slow, building an insistent rhythm, feeling for the flutterings and tightening of her muscles around him. She was moaning now, close, and he moved faster, letting himself chase his own release as he reached down between them and touched the part of her that brought her shuddering to her peak.

She cried out, fingers clutching his shoulders, and he remembered just in time to withdraw.

Twenty-Three

TO HESTER, THAT FIRST night together was their wedding, in all the ways that mattered. He'd cleaned her, cared for her, held her, then kissed away her soreness... And so, if that was the wedding night, it made sense for the weeks that followed to be their honeymoon.

If it really had been, she could've thought of none better. Sailing with Lucian on a calm and drifting sea, with no society or callers to take up their time, and no duty upon them but the work they did together, equal partners on that vital task... What better marriage could there be? They took every breakfast together, and often their dinners too, where it would not have caused Captain Moore suspicion. In short, every moment of every day was spent in happy companionship and every night in each other's arms.

The crew were told young Trunkton was sick again and had been moved back to his guardian's cabin. Willsly knew the truth—had known it all along, try as hard as he might to protect them from it. He said nothing to Hester, and if he spoke any word of censure to Lucian, Hester didn't hear it. But the loyal valet sighed as he went about his work, and there was an anxious, sympathetic look in his eyes when he met hers, the frown of a man shaking his head, saying, *I did what I could; it's out of my hands.*

She was too happy to worry, at first. Every moment of her days was a dreamlike bliss. To sit on the bed and work together with her back against his chest, him with notebook in his hand, her with paper on her knee... To lie with her head upon his lap and be lulled to a doze by his hand on her hair and the motion of the boat... To look up with tired eyes from her writing and meet his look from where he sat at his desk... To be teased over breakfast, his scalding humour rousing her to indignant mirth even as he buttered her roll for her and filled up her coffee cup without her needing to ask...

And they talked. Not just of the work and their frustrations with it or the minutiae of their journey, but of their lives, Lucian gradually revealing himself. She came to understand that much of his earlier evasion had been due to natural humility as much as the necessary secrets he kept. He really couldn't understand why she found every detail of his childhood and youth so fascinating.

As he'd once warned her, there was little excitement in the story of his life, but she listened to the descriptions of his home and his sports and his boyhood pursuits and tutors and accidents and joys as though he was telling a fairy tale of dragons and immense heroics. And he hadn't been quite honest before when he told her there had been no tragedy in his life, because she soon learnt of his brother, Robert, two years his senior, who'd died at fourteen in a fall from his horse.

"A bruising rider," Lucian told her. "Mad for it from the moment he first sat in the saddle. I've a friend who has always reminded me of him—one of those men with that rare affinity for the horse. Many men think they can ride, but few truly can, not like Robert Grey or Drew Ashley."

But Robert's horse had fallen, and the boy been crushed.

"Neither of their faults, really," said Lucian, stroking her hair absently as she lay on his chest, afternoon light coming dust-spotted through the window. "Just a patch of muddy ground and the slip of a hoof. I saw it happen."

She lifted her head from his chest, but he smiled at her, shaking his head minutely to let her know the sympathy was welcome but unneeded. He arranged her again on his chest.

"The thing is, you see," he continued, "that Robert was my father's heir. I was never meant to be duke, not really, though I've had from the age of twelve to be prepared for it. I was the more bookish, or the more stupidly dreamy, with an interest in history and ancient things. I read all the stories of the great explorers and thought discovering abandoned tombs would be the perfect life for me, but when Robert died, my father changed the course of my schooling, and it was all languages and politics and being taken to a great many parties and dinners and places boys seldom went so that I could learn the ways of society and how to talk to anyone. And, most importantly, how to listen and how to think."

"So he was training you to be a spy even then?"

"I think so. But also training me to be a politician—his type of politician, of the Royal Court. But politics and spying are fairly similar. They're both about secrets and manipulation and knowing more than anyone suspects."

He said it very dryly, but she heard the bitterness.

"You know," he said, "your brother said something that struck a chord. He said we each end up pulling the plough we can best bear. I think I've spent my whole life feeling I'm hitched to the wrong one—my brother's plough. I've been living his life. So I suppose it's no wonder I'm adept at disguises. My life has been one."

He'd laughed at himself then, made a joke that he was getting old and prosy and self-indulgent and would soon be writing his memoirs to better bore subsequent generations, and then he'd rolled her onto her back and kissed her in a way that revealed the tremors of emotion that still wracked him, the regret and the grief. They made love—for love it was—and on the next day, when the ship's slow progress had brought them no further than Oporto, they put into harbour to re-provision.

The winds still blew against them. With no hope of progress, they took a villa on the edge of the town and spent three weeks among the olive groves, receiving scant news of the hard-won victory at Badajoz and silently praying that a young lieutenant of the Army Guides hadn't been among the thousands slain. The battle that finally broke the siege was rumoured to have been savagely costly, and the lists of the dead hadn't arrived at Oporto before the winds took them from it.

They reached England as April was ending, anchoring in the Channel so as to make their final approach into Portsmouth by daylight.

"I'll send a messenger to London as soon as we land," Lucian said as the final dawn broke, "but I'll accompany you to Rowlands and make every necessary explanation to the Parlings. And we'll look at your parents' notebooks. But I...I cannot stay long. There's a moon tonight, and I must make use of it to travel to London and be there by dawn tomorrow. The information is too important for delay."

It was the closest they'd come to mentioning their separation. Hester nodded, her head pillowed on the muscle of his arm. They'd lain silently in Lucian's bed through all the dark hours of the night. Neither had slept.

"I hope my parents' notes are easier to decipher than Wren's," she said.

They'd finished the task the day before, and what they'd

found was of great interest, though it hadn't given them the answer they sought. In amongst general notes pertaining to his work had been a list of suspicious incidents—messages that had been late to arrive or had arrived incomplete, couriers and messengers who had been lost in areas where little enemy presence was known, occasions when the French had seemed to know the intentions of the British almost before they did, and when more than luck had seemed to be on their enemy's side. But there was no name, no culprit pin-pointed, just a pattern that confirmed their suspicions of a traitor in their midst.

"We got there in the end," said Lucian. "Or you did." He leant down and kissed her forehead. "I think there's no code you couldn't solve."

She smiled away the compliment, knowing it was far from true, though deep down she glowed at his praise. "My parents' notes *should* be easier. I'd begun to look at the ciphers they're written in before my governess duties took me away from home. One notebook was very easy and proved to be nothing more than a country diary. I think they were mostly just entertaining themselves with their ciphers, or practising." She paused, looking up into the dawn-shadowed beams of the ceiling that lay beyond the glint of his eyes. "I hope there is something actually helpful to be found in their other notebooks. What will we do if there's not? Knowing there's a traitor, but with no idea who it might be, is the most dangerous position of all to be in, is it not? He will surely want us both dead."

His arm tightened around her. "Not you. He'll know nothing of your involvement."

"And almost everything of yours."

"Ah," he said, smiling, "but I have Willsly to protect me."

"Even *you* cannot joke about this!"

"I'm not joking. But, yes, I refuse to let anxiety get the better of me. What good would it do? It's hardly the first time I've been a target."

"That time you said you were poisoned. It had nothing at all to do with brandy, did it?"

"I haven't been victim to that drink since the tender age of thirty. It was time to grow out of such behaviour, you know."

She pushed his bare shoulder. "Oh, do be serious!"

"I'd rather not be, not now, with you in my arms, in the last hours of this last night. I'll not talk of death and murder; there's sorrow enough to come. Talk to me of something else. Tell me... Hmm. Tell me when you first realised how impossibly attractive I am."

She lifted herself on her elbow, switching positions so that he lay on his back. His dark eyes glinted with more than the lantern light. They held the stars of the night sky. They held her heart itself.

And a great deal of familiar amusement.

"Are you?" she said. "I hadn't noticed. But you are certainly *impossible*."

He smiled, lightly pinching her chin between his thumb and forefinger and drawing her down for a kiss. "You," he said, the amusement in his voice replaced by something that made her throat ache, "are the one who is impossible. I never believed any of this was possible. To feel this much... To find this perfect accord..." So close, all she could see was his eyes, and the hard lines—the softness—of his mouth. "To find you, the other half of my heart."

He kissed her, and they said with touch all they could not speak, both knowing this was the last time they would be together as one. How ironic that words were her domain and yet words now failed her. *I will miss you* was not enough. *I love you* was said better with every look and touch. *This parting will kill me* could only wound the one she never wished to hurt.

They dressed as the grey dawn crept into the cabin, unalterable reality forcing an end to their last night. They sat together on Lucian's bed, his arm around her as they watched the Portsmouth wharfs come distantly into sight, the ship making its slow and careful entrance into the busy harbour.

"Don't," she said, hearing the breath Lucian took to speak. "You're going to say you'll marry me anyway, and the devil take the Regent and his threats. I can as good as hear your thoughts. But don't say it. Because I'll not marry you."

"Hester—"

"No! I will not ruin you, and not just you, but all those who depend upon you. All the thousands of tenants on your estates, all the hundreds of staff in your employ. They'll all be hurt if the house of Cumbria falls. Your cousins and aunts and uncles. And your mother! What happiness would we have, Lucian, with your mother heartbroken and the ashes of your life around our feet? Resentment and guilt. That is all we'd have—at best. Or you with your neck in a traitor's noose. And I'd rather have nothing at all than that."

The arm around her shoulders was iron, but the steadying breath he took was pure pain. "I will find a way," he said, little more than a whisper. "I will find a way."

She shook her head, fingers pinched painfully against each other to stop her tears. "I've said it before: a little hope can be worse than none. Let's not torture ourselves but make a clean break. We'll say goodbye to each other and to all of it. And...and you will marry as you must. I'll not hate you for it."

"Yes you will. But not as much as I would hate myself." He prised her rigid hands from their grip on each other and lifted them to his lips. "Hester, you are my wife, my only wife, in every way that matters—"

The crashing rattle of the anchor chains came from all around. Shouts from the sailors. A cheer for the journey's safe end.

The duke—her duke—stood from the bed, and the look in his eyes, the cold iron in the way he held himself, made her think of the ship's anchor, plunging down into icy dark waters, holding fast in the blackness even as the water closed chokingly over his head.

"Come," he said, holding out his hand. "It's time for Harry Trunkton to make his last journey."

Twenty-Four

How pretty the Parlings' house looked in the spring sunshine. Ancient Rowlands, stone aglow, the neatly tended flowerbeds abundant and bright with daffodils. What a place to kill oneself.

Lucian wasn't often given to melodrama, but even that statement seemed insufficient. He would leave Rowlands having terminated everything he wished for in life. From the carriage ride to London onwards, his days would be nothing but hollow habit, a cage of time.

The carriage—one of his own, the one he'd first journeyed to Rowlands in, and which had been waiting for him in storage at an inn ever since—bowled up the gravel drive. Too fast. Not fast enough. His heart was in the same curious state as time itself: standing still, then galloping painfully onwards. Hester sat opposite him. By unspoken, mutual agreement they had not touched since leaving his cabin on *The Ondine*. It would be like wilfully touching fire: stupid and agonising.

Hester sat looking out of the window, lips pressed together, her cheeks pale, but her chin held defensively, almost aggressively up. The brim of a bonnet—bought in Portsmouth—hid much of her expression from him.

The boy Harry had been seen leaving *The Ondine*. The boy Harry had climbed into Lucian's carriage. But her dress had been waiting inside it. That same dress she'd first worn when she arrived on his ship, folded neatly by Willsly upon the seat, though it looked a sad and drab thing indeed. Creased and unloved, a grey little governess's dress, made to hide her.

He'd wanted to burn it.

The clothes she'd discarded were stowed under the seat. Willsly would deal with them, would fold them away atop the bright banyan and the black silk dress coat bought in Lisbon. Lucian supposed they'd travel home to London with him. They'd be put in storage somewhere. And haunt him evermore.

The carriage stopped before the steps. Hester's thin white hand was at once upon the handle of the door, and she sprang from the carriage as though she'd been suffocating inside it. Heart-aching, Lucian followed her out.

Willsly had been riding with the driver and was now superintending the footman who'd come forward for their luggage. It was mid-morning, and they weren't expected but the butler had heard the carriage and was waiting at the door, all his training not adequate to mask his surprise at the duke's arrival or Miss Littleton's return.

"Your Grace." He bowed low, beckoning them into the entrance hall, eyes darting to Hester. She stood with the brim of her bonnet low over her downturned face. Lucian gave no explanation.

"Is Miss Parling at home?" Lucian asked.

"Yes, Your Grace."

"If you'll permit us to wait in that little parlour across the way, be so good as to ask her to meet us there."

"Of course, Your Grace." The butler bowed again and led them to the room, promising refreshments before going to convey the message to Miss Parling. Hester walked to the window and stared out of it, her back very straight. With a sudden movement, she tore her bonnet from her head and turned to him, a burning look in her eyes. But whatever she'd been about to say or do was abandoned. Her eyes went past Lucian, and he turned to find Miss Parling in the doorway, face very pale, lips parted in stunned surprise.

"Hester? Hester! Good God!" She swayed, reaching for the doorframe as Lucian stepped forward to support her. She glanced up at him, noticing him for the first time, her eyes widening yet further as she recognised him. "Your Grace!"

Hester had come forward, and she took hold of her friend's hands. "It's me, Jane," she said, smiling through tears in her eyes, a grimness to her voice where there ought to have been joy. "I have come back."

"I thought...I thought you were dead! I have feared...! Oh! You cannot imagine!"

"I can," said Hester unsteadily, Jane throwing her arms around her neck and beginning to sob. Hester's tears finally overran her eyes too, and Lucian half turned his head, hardly able to bear seeing them when he could play no role in soothing them. "I can imagine what you've suffered, Jane, and I'm sorry. But I'm...I'm quite well."

There was much confusion for a few minutes, both the women crying—Jane more than Hester—and both attempting to say quickly what needed hours to tell.

"Miss Parling," Lucian interrupted gently. "Could I request that you convey Miss Littleton to her room and allow her to freshen herself after her journey before meeting the rest of your family? In the meantime, I will speak to your father and explain the whole. Later, if you'll grant it, I request a few moments of your time."

Her cheeks flamed, and she looked away, clearly fearing a renewal of his offer for her hand. She murmured an almost inaudible acquiescence before leaving the room, Hester at her side. But Hester would soon set her fears at rest, he was sure.

He walked over to the window Hester had stood at moments before and surveyed the pretty lawn, wondering which direction the Littletons' cottage lay and determinedly thinking of nothing else at all. When a maid arrived with tea, he asked to be taken to Mr Parling, and, after a deep curtsy that nearly unbalanced her, the stammering girl conveyed him through the house to a bright morning room, where he found the master of the house behind a newspaper.

If Lucian had been unused to making reports of things as complicated as an entire country's political or military situation, he might have quailed at the task of summarising the events that had taken place since he last quitted this house, but he unfolded the story in his usual brisk, clear way. And Parling, too awed by both his visitor and the strangeness of the story, didn't interrupt, but listened in silent astonishment, the deepening crease between his brows explained by his vehement exclamation as soon as Lucian's tale was told.

"The impudent folly of the girl! To foist herself upon your notice in such a way! I hardly know how to apologise, Your Grace. But that you have been so incommoded and put in such an embarrassing position and so sorely inconvenienced by a girl who, though she's of age and no longer my ward, is one I find myself still, in some measure, responsible for—"

Lucian held up a hand. "If my account suggests I lay any blame at Miss Littleton's feet, then I've failed in the telling of it. Miss Littleton at all times behaved in an admirable manner, with great sense and great courage. She has suffered a trial, Mr Parling, and all that is required from you and your family is your sympathetic care. And your discretion."

"Well...well of course, we've not advertised her absence to the world. To the staff, and anyone who has noticed her gone, which fortunately, is hardly anyone at all, for she was never really in society, you see, we've said she was offered a new governess position, with an immediate start date, owing to some urgency or other at the employer's household."

Parling looked as though he expected some praise at this genius stroke of deception. Lucian, not in the mood to flatter a man he was liking less by the minute, merely inclined his head.

"As I briefly mentioned, I had the good fortune to meet Mr Charles Littleton while in Lisbon."

Flustered, Parling glanced away. "Ah, yes! So you said. And he was well, you said?"

"Quite well, you'll be relieved to hear."

Mr Parling nodded quickly.

"As, so I believe," Lucian continued, "will Miss Parling be."

Parling was wise enough at least to know when the game was up. "So he or Hester has told you of his hopes, I suppose? They've never been encouraged by us, Your Grace. The upstart puppy has twice had the presumption to ask me for my daughter's hand and twice been denied it."

"Yes, just as I imagined, you are indeed a fool."

Jaw slack, Parling stared at him.

"Mr Charles Littleton," Lucian said calmly, "is such a young man that any parent of sense would wish for a son-in-law. All he needs is a little assistance to start his way in life. Given that, he'll surely exceed most of us. Indeed, as he's already a lieutenant in one of Wellington's most valued corps, he may not even require my assistance at all. But I still mean to give it. Jane is twenty-one soon enough. She'll marry the boy one way or another. I advise you not to make an enemy of either of them, Parling. You will look stupid, injure your family, and lose the regard of two very fine young people. And, though I hardly feel it compares in importance to the esteem of your own daughter, you will also lose mine." He reached for the tea which the maid had brought and took a sip. "Have I been clear?"

"P-perfectly, Your Grace," huffed Parling, still with pride

enough to take offence at being ordered about. "But, may I remind you, you yourself have offered for my daughter."

"And was not accepted."

He startled. "That is not what she said!"

"I believe she's been rather too frightened by knowing your obvious wishes to speak her true mind. And," he added meditatively, "without knowing whether Charles was alive or dead, she may have been sensible enough to wish to keep her options open." He lifted his cup in a mild salute. "Your daughter is no idiot. I congratulate you."

"And you would back out, would you?" accused Parling, worked up now. "You would embarrass the girl and jilt her and let all the world know that she has lost a duke. And for her prize she ends up with a lieutenant from the ranks!"

"I do not gossip, Parling. If anyone knows of the offer I made your daughter, I believe that must have been your own family's doing. But, yes. I will back out. There can hardly be any shame or dishonour attached when a prior engagement exists."

"There is no engagement!"

"Are we to quibble over words, Parling? A prior attachment. An engagement. It matters not. Please don't embarrass yourself by clutching at my boots, sir. You are about to gain a very fine son. And, more importantly, you will secure the lasting happiness of your daughter." He put his cup down and stood. "I call it a very fine deal. Now, please ask Miss Parling to attend me. I'm not so disreputable, you see, as to not wish to jilt her to her face."

Twenty-Five

Hester stood before the long mirror in the room she shared with Jane, repeatedly smoothing down the front of her dress as though that could make it fit any better.

It was her best, an old one of Jane's that the girls had altered together a long time ago. It was some ridiculous instinct of vanity that had prompted her to change as much as the musty sea-salt smell of her own garment.

Now she frowned, miserably dissatisfied, some astute corner of her mind knowing that this small discontent was all the vent she could safely allow herself. There was a cage around her heart, though her stays were as loose as they could be. She had little need of them. But the stiffened material still made itself known against the base of her thin ribs. Her skirts felt both cumbersome, like ropes tangled around her legs, and insubstantial, air creeping up underneath them like a hand trailing up her leg.

Not his hand. Never his hand again. And what would he make of her, looking like this? She'd hidden, scrunched up in the carriage. Now she wore pale pink muslin that swept to the floor but Harry's face stared out of the mirror, browned by travel, the freckles more prominent than ever. The circlet of miniature silk roses Jane had arranged in her hair did nothing to stop it looking like a boy's.

"We will have the hairdresser call tomorrow," Jane had

promised, biting her lip in anxious sorrow. "He'll be able to...to...neaten it up, you know, and then I'm sure it will look just the thing! Very modern, very daring. Just like—"

"Lady Caroline Lamb," Hester had supplied dully. For a moment she was back in a tiny wooden room, the floor pitching strangely beneath her feet, the air pungent with tar and wood and seawater and wet rope, lantern light glowing in the stuffy, heaving space, and Lucian...Lucian behind her...Lucian's hands on her neck, running into her hair...lantern light glinting on scissors, on dark eyes...

A prick of tears. Her chest lifted on a sucked-in breath.

"Exactly!" Jane had said with unconvincing brightness. "Just like Lady Lamb!"

"I am a beanpole in a sack." She stared at her reflection. "A *short* beanpole in a sack."

But Jane had been called away in the middle of promising the contrary—called away to talk to *His Grace, the duke*, the maid had said, conveying the message with a whisper of awed excitement. And Hester was left to survey her disappointing reflection in the mirror and chastise herself severely for the ridiculous flicker of jealousy that accompanied the thought of Jane in *His Grace, the duke's* company. *She* wanted to be there. *She* wanted to see him, and hear him, and soak up every last moment of his company before he left forever. Instead, she stood upstairs, further away from him in this large house than she'd ever been on board even the majestic *Ondine*.

He would see Jane's beauty, and then he would see her in this dress, and perhaps at least it might make the parting easier for him. Back in England, surrounded by the most beautiful and elegant ladies the *ton* could offer, might he not soon come to be glad he hadn't been free to make her a rash promise of marriage?

She was not insensible enough to believe he did not love her, the last weeks had given her too much evidence of that. But that he might love the Hester of Lisbon and *The Ondine*, the outrageous Hester in boy's clothes, the co-conspirator in his urgent decryptions—that was one thing. But to love the Miss Littleton of Hampshire, the quiet governess in her sober dress, the skinny, drab little portionless female whom no one regarded... For him still to love her when he was back in London society in the company of dazzling beauties and foreign princesses and aggressively courted by all, with the Regent in his ear and dining with his mother and her expectations, and in his club with his friends, and at the theatre and the opera, with his favoured Cyprians or widows only one crook of his finger away... No. She could not expect that. She didn't even wish it; at least she told herself she did not wish it. Better he forgot her and found happiness elsewhere. *She* would not forget. But such happiness had never been in her future.

She turned from the mirror, about to look for her parents' box of notes where it was stored under her bed, when Jane came beaming into the room, smiling and breathless.

"Oh, Hessie! He has released me! And he spoke of Charles... He said... He said Charles said..." And she burst into tears of joy.

Smiling, despite her own opposite feelings, she pulled Jane down to sit beside her on the bed, saying laughingly, "Tell me what my brother said to make you cry, dearest Jane, and I promise to scold him for it."

Jane laughed back, wiping her eyes. "Oh..." She sighed dreamily. "Hessie, apparently he said to the duke that...that I was his heaven waiting here on Earth, and that he would not quit this sphere until he had returned to me! Is it not pretty? And I believe it like I've never believed it before—that he *will* come back to me. He must. And the duke agreed with such certainty that I can't help but believe it!"

Hester, well able to imagine Lucian capable of making anyone believe almost anything if he chose to, could only smile.

"I'm glad of it. And I'm certain too," she lied, wishing it was truth. But she'd seen Lisbon, had seen the naval ships, the cannon balls being unloaded, all the various soldiers around the town, some shining and neat and newly arrived, and some faded, limping, one-legged on shuffling crutches. She'd seen street hawkers selling buttons scavenged from dead men's uniforms. She'd seen scavenged teeth.

She'd seen a man die, had his blood on her hands, smelt it fill the carriage air. And she'd seen Charles himself, hardened to sinew and bone from the rigours of his soldier's life. It was all too real for Hester to be able to share Jane's certain dream, as much as she longed to.

"What a wedding you'll have," she said gamely, "both of you too sick with joy to stand up, too giddy with happiness to speak your vows, and crying too hard to see each other's faces."

Jane laughed. "I might! But Charles is too strong to be so overcome."

She squeezed Jane's hand. "He is. And he will come back."

Jane sniffed valiantly, but it was no good, she started crying once more. Hester got up to get a handkerchief for her from the dressing table. Jane took it with a watery smile.

"And are any of these tears grief for not being a very grand duchess?" teased Hester, attempting to shift Jane's mood to lighter topics. "I can guess how your family have spent the last weeks filling your head with thoughts of carriages and gowns and very great houses. All the jewels, Jane! A tiara for you, and a little page boy in livery, and a gold and cream phaeton pulled by the prettiest matched greys, with ribbons in their manes. I can see it exactly."

Jane laughed. "There's nothing I would like less! My Charles and a little cottage as your parents had—*that* has been my only dream. I'd hate to be a duchess! All the pomp and fuss. Those huge houses and estates to care for, and all of society's eyes upon you!" She gave a dramatic shudder.

"Yes," said Hester, sitting down on the dressing table stool and pushing her finger into the bristles of the hairbrush there. "Just think. It would be awful."

There was a pause. Then, "You love him, don't you?"

Hester looked round so sharply it cricked her neck. Heat flooded her face, making her emphatic "No!" sound just as absurd as she knew it to be. Jane just looked at her, sympathetic.

"Yes," admitted Hester, picking up the hairbrush and absently playing with it once more, pressing her palm against the sharp bristles. "Yes. I do. How stupid of me."

"No." Jane shook her head. "Because he loves you."

Hester looked up.

"It seemed obvious to me, even in the brief moment I saw you together in the room—half fainting as I was! And when I spoke to him just now, in the way he hardly mentioned your name even when it would have been most natural to do so, and then, when he did...the smallest pause and the careful way he said *Miss Littleton* as though...as though your name was precious glass or something hushed and miraculous in an ancient church..."

Hester gave an awkward laugh, protesting. "Jane..."

"Yes, yes, I am romantic and foolish, but tell me it's not true. Tell me—and I'll not believe you!"

"Then I shouldn't bother to tell you anything." Hester gave a crooked smile. "You already know it all."

"It is true, then?" Jane breathed, eyes brimming with a joy that made her stand from the bed and come hurrying to kneel at Hester's feet, her hands gripping Hester's knees. "It's true? You're to be a duchess?"

A blow like the crash of a sea wave against *The Ondine's* prow swept cold over her. She swallowed. "No, Jane. I will not be a duchess."

"But..."

"I do love him. And he does love me. But we cannot marry. You of all people must understand. In a world where some people think Charles not good enough for you, can you believe Hester Littleton a fit match for the Duke of Cumbria?"

"Of course you're good enough! And if he thinks so, who cares what the rest of the world thinks! A duke can do anything!"

Not this one, thought Hester, but she couldn't tell Jane his secret.

"He asked me," she said instead, more or less truthfully, "and I refused."

Jane stared up at her, horrified.

"So do not hate him, dearest Jane. If you love me, do not hate him. And please don't berate me or tell me that love will conquer all, for it does no good. But know..." Her composure began to fail her, and tears, long held back, began to blur her eyes and break her voice. "Dearest Jane...know that I am very, very unhappy...and in great need of a friend."

A fit of desperate crying did nothing to improve her looks. But she didn't see Lucian when she first went downstairs. Mrs Parling, Georgina, and Elizabeth were all waiting in the drawing room. Jane went first into the room, holding the door half-closed to mask Hester from view.

"Well, Mama, girls, did I not say I had a surprise for you? Here it is!" And she threw the door open, taking Hester by the elbow and pulling her forward.

The dramatic entrance wasn't necessary to add to the excitement of the moment. Mrs Parling almost screamed, and both Georgiana and Elizabeth actually did. Hester winced at the noise, and then there were three pairs of arms attempting to fling themselves around her and a babble of tears and exclamations. She bore it smiling, a little moved, though she knew the exuberance of the greeting had more to do with the novelty of her sudden absence and reappearance than true affection. Life could be very slow in the Hampshire countryside and here was something exciting indeed.

They sat, and Hester told an edited version of her story, or attempted to, but was so much interrupted she'd barely got as far as finding herself on board *The Ondine* before the door opened and the gentlemen came into the room. Lucian bowed very properly, including all the ladies, but addressing himself mostly to Mrs Parling. His eyes only met Hester's for the briefest moment before Mrs Parling claimed him, begging him to sit beside her so that she could smother him with overdone gratitude for the return of *their darling little Hessie.*

Mr Parling gave her a very hard look. He shook her hand stiffly, then, in foreboding tones, said he would talk to her in private later. The scold coming her way she could well imagine, and it was inevitable that the days of her comfortable residence at the Parlings' home were coming to an end.

Lucian's ruse might have saved her in society's eyes; her secret was safe from the world at large. But Mr Parling knew. Mr Parling wouldn't forgive or forget that Miss Littleton had disgraced herself, had travelled abroad alone with an unmarried man, and worst of all, had left Rowlands with a duke proposing marriage to its finest daughter and returned with that same duke retracting his hand. That it was all *her* fault, she knew Mr Parling was sure.

Hester nodded at the veiled threat in his promise, said, "Yes, sir," and went to sit in a corner. With the duke in the room, no one had ears for her version of the story.

Tea and cakes were brought. Jane served very prettily. Conversation flowed eagerly—the bulk of it from two quite silly girls and an almost as silly mother. But to any observer looking in through the window it would've seemed a very happy afternoon party. Hester said little, and though she tried to act normally, found she was often forgetting to smile. Lucian hardly looked at her. When he did not, she longed for him to do so. And when he did, she felt wretched with self-consciousness at how she must look with Jane and her sisters as pretty and plump as snowy white birds next to herself, a little brown stick.

And yet...Lucian, though he smiled often, never did so with the smile she knew best. And though his conversation was ready enough and lively, he didn't laugh, or venture any of his dry wit. And when he had occasion to pass near Mr Parling, he spoke some words into that man's ear that made him turn purple with suppressed anger. Lucian briefly met her eyes, and her heart swelled, certain that he'd saved her from any immediate scold.

It was only a few minutes after that when Lucian put down his teacup, politely declined another refill, and said, "Miss Parling, I see you sitting over there with your eyes going to that window, and I sympathise—it's a glorious spring day, is it not? Would you do me the honour of guiding me around the garden? I didn't get a chance to see any of the grounds when I was here last."

Mr and Mrs Parling exchanged a glance, hopes rekindling at this mild suggestion. Eagerly, they encouraged their eldest daughter to acquiesce to such a delightful scheme—a wonder they hadn't thought of it themselves!—and just as eagerly, they found at least three solid reasons between them as to why the youngest daughters couldn't possibly go too.

Lucian watched these arrangements being made without comment. Hester watched him, wondering what else he could have to say to Jane.

But when Lucian stood, smiling at Jane and gesturing for her to proceed him from the room, he added quickly, too quickly for either master or mistress of the house to intervene, "And of course Miss Littleton ought to come too." He looked at her, the hint of a wink gleaming in his eyes. "I feel sure you need as much fresh air as possible after so long confined to a ship." And he held the door open for her to slip through in Jane's wake.

Hester and Jane went upstairs to change their shoes and put on their coats and bonnets and gloves and everything else that seemed necessary for a short walk around a garden in the spring sunshine. Tying the ribbon beneath her chin, Hester thought ruefully of Harry Trunkton's beaver hat and the ease with which it was both donned and doffed. And she thought with something a little more painful of days spent in the warm sun and dappled shade of olive groves on a hill above Oporto, wearing nothing but trousers and shirtsleeves, or often, far less.

They said little as they got ready, but Jane sent her many a speaking glance. Hester pretended not to notice them because she had no answer to give. She didn't know how she felt. *Yes*, she wanted to walk about the garden with Lucian and steal any scrap of time alone with him that she possibly could. But *no*, she knew it wasn't wise, and *no*, she didn't know if she could bear it, and *yes*, she really was trembling as she walked back down the stairs, heart stopping at the sight of him waiting in the hallway in his dark hat and coat.

He smiled up at them—or rather, he smiled up at *her*. It did nothing good to her faltering heart, and Jane breathed a silent laugh as she tugged on her arm and forced her onwards down the stairs.

When they got into the garden, Lucian offered an arm to each lady, but Jane held back.

"Do please accept my apologies," she said, smiling, eyes flashing to Hester with a twinkle of mischief, "but I've just remembered I have an urgent message for the cook. And, do you know, I've the strongest notion it's going to take me a very long time to find her!"

Lucian smiled. "Then you must leave at once, Miss Parling. I quite understand."

"I thought that you might."

Hester didn't know whether to laugh or box her ears, but she settled on the former as Jane passed her on her way around the house to the kitchens at the back.

"As hard as it is to imagine the fair Miss Parling doing anything as unladylike as winking," said Lucian, "I believe she just did exactly that, Miss Littleton."

"I think you're right, Your Grace."

Lucian held out his arm for hers. "Will *you* accompany me, then, Miss Littleton? We had little chance to get acquainted on my last visit. But I've the strongest suspicion we might get along quite comfortably, once we get to know one another."

"Is that so?" she said, laughing, her awkwardness melting away. It was Lucian at work, she knew, manipulating her mood with his usual skill, but she didn't mind it. It was comforting to be in the hands of an expert and let him take the tiller of these last hours of their friendship.

"Miss Parling has more about her than I thought," Lucian said in his normal voice as they headed away from the house.

"She's not stupid, you mean? Poor Jane. Everyone assumes she must be because she's so beautiful *and* so soft-hearted. But she's far from it."

"I'm glad for Charles's sake."

"And growing envious perhaps?"

She said it teasingly, though she knew it was a weak, fishing sort of comment, prompted by nothing good. Lucian looked at her, surprised, his "No!" vehement enough to make her feel very silly indeed.

"I'm sorry," she said in a small voice. "I'm not at my best today."

"Of course you're not. How can either of us be? But if you love me, bear it with me. Let us be...be gentle with each other, and honest, and open. It is a grieving, terrible *mess*—" He broke off, steadying himself. "I must leave for London soon, whatever progress we make with your parents' notebooks. If you allow it, I must ask that I can take the notebooks with me. The work will have to be finished without delay."

She felt a pang at losing them and having strangers' eyes pore over her family's words. But she understood the importance. "Of course. If there's anything of use in them—and I'm not even sure there is—then of course it must be found out at once. In London. By the most skilled people you have, and where you can report it immediately to those who must know it."

He gave a hollow laugh. "I believe there are few more skilled than you. But they'll not clear you for the work."

"No. I am a woman."

"Not only that, but they'd need to know they could trust you, and that takes time. It's irrelevant anyway. We've already decided to keep you out of the business, for your safety's sake."

"Yes." She had no desire to have the eyes of Lucian's employers turned upon her. Men who could control a duke were a frightening prospect.

"So," said Lucian softly, "as I'm to leave soon... It is too much to ask, I know, that we be as we were. Our hearts are too heavy. But if we can avoid our sadness becoming bitterness... If we can try to find some happiness in this time we have... Is it stupid that I want to laugh and be merry with the cliff one step behind my back? But it would be more stupid to lose these hours to gloom and despair."

She squeezed his arm against her side. "No. You are right."

"Then...I've a mind to take a very long walk, Miss Littleton. Perhaps we might even get lost somehow and not find our way back for hours."

Twenty-Six

Perhaps Lucian was cruel to try to force Hester's spirits to brightness, but he hated to see her so sad and quiet as she'd been in the Parlings' drawing room. And maybe he was selfish too, for the fact her pain was his own doing was more than he could bear, and removing the evidence of that pain was as close as he could come to removing the fact.

But, in truth, it was all simpler than that. He couldn't be anything other than happy in Hester's company. His mood lifted with every step away from the house, with every word spoken by her beloved voice, with every press of her arm against his side. This feeling of delight in another person's presence, this intoxication of spirit at their very existence, this adoration and craving... It was all of it love, just as was the urge to protect and possess her, to claim and own and boast of her.

Tomorrow would be hell; he'd tasted it already, their parting coming by degrees—a night onboard *The Ondine*, a silent carriage ride, the turning her over into her friend's loving care... It was coming with creeping steps, the leaden footfall of a condemned man mounting the gallows steps.

But *now*... Now the sun was shining and there were butter-yellow primroses along the path, and he was alone with Hester, the white-washed wall of her childhood home growing steadily closer ahead.

"It's empty at the moment," she said. "The tenants who took it on after my parents died moved out over a year ago. Since then, it's been intended for Mr Parling's steward, now that he is married, but the man wants to do a vast deal of improvements and enlargements—mainly at the insistence of his wife, so it's said. The architect and builder have been forever coming and going and drawing up plans and costings, but they're never quite what Mr Dipley—he's the steward—or, more importantly, what *Mrs* Dipley wants. So the whole project has been at a standstill these last twelve months. This, I assure you, is a humane summary of the whole. I'm not cruel enough to subject you to the full story and all its attendant dramas. But if you'd been resident at Rowlands you would inevitably know it. It's been the greatest topic of discussion in these parts for some time."

"Ah-hah!" said Lucian. "Now I know why you hid in my trunk. The mystery is solved. It was to flee the tedium of the Dipleys and their improvements."

She laughed, a delightful sound. "So I am excused, my circumstances mitigating."

They'd approached the cottage from the back, and now their path led them around the curve of a well-clipped hedge, the gardener clearly still at work, despite the Dipleys' dithering. At the front of the house, kitchen garden beds of mixed fruit, vegetables, and flowers were split by a neat flagstone path to the heavily porched door. It was an elegant house, symmetrical, but small.

"And there is the duck pond," said Lucian with a strange twist of his heart, looking behind him to where the water, edged by drooping willows, was clearly seen at the base of a small, sloping lawn.

"Yes," said Hester with a rueful smile that clearly showed her heart was twisting in a similar manner to his own. "And look! The swans and their cygnets! How many this year..." She counted them as they crossed the pond in stately procession. "Five! Not as high as some years, but a good number."

"It's a pretty house," Lucian said when the swans had sailed out of sight. They both looked up at it for a moment, sun catching on the diamond-paned windows.

She gave him a dry look. "And how does it compare to Thornley Castle, Your Grace?"

"Very charmingly, Miss Littleton."

She breathed a laugh, then opened the latch gate and walked up the garden path, hunting for a moment underneath a white-washed stone before looking back at him with a key dangling from her fingers and a very impish smile on her face.

"Would you like to see inside?"

Whether they ought to trespass or not, he hardly cared. The building had been empty a year, and he very much *did* want to see inside. He followed her with nothing but the wry shake of his head.

As expected for an untenanted building, it was not currently very homely. The rooms were almost empty except for a few items of heavy wooden furniture here and there, some of them under covers but others left to grow dusty.

"I remember this bookcase." Hester trailed her fingers over a shelf, heedless of the dirt that marred her glove. "It used to be in the study, not here in the hall. But I suppose the study has been returned to its proper purpose as a morning room."

Lucian made no comment, letting her remember, time turning back with every step she took. They only looked briefly into the downstairs rooms, then, without a word, she led the way upstairs.

"My parents' room," she said, pointing to a door at the end of the landing. "And Charles's. And this was mine."

The bare floorboards creaked as they walked into the little room. The paper on the walls was faded but dry. The low, bright window stood in a deep recess, the ledge boarded with aged pine. She sat down upon it, looking into the garden as, he supposed, she'd often used to do.

"How strange it is," she said. The edge of a willow tree was in view, but not the rest of the pond. Countryside stretched beyond the cottage's garden, a distant church spire just visible above budding trees.

"If I could draw, or paint, I'd capture you here, just like this," said Lucian.

She looked around, pulling the face he'd known she would, as though the wish to capture her likeness was absurd. She stood up as he stepped closer but stayed still, meeting his eyes, the air of the silent cottage hushed all around them. He reached out and drew the bow of her bonnet free.

"These clothes don't suit me," she said quickly, as though unable to keep the thought back any longer.

"Not as well as your Portuguese robe," he said, smiling. "Or...nothing at all."

But she didn't smile back. "I feel ridiculous. And that you...you must think so too."

"Find a woman in a dress ridiculous? Why?"

"Harry's clothes suited me better."

He lifted the bonnet from her head and put it on the window ledge. Then he put his crooked finger under her chin and made her look at him.

"What nonsense is in your head, Hester? That I don't find you attractive when you're *not* a boy?" Still holding her gaze, he began to run his finger down her throat. "If you have any idea how the sight of all this skin has tormented me these last hours, you wouldn't think so. Harry hid it with a neckcloth. Hester taunts me with it bare." He found the hollow of her throat, felt her shiver under his touch. His hand moved slowly down the slope of her chest to the line of her dress.

"The only fault I find with this dress is that it is on you and not the floor." Then he let himself look down her body, flicking his eyes back to hers with a grin. "And there are many elements of a lady's dress far superior to a man's. Stockings." His grin deepened. "Garters. Are you wearing them, Hester?"

Her cheeks were flushed. She whispered, "Yes," and he stooped to gather the hem of her dress, slipping his hand under the fabric to cup her calf. As he stood, he ran his palm up until he reached the little ribbon tied above her knee. He rolled the knot of the bow between his finger and thumb. "So you are."

With a heavy, trembling breath, she sank back against the wall behind her. He stepped into her, still toying with the ribbon of her garter, teasing it free beneath her skirts.

"I thought," he began, with some difficulty due to the tightness in his throat, "I thought when we left *The Ondine* I'd never get to touch you again."

"I know," she whispered, her hands coming to his neck and pulling his forehead to hers.

"I shouldn't... This is madness..."

"I know," she whispered again.

"You should be in a bed," he said, his own voice hoarsened to a near whisper. One hand swept into the familiar short strands of her hair, while the other, under her skirts, left the garter bow and travelled up to her hip. She moaned, pressing into his touch. "The Queen's bed at Thornley. It's bigger than this whole room."

"I don't care. I want only you. This last time... Please..."

She kissed him, feverish, shaking, and he kissed her back in the same way, all reason overwhelmed, fire in his blood, and aching loss, and pain and pleasure both, just opposite ends of his desperate need.

"One benefit of skirts..." he murmured, his hand between her thighs, finding her ready and hot. Her own hands were at his falls, her touch as urgent as his, no time to waste, because this was a stolen moment. There might be a voice in the garden, a tread on the stair, but they had to have each other, had to, had to be together this one last time...

He lifted her, holding her against the wall, her legs around his waist, and pushed into her ready heat. "Hester, Hester..." He hardly knew what he said. "Dress or no dress, boy or girl, now or decades hence, I only want you. You, Hester," he breathed, "other half of my soul. Only you."

Twenty-Seven

IT WAS A SORT of prayer, but to which gods, Hester didn't know; it was an animal-like calling to the world. *See? See what we are to each other? How can you part us now?* But the world cared as little for them as it did for all those other tragic lovers. They were cruel and ancient, the gods who watched over such things. Roman gods and Greek, and older still. Shakespeare knew it when he penned his tragedies. Humans were merely sport.

Then...an end came...yet another end in a misery of endings. She was back on her feet. She was in Lucian's arms, but for the last time. The way he held her told her that. She did not want to feel it.

"My...my reticule." Neither had their breath back. Both were still trembling. "I left it in the hallway..."

She moved away from him, not looking at him, smoothing clothes. He followed her down the stairs, a question in his silence. No, an apology. It was him who was leaving. He knew why she couldn't meet his eyes.

"You will despise me for leaving..." He'd said that once, and, as always, he'd been wise. As the moment drew nearer, the pain increased to the agony of an animal in a trap, lashing out at everyone, heedless and stupid. *How can you leave? How can you do this to me?* But she refused to say it. Would not, could not hurt him. So she kept quiet and hunted for her reticule and

pulled a notebook from it.

"This was the last one—the one I saw my father writing in shortly before he died. I remember it well because I gave it to him as a present, bought it on a visit to the shops at Portsmouth. It was his birthday and— No matter. I am prattling on. But here..." She turned to the last page that had been written on, sitting down on a large wooden chest in the hallway as she did so. Lucian sat down beside her. "This would be the last entry before he died. And my mother's hand is the one above it. It seems they took turns writing in it."

Lucian took the notebook and studied it silently for a moment. The rows of numbers were written at a slant, written quickly, by authors very familiar with the code they used.

"This is what I deciphered from the first of their notebooks I looked at years ago, shortly after they died." She passed him a folded piece of paper, yellowed with age.

"*Only one apple tree in blossom*," he read out loud. "*Starlings nesting. Very noisy. White butterflies only. Cabbage beware!*" He smiled sadly. Words from a dead hand.

"As you see," said Hester, "it's only a country diary. I fear this notebook may be the same, and that I've excited your hopes for nothing."

"Nothing you do could ever be nothing," Lucian said, so quietly she felt it was only meant to be his own thought.

"The code used is somewhat different, however," she continued, forcing herself on. "I looked at it quickly while you were with Mr Parling, and I think I've mostly figured out the method. It is very like Wren's, you see. I believe they taught him the trick of it."

"It's very likely," Lucian agreed. "Swan—or perhaps I should say The Swans—were the best codebreakers we had. Much of what we know is based on their work."

"Here is the key for Wren's." She took out another piece of

paper, and a fresh sheet, and a box containing pen and ink.

"You've come prepared, I see," said Lucian, smiling ruefully.

She glanced up at him, her gaze going past the smile to the bleak shadow in his eyes that it didn't mask. She looked quickly away. "Yes. Well, I knew you hadn't much time...and it would be difficult to get some privacy to do this work at the house. So when you arranged this walk, I packed these things when I went upstairs to change. I thought it was perhaps why you arranged it so neatly—getting us alone, away from the house..."

"I should pretend I was thinking of work, but I was only thinking of you, Hester, and my selfish desire for your company."

He reached out and swept his thumb over her wrist, taking her hand in his.

"Will you stay for dinner?" she asked softly.

"I should not. But will I? It'll be another hour in your presence. But will it be worse to see you across the table and be able to take no more notice of you than the first time we met?"

She managed a smile. "You didn't know I was there."

"What a fool I was. But in my defence, how could I have known? I didn't know a creature like you could exist; how should I have been on the lookout for it?" He pressed her hand to his lips. "I didn't come to Rowlands thinking to find the other half of my soul. I didn't know I had lost it—until I found it."

"Lucian..."

"I know."

"I love you."

"I know." He kissed her hand again. "And I you. So much. Oh God... How can I..." He dashed his other hand across his eyes, then took a ragged breath, pinching his forehead. "No," he said quickly, "No, you are right. We must work."

Letting go her hand, he picked up the notebook once more.

She allowed herself one last look up at this face, at the stark misery there that echoed her own. She watched him blink back tears, once, twice, forcing himself to focus on the page. Summoning all her will, she did the same.

It was comforting in a way, the murmur of their voices, the reading out of numbers and the suggestions of meaning. They had enough lines of attack, enough knowledge of the secret ways and mazed back alleys that the citadel soon fell open. But Hester's heart sank with every word they discovered.

Lucian read it aloud when the entry was complete. "*The blackbird called in alarm among the foxgloves. They are growing right to the door, and I fear will soon be inside the house. The apple of the tree is very nearly ripe.*"

"It's as I thought," she said, wretched with their failure. "I'm sorry. It doesn't help you at all. And I was so sure—"

"No," Lucian interrupted her softly, still looking at the paper. "Look...a blackbird. And the first one mentioned a starling. We're all birds, you see—Raven, Swan, Wren. There are a dozen of us at least. I don't know them all, but I know there is, or was, a Blackbird. I know there's a Magpie. I worked with him once. Maybe there's a Starling too. This could all be some other kind of code, or riddle... A way of hiding things even if someone managed to break the cipher."

Hester stared at the paper. "You're right. You must be, because look—it mentions foxgloves and apples in the same entry. But foxgloves flower in the summer and apples don't ripen until the autumn when the foxgloves are finished."

"The apple of the tree..." Lucian read again. "Why phrase it so strangely?" He looked up sharply. "There *is* a famous apple tree, of course, in the Garden of Eden. The tree of knowledge. *Knowledge.* They could be referring to the Paris Cipher. *The apple of the tree is very nearly ripe...* They may have almost broken it."

"And that is why they were killed."

"Speculation. But it's very possible. And it fits with what we know of Wren's suspicions." Lucian studied the paper again. Hester felt sure his attention was now on the line that was sending chills down her spine. "The blackbird and the foxgloves..." he murmured, "and the foxgloves growing right to the door..."

"They knew," Hester said quietly. "They knew someone was coming for them. This other spy, Blackbird, must have given them warning. *The foxgloves will soon be inside the house.* That is what killed them. Foxgloves. It's poisonous, is it not?"

Lucian met her eyes, his look full of sympathy.

"It is, though it affects the heart, not only the stomach. Foxglove might well be the code name of their attacker, not the method he used."

"Then who is Foxglove?"

Lucian shook his head. "I've no idea. I've never heard a code name that wasn't a bird. But if I can work it out..."

"Then you have found the traitor."

He nodded, standing up abruptly. "May I take this notebook? And the others? I will work on them on the way to London and see what other clues they might hold."

"Yes, of course." She stood up too. "You have to go now, don't you?"

He looked at her, and she saw the effort it took him, just as she saw the cold iron stealing over him, as though he was a knight, buckling on piece after piece of armour, transfiguring himself from the lover that arose at dawn from his maiden's bed to the faceless soldier hidden under plate metal. But the knight's lover would wave him off to battle in despair at not knowing if she would see him again. Hester already knew her answer. This was an eternal goodbye.

They walked back to the house hardly speaking. What was there to say? Their snatched few hours were crumbling around them, already a disbelieving dream, dew burnt off a spider's web until it was lost to sight.

At the house, Lucian called for Willsly, and the bustle of departure began. He spoke to Mr Parling, he made his leave of Mrs Parling and Jane and Georgina and Elizabeth. The carriage was on the drive; the horses were tossing their heads. Willsly stood at the door. He looked at Hester, smiled grimly, and the blunt sympathy in his look was a stab to the heart that nearly made her faint. Willsly couldn't stop this, even Willsly, dear, dependable Willsly... Even he knew this was the end and there was nothing, nothing to be done, oh God...no, no, no, no...

Jane's fingers found her own. Lucian stood before her.

"Goodbye, Miss Littleton. God be with you."

He climbed into the carriage and was gone.

Twenty-Eight

LUCIAN WORKED ON THE notebook like a madman, never looking out of the carriage window, working by swaying lantern light as night fell, never stepping out to stretch his legs as the ostlers flew to change the horses at every stage. He worked until his hand cramped and his eyes blurred with grit and his head ached, and, devil take it—he could take no more.

"You'll find a way," said Willsly softly from where he sat in the carriage across from him. He'd been sitting there the whole time, except for at each change of horses, silently passing fresh paper, or ink, or adjusting the lantern light, or whatever else his ashen master needed. "Through it or past it, you'll find a way. You always do."

Lucian looked up but didn't trust himself to meet the other man's eyes. He nodded but made no reply. He didn't trust his voice either.

It was dawn, and Willsly moved to extinguish the lanterns. Before long, they were rattling through London streets. Lucian frowned at their route, realising they were headed to his London home. "I told the driver Carlton House, not Cumbria House."

"And I told him otherwise," said Willsly imperturbably. "You need to shave and dress. And eat."

"Eat bread and sip my coffee while this traitor walks among us? Why not get me a newspaper too, Willsly. I seem to be at leisure!"

"You won't do your message any good fainting away in the Regent's arms. He won't be awake at this hour anyway, nor Ryder, nor anyone else you need to see. And he's that exquisite a fop anyway," muttered Willsly to himself, deprecating the prince's air of fashion as always, "that he'll probably refuse to see you if you turn up looking like that, with that crumpled neckcloth and your hair nearly pulled out from clawing at it so. You look a worse ruffian than young Harry ever did."

Not knowing whether to laugh, scowl, or weep, Lucian instead irritably shuffled the papers on his lap and assented with sulking bad grace to his servant's wisdom.

Three hours later saw him admitted to Carlton House. Another hour passed in waiting, striding furiously up and down the dreadfully elaborate decor of the room to which he had been escorted. He stopped abruptly at a light knock and assumed a nonchalant air upon a blue velvet sofa as the door opened, but it was Lord Gant who entered the room.

Lucian stood with a small bow. "Gant, how goes it?"

"Cumbria!" said the older man with a smile. "I heard a rumour in the corridors you were here but didn't believe it, knowing you to be surely among our Portuguese friends."

Lucian smiled. He knew Gant personally only a little. Like his father, he'd been one of the King's closest advisors, and though his auburn hair was now grey and he was far from the usual sort of hard-drinking, sin-abetting companion the prince chose to surround himself with, he held considerable sway, being one of the few voices of reason the prince would listen to. It was said that it was Gant who'd held the monarchy together during the last difficult years of the King's illness. It was said the entire country had a lot to thank him for.

"You know how it is, Gant, one gets an urge for good roast beef that simply cannot be denied, and thus," Lucian said smiling lightly and making an airy gesture, "one is compelled to return home."

"Ah, you come to take beef with His Highness, do you? Well, I dare say he's as up as ever for a rump and a dozen, though it's a little early for it. But you're...hungry, eh?"

Lucian just smiled at the questioning note. Though Gant wasn't one of the small circle who knew Lucian's true role, he undoubtedly suspected it. Little went on that Gant didn't know.

"Well, perhaps you'll get some breakfast at least," Gant said. "Come, they're on the terrace."

Gant led the way, bowing his farewell and leaving Lucian alone with the Regent—who was bundled in an admirable coat, grimacing at the cold morning breeze—and the Home Secretary, Ryder.

"Your Highness." He bowed deeply. "Ryder."

The other man nodded, and the prince said, as they walked away from the house and into a deserted part of the garden, "This'd better be good, Cumbria. I don't get hauled from bed in the middle of the night for nothing."

"We've broken the Paris Cipher, Your Highness."

He nodded. "Yes, I heard as much from the man you sent. It's damned good news."

"And in doing so have discovered evidence of a traitor—one who has likely been operating under our noses for eight years or more."

Both men went very still.

"What manner of traitor?" asked Ryder.

"British, working with the French. Interrupting our intelligence efforts and therefore impeding our military. Attempting to prevent the breaking of the Parish Cipher by assassinating those who grew close to doing so: agents Swan and Wren, to my knowledge. Perhaps more."

Frowning, Ryder said, "And who is the rat?" His frown deepened. "A big one, I'd wager, to bring you here at so unnatural a time and at risk of exposing yourself in doing so. Am I right?"

"Yes. I became aware of his identity yesterday evening and only confirmed my first suspicions on my way back to London."

"Then who the devil is it?" exclaimed the Regent. "Stop talking in riddles for once and give me a name. I hate all your spying lot's fiddle-faddle way of talking! And *do* tell me he's already behind bars, otherwise I'll be damn sure to ask why you're here wasting time talking to me."

"I have not given the order for arrest, as my evidence is not of a kind to hold up in court."

The two men exchanged a glance.

"Well?" prompted Ryder.

"It is Lord Gant," said Lucian, his statement producing the exact reaction of disbelieving shock he'd been expecting.

The Regent narrowed his eyes. "That's a weighty accusation, Cumbria. A very dangerous accusation."

Ryder looked at Lucian more thoughtfully. "He's certainly a man who has access to much information—and many resources. But the likelihood of it being him... I've never known a man more loyal. Your Grace, Cumbria, you must be mistaken."

"What's your evidence?" snapped the Regent.

Lucian gave an apologetic smile. "It's not really evidence at all. Red hair, a name, and a reference to a poisonous foxglove."

The Regent stared before turning away with an angry gesture. "Fah! More spy talk!"

"Gant...it is French for glove, is it not?" asked Ryder.

"Yes."

"And red hair like a fox?"

Lucian inclined his head.

"Raven," said Ryder, "you've long been one of my best assets, but you need to do better than this. Gant is...not quite untouchable, no one is. But—"

"Yes. I'm aware. He's the country's favourite uncle. And as good as a second father to you, Your Highness."

The Regent turned. "Right now, Cumbria, it's your own neck you're making a noose for, making accusations like this."

"I know," said Lucian. "I am certain of my suspicions, but entirely unable to prove them. A coded note in an obscure notebook written by a hand that no one can even stand up in court and claim as Swan's—given Swan, just like Raven, does not exist—is no evidence at all. The flicker of suspicion—immediately suppressed—that I saw in Gant's eye when he found me here just now, is likewise not evidence either. But I have a plan to get you proof of an undeniable kind—and to do so in a way that will remove any chance of political unpleasantness falling upon anyone here, should my efforts fail."

Ryder pursed his lips, the Regent still scowling but listening intently.

"Go on," said Ryder.

"How does Thornton fair negotiating with Sweden?" Lucian asked Ryder. The man's brow creased at the unexpected question.

"He's there, but it seems likely to be a protracted affair."

"One that might benefit from some additional diplomatic assistance, perhaps? Such as myself and a messenger from the Regent himself."

"You and Gant go to Sweden?" barked the Regent. "Whatever for? What does this have to do with anything?"

"I will take him on *The Ondine*. The fact he goes with me, guessing as he does something of my true role, will raise his suspicions. You know how good I am at reassuring people and gaining their trust. I can just as easily do the opposite. A few clumsily put questions will convince him I know his secret. I'll put him in a panic."

"And then?"

"If I'm right, he'll try to kill me. It's his usual method. And what better place than at sea, with no one around to bear witness or interrupt him? All sorts of things happen at sea. Accidents and illnesses of every kind."

"And if you're wrong?" asked the Regent.

"Then we'll have a pleasant voyage, do our duty in Sweden, and hopefully arrive home some months hence with a peace treaty in our pocket and no one will be offended by any unfounded suspicion."

"I still don't see how him killing you helps," huffed the Regent. "You'll be dead, for one thing! Can't very well stand up in court if you're at the bottom of the sea."

"Well," said Lucian, smiling faintly. "I admit my preference would be to survive the murder attempt. But whether I do or not, the attack will be enough evidence for Ryder." He met the man's eyes. "You would know how to move discreetly if you were certain Gant was the man. If I don't survive the voyage and Gant does, you'll know the truth. And...if I *do* survive an attack, then Gant will not. *He* will die at sea. And you know...all sorts of things happen at sea," he wryly repeated his earlier words. "Accidents and illnesses of every kind. Gant will be gone in a tragic accident and no public scandal raised, everyone's hands clean but my own."

Ryder nodded slowly. "It's a mad plan, Raven. I can't like it."

"All the risk falls on me."

The Regent was shaking his head. "And you're happy to be bait, are you? Just like that? Sail away on your pretty boat and wait to feel the knife between your shoulder blades? You're mad, Cumbria. Oh, not like my father, no. But like...like Sampson, is it? In Shakespeare, except you're biting your thumb at death, at all of us, the way you always have done. There's that rebellious streak in you, hide it as you like with your cool sarcasm and your smiles. You look the gentleman, Cumbria, always have, but you're a mad rogue at heart."

"Which is why you like me."

The Regent was forced to laugh. "Like you! Part of me does, damn it. How do you manage it, eh? I don't know."

"It is what makes him so useful, Your Highness," said Ryder. "And one of many reasons why I'm loath to approve this. I've never known you to be wrong, Raven. Which makes this a suicide mission. He killed Swan, you say? And Wren?"

"Likely Blackbird too. I've not heard any news of him in many years. Did he retire, Ryder?"

"No. He's dead. Died a week before Swan did. Damned fishy business, but we thought we caught the culprit. Little French spy, found with papers in his pocket but shot dead in the capture."

"Convenient."

"Mmm." He stared fixedly at Lucian. "There's something else at play here, Raven. What aren't you telling us?"

"His Highness is as astute as ever with his introduction of Shakespeare's Romeo and Juliet. You see, I happen to wish to marry someone who I'm not presently permitted to."

"That Parling girl?" said the Regent. "Aye, aye, I know all about that, annoyed as I was when you took yourself off to Hampshire without my permission. But you knew what you were about. I remember her—half of London remembers her. The male half, at any rate. She's not as useful to me as that princess or whatever she is from Buenos Aires, or that Spanish gal you picked out Ryder, or even that damned merchant's daughter—what's his name? The one we need for his gunpowder and things?"

"Markham, Your Highness."

"That's it. One of *them* is who you should have, if you've really any duty to me, any gratitude for the advantages my family has given yours. But a face like that Parling chit's has its own advantages. Beauty like that opens doors even you can't, my silver-tongued duke. Makes men talk. Could catapult you to the top of society. So, cross as I am with you, you have my permission."

Lucian bowed. "Thank you, Your Highness. But it is not Miss Parling whom I wish to marry."

"Who the devil is it, then?"

"A friend of Miss Parling's. Miss Littleton."

"Beautiful, I take it?"

"You wouldn't think so."

"Rich? Though I've never heard of the family. Have you, Ryder?"

"I have, but..."

"She is not rich, Your Highness. She is, in fact, rather poor."

"Good Lord, not some serving wench? Some pot girl? A maid? If you've got her with child, do the necessary, Cumbria, but for the love of God, don't go mentioning marriage."

"She is a governess, Your Highness."

"She is Swan's daughter," said Ryder, eyeing him thoughtfully while the Regent recovered the ability to talk. "You worked it out, did you? And this boy who I've heard reported in your company... Good Lord," he breathed, "and here I was, thinking you'd taken to the trouser line."

"A governess!" exploded the Regent, having sufficiently regained his faculties. "Throw away the Duke of Cumbria on a governess! After everything my father did for yours! This is the gratitude you show, is it? And you know as well as I do that half the lands my father made a present of were carved from our own. Royal land, to be governed by a governess! No, dammit, I'll not hear of it! Marry her and you'll be Cumbria no more!"

Lucian inclined his head in polite acknowledgement of this, and said calmly, "I'm glad you are sensible of the value of gratitude returned for gifts—the gratitude one is forced to feel. Even perhaps against one's will." The Regent's eyes flashed dangerously, but he continued. "Let me present my likewise case to you. I will risk my life to gift you freedom from one of the most dangerously situated traitors imaginable, at no trouble or risk or even cost to you. Your gratitude to me, if I survive the task, may be adequately and entirely expressed by permitting me to marry how I choose. Something I feel you might sympathise with, Your Highness."

"You bring my wife into this, do you?"

"I bring your sympathy as a man."

Ryder, motivated not, Lucian was sure, by any romantic sentiments but by a wish to remove Gant in a manner so comfortably convenient to all except one, entered the fray, and the Regent was gradually brought to approve the deal.

"I'll have it put in writing," Ryder murmured in Lucian's ear as he escorted him from the Regent's presence. "And Raven...keep your wits about you. If you're right, Gant is a killer, and he's already got your scent."

"I know."

They made their bows, but Ryder paused before turning away. "She's worth the risk?"

"I risk nothing. You see...without her, I'm already dead."

With another bow, Lucian departed.

Lucian sent word for *The Ondine* to be brought to Dover. Within another week, it was provisioned and ready, and the Duke of Cumbria and Lord Gant set sail for Sweden in the face of changeable weather that promised neither to be with nor against them.

The two men lingered over their port after their first evening's dinner, the captain already having returned to his duties.

"So, Cumbria," said Gant, leaning back at leisure in his chair, the small port glass held delicately between two blunt fingers, "we can finally speak man to man after a week or more of smiles and diplomatic flattery—not that I resent you for it, I'm sure it's nothing but preparation for the task to come. Though, as a man who's spent decades smoothing His Highness's flighty temper, not to mention a King's ravings, I'm sure I need little instruction in the art of fielding my tongue. But I'm at heart a straightforward man. So out with it. Tell me the truth. He's annoyed with me, is he? The Regent? And this is my punishment, sending me off to talk tripe and puffery?"

"Not at all."

"Then it's as I feared. He's got some expensive scheme in mind and wants me out of the way before I can put a stop to it. Let me guess... He's sick of Carlton House, finds it too small even after all he's poured into it, and wants to...let's think...knock down Buckingham House and replace it with a Turkish Palace? I wish to God he'd never laid eyes on that fellow Nash."

Lucian smiled. "Almost as much as the Treasury regrets it, I'm sure."

Gant chuckled. "That's about the top and tail of it."

It was interesting, Lucian noted, how the thought that every mouthful might be poisoned leant a certain piquancy to the taste of food and drink. They were sharing the same bottle, and he was sure he was safe—currently; Gant wouldn't act yet. But still, he imagined odd flavours, try as he might to ignore the thought.

"If Prinny *is* planning anything," Lucian remarked, "I suspect it'll be to the gardens. He thinks they're snuck full of foreign weeds."

Gant looked at him for a moment. "Is that so?" He sipped his port. "Said as much, did he? You did disappear off into the gardens for quite some time. Ryder too. Never knew he was a gardener."

"We all have hidden depths. And Ryder has a fairly strict policy against invasive plants. Likes to cut them out, root and all. As for me, it's the poisonous ones that give me qualms. I knew someone, you see, who died after an accident with some foxgloves. I've had an aversion to them ever since." Lucian shrugged. "But, in truth, it was you we met to talk of."

A little sharply: "Oh?"

"This trip, of course. This is no punishment, Gant. You know the Regent has long wished you to retire. I believe he sees a shift away from the palace and into diplomacy as something that might ease your path, show the public that court can run smoothly without you there. He's fond of you, you must know that. This trip is a reward, Gant, to repay you for all you have done for him. And our country." He lifted his glass. "To you, Gant."

The man chuckled. "I can hardly drink to my own health, Cumbria."

"To duty, then. To long service. And loyalty."

He drank deeply, and did not die, not then. The poison found him some days later, when *The Ondine* was far distant from any shore.

He was preparing himself for bed, the ghost of Hester no less present in the room than it had been when he first boarded at Dover. *The tooth powder,* he managed to think as the first wracking pain tore through his gut, *that's where he's put it. Very clever.*

Then the brush fell from his hand, and he lurched, buckled with pain, knocking the basin from the stand. It was fast acting.

Far faster than he'd anticipated, not the slow decline of Hester's parents. He'd made sure to find that out, attempted to identify the poison.

But...God... Gant wanted no slow death this time...

Agony after agony ripped through him. He vomited blood and trembled, half falling against the wall of the rocking ship before another wave of pain wracked him and brought him to his knees, sweating and shaking.

The door... If he could get to the door, to his dressing room, find the case of emetics and antidotes...

Too late, terror said, blunt and stark.

If he could ring for Willsly, wherever he might be—not keeping guard, not right outside his door because Lucian hadn't told him the real reason for this trip. If Willsly had suspected Gant, he'd have kept too close an eye on the man for him to act, and Lucian needed the proof, needed this proof, the fatal evidence... And God, at what cost...

In the moment of dying, he discovered how much he did not want to die. *Hester.* Vision flickered behind darkening sight. His risk was all for naught...but at least she'd be looked after. He'd changed his will before he left England, secured an annuity on her if he died; she'd want for nothing...nothing but him...

God dammit, if he could only get to the door, if he could only ring the bell... But his strength had deserted him, he was sweating on the floor, spasming with pain as more blood came from his mouth.

Crawl... Crawl a little further...

God damn it. Devil take him if he gave in now...

My heaven is on Earth and I will not quit this sphere...

On knees, head swimming, vision blurring...

Was that a bell? The final bell, tolling for him... Or maybe it was the latch of the door. He saw the toe of a boot.

"Your Grace!"

Ah, Willsly, he said. Or tried to say. *Remember that time I was poisoned, and how well you kept your head? Be a good chap and keep it now...*

Twenty-Nine

"They say the rose is related to the apple tree, and the bramble," Hester said to the three girls in her charge, none of whom were listening.

It was a hot day in late July, and, after much entreating from the young ladies, Hester had consented to move their lesson outside and have some rugs spread in the shade of one of the venerable beeches at Beaford Court, her current place of employment. But the three Miss Carters had scarcely sat down before they were off among the flowerbeds, picking roses to try in their hair.

They were frivolous girls and cared for little but their own amusement, but they were good-natured and as kind as spoilt girls aged eight to fourteen were ever wont to be.

Hester sighed as the girls moved deeper into the garden, giving up the attempt at a little botany to replace the abandoned geography. She sat in the shade, listening to the giggles coming from among the roses and idly turning the globe that stood on the rug beside her. Asia. Africa. Spain, Portugal... Her finger trailed over the familiar shape of England, lingered a moment in that southeast corner that held London, then she stood and walked resolutely in the direction of her wayward charges, the bright sun filtering sharply around the peak of her bonnet and momentarily dazzling her sight, painting the flower beds in gaudy colours.

There were foxgloves among the display, tall and brown and gone to seed, and she tried not to look at them, pretending to ignore the sharp catch in her chest. Three months and no word. Not that she expected any. But even in the society sections of the newspapers, which she now perused with more diligence than she wished to admit, his name was never mentioned.

But there was equally no mention of his marriage. Or worse—his death. He'd gone on another mission, she supposed. Was perhaps back in Lisbon, or wherever else his work had taken him. Courting nobles and diplomats and dark-eyed condesas... No. He would not.

Folded very carefully between papers in the trunk in her bedroom on the very top floor of this grand house, was a brightly coloured Portuguese shawl. It had been waiting for her on her pillow when she stumbled to her room at Rowlands, eyes blurred with tears, the sound of departing wheels in her ears. There'd been no note, but of course she knew, and besides, on top of the shawl was the novel he must've taken unknown to her from *The Ondine*. That ridiculous novel of Angelica Thorogood and Lord Bravecourt, exactly as she remembered it, the marble covers worn at the corners, but now with a note inscribed on the flyleaf in a very familiar hand.

How does it end?

She'd made herself finish the book, bitterly, over several evenings, trying not to cry. And of course it had ended happily. The hero prevailed after hard trials, the villain was brought to justice, and true love won the day. Angelica and Bravecourt married and lived happily ever after. *Good for them,* Hester thought, closing the book with a snap and fighting the urge to hurl it across the room. She'd never opened it since, and it lived in the same trunk as the unworn shawl, buried deep in a corner.

"Girls," she said, coming upon the admittedly pretty scene of the three sisters wreathed in roses. She smiled, but said sternly, "You have spent long enough in the sun. Remember what your mother said."

"I have my bonnet!" cried the youngest.

"Oh, to be forced to sit in the shade on a day like today of all things!" said the next.

"Harry rides all day in the sun," said the eldest, talking of her brother, a sporting mad youth of eighteen. "He rides all day, wherever he likes, and no one is scolding *him* for getting brown."

"It is different for Harry," said Hester primly, thinking: *And how! Oh, to be Harry again!* "And besides..." She leant in and whispered, "I heard your mother say he was looking as coarse as a farmer. So perhaps it's not so very different after all."

The girls giggled, and Hester felt fairly sure this confidence would be betrayed immediately once they spied the unfortunate young man. She felt no guilt. They were a loud and boisterous family and affectionately insulted each other to their faces all day long. It was a happy home and the most comfortable position she'd yet held.

She half suspected Lucian had played a hand in securing it for her. A letter from the mistress of the house had arrived for her only ten days after Lucian had left. *A mutual friend had recommended her,* Lady Atherington had written. And other than smiling significantly on the two occasions Hester had braved the topic, she'd communicated no more.

A shawl, a book, and comfortable employment. These were all the tangible signs left, all the outside world would ever see. But on the inside... Oh, on the inside...? Like an earthquake had shaken her near to death. Rearranged the whole. Mind and heart and self an unrecognisable landscape of breathtakingly sharp peaks and many, many dismal lows. Dark, torn rifts... A landscape of scars and pain and...

She would not cave to it, not here in the sun with the girls around her and rose perfume in the air. Fixing a smile to her face she chivvied them back into the house, brandishing the promise of tea and cake the way a drover uses his cudgel: expertly and without remorse.

The light was dim and cool inside after the sunshine. The girls spilled through the door into the sitting room in a chattering mass, and Hester took a moment to pause and breathe as she undid the bow on her bonnet and pulled the neat straw creation from her too-hot head.

"Miss Littleton."

She looked up at the stout little porter and smiled. "Yes, Tomas?"

He seemed somewhat thrown, the usual garrulous manner he took with her absent. Hesitantly, as though he wasn't quite sure he believed it, he said, "There's a gentleman here to see you, miss. A *gentleman*," he repeated, "to see *you*, he said, not mistress. And so grand and high-like that I fair forgot my own name and forgot to ask him his! Forgive me, miss, but he wouldn't come in. He's waiting by his carriage at the front steps."

Her heart gave a stupid lurch, and she furiously hushed it as she hurried to the front of the house. Then slowed. Stopped. The door was ajar, and from this angle she could just see the edge of a magnificent lacquered carriage. And a hat. A dark, very elegant, very beautiful beaver hat.

She made herself take a breath and walk forward, but her brisk steps again faltered because as she drew level with the door and the figure of the man revealed himself, she found each step getting slower, and slower, as her mind tried to keep pace with what her racing heart cried.

"Lucian...?"

Lucian it was, standing on the gravel drive at the foot of the stairs, dressed every inch the duke—no wonder poor Tomas had been thrown—standing tall and straight, a smile pulling up the corners of that stern mouth, a smile that grew and grew as he stood and watched her stupefaction.

"Hello, Miss Littleton."

"But how...? But why...?"

She was too frightened for joy, terrified that his being here meant she would have to watch him leave all over again. And she'd not yet recovered from the last time. Never would, never could watch him leave again...

"I've come to take you on a little holiday. There's to be a wedding, you see. One you'll very much wish to attend."

She stared at him.

"Charles," he said, smiling. "Charles is coming home. Injured, but out of danger. I had word from Lisbon—I asked someone to keep an eye on him. He ought to be arriving at any moment now, if not already."

"Charles..." she repeated. But it was too much to take in. She looked at Lucian, truly looked at him now the moment of shock was passing.

She came rapidly down the steps. "What has happened?" Hardly knowing she did it, she reached out a hand and touched his cheek. A tremor went through him, but even that she barely noticed. "Lucian, you're so thin..." He was gaunt, his athletic strength withered, his cheeks hollow, lines of suffering around his eyes. There was a smattering of grey at his temples that hadn't been there before. "What happened to you?"

He smiled crookedly, taking her hand from his cheek and holding it between his. "A little bad brandy."

"Poisoned!"

"Hush, dear one." He let go her hand and nodded towards the house behind her. "We have an audience."

She turned and found three small faces agog at one of the windows and Tomas sheepishly ducking out of sight behind the door.

"We'll have plenty of time to talk," he said softly. "It's a day's journey from here to Rowlands. Ah—and we can set off at once, see—here's a footman with your trunk."

She stared as the liveried man carried her belongings from the house. "But... How..."

"Lady Atherington is an old friend," Lucian said, smiling. "I wrote to ask her permission for you to take a small holiday. If you wish it? Charles means to marry Jane without delay, you see. And I thought you might be more comfortable with me than on the stage. But if you'd rather the stage, or perhaps, knowing your inclinations, inside your own trunk..."

"How can you be so ridiculous!"

But for once he wasn't joking. "I wasn't sure...if you would be happy that I have come."

"Happy! What a feeble word! Next you will say it is *nice* to see me! That we will have a *pleasant* journey!"

"All very true. But...Hester...if you'd taught yourself to hate me to survive these past few months, I wouldn't have blamed you."

"Oh, how can you!"

"Do I venture to hope from the way you're glaring and huffing with anger that you do *not* hate me?"

"Of course I do not!"

"Then go," he said, ushering her gently towards the house. "Check you have everything you wish to bring with you and say goodbye to your charges. But warn them, with your utmost pedagogical authority, that you don't have time for a full explanation, and that their one hundred questions will have to wait because the very grand man with the marvellous equipage wishes to whisk you away immediately."

Darkly muttering something about impossible men and other things even less coherent, she did as she was bid. A confused and dreamlike whirlwind of fifteen minutes ended with her stepping into the beautiful interior of the Duke of Cumbria's best travelling coach and being, as promised, whisked away down the drive by four matched blacks of a quality that left the young Harry Carter—spying them flying down the road as he rode home across a field—staring after them, mouth agape. Hester waved, entirely unheeded, as his eyes were fixed on the equines, and supposed to herself that he'd be describing the horses to all his acquaintance for months to come.

She sat back on her seat and looked at Lucian sitting across from her. A smile still curved his lips, growing again as his eyes held hers.

"Brandy," she said severely, in an unromantic manner that would've appalled Miss Angelica Thorogood.

Lucian scratched his jaw and took off his hat, setting it down on the seat beside him. His gloves soon found their way inside it, and then he ventured the risk of meeting her eyes again.

"The last time," he said. "I promise."

"Foxglove?"

He paused. "Dead."

She let out a breath. "Lucian...tell me what happened. What have you been about?"

"Luring a fox from his hole." But at her quelling look, he grew more serious and quickly outlined what had passed since he left Rowlands, though she suspected he left out much.

"Lord Gant," she breathed. "Whoever would've thought? What made him do it? Did he reveal his motive?"

"Not in person. It was discovered afterwards by those who combed through his effects and personal networks. It seems the King's illness, and the Regent's profligacy, had long disillusioned him with the monarchy. He became a fan of the radical ideas in France, secretly supported the revolution, and thereafter supported Bonaparte, becoming more and more fanatical in his devotion with every passing year and every French success. A devotion that was, I suspect, greatly aided by what he'd been promised for his support."

"Which was?"

"Once England was won and our monarchy disposed of, that he would rule in its stead."

Hester sat back, stunned. "No small aspiration!"

"Quite."

And so *that* was what her parents had been murdered for. And that poor man in Lisbon, and probably many more.

And very nearly Lucian himself.

She studied his face for a moment. "Are you well, Lucian? Are you really recovered?"

He smiled ruefully. "Almost. It was...precarious...for a while. I spent two months recuperating in Sweden before the doctor gave me permission to travel home."

"Good God..."

He leant forward and grasped her hand. "I am here, Hester. And in a few more months, I'll likely be as well as I ever was."

"You said he was dead? Gant? Foxglove? I'm glad of it. I shouldn't say so, but I am. Can you tell me how it happened? It's ghoulish that I want to know, but I was there when my parents were taken ill... I watched them sicken and die..."

Lucian squeezed her hand.

"I didn't see Gant's end. Willsly was...the witness. He saw Gant go overboard. A freak wave at the moment the boat happened to pitch steeply. These things happen at sea, you know."

She met his eyes. "Yes. I suppose they do." And then, quietly, "Willsly is always to be relied upon. And you said he was the one who found you?"

"That's right. And gave me the emetic that saved me."

"God bless him," she said reverently. "How can we ever repay him?"

"I often try," said Lucian wryly. "He knows he has a rich farm awaiting him any time he chooses to retire from my service, with enough income to set him up as a country squire, if he chooses. Or a position in any career, or even just a house and a pension, if he thinks idleness would suit. I've promised him everything I can think of over the years. But he just goes, *'Aye, and where would you be without me?'* And when I pester him, *'Ah, sure, I'll think on it a while,'* and goes back to blacking my boots and whistling while he does it."

"He's right though," Hester said, laughing. "Where would you be without him?"

"I dread to think."

But the sombre edge to his tone didn't last. He began to smile again, toying with her hand in his. "I do know where I'd *like* to be, right now."

"And where is that?"

"On that seat beside you."

She met his eyes, her heart skipping.

"If you permit," he asked.

"I do."

He moved to sit beside her.

"And...greedy as I am, now I'd like to put my arm around you...yes, just like so," he said, acting to fit his words. "And you snugged up against my side where you fit so perfectly... That's it."

A tremor ran through her, and she turned her face to his coat, eyes squeezed shut, pressing her face into the solidity of his chest, the weight of his arm holding her tight.

"Hester," he breathed, hand on her hair. "Hester, my love..."

She tipped her face up to his. "What happens," she whispered, "after the wedding?"

His eyes glowed. "I suspect that's a private matter for your brother and Miss Parling."

"Oh, how can you joke!"

"Because I'm a coward. Because I hope for too much... But, Hester, my love, after your brother's wedding, I'm very much hoping to take you to your own."

She could not move. "Do you mean...?"

"Yes. Marry me, Hester."

"And the Regent...?"

He touched her cheek, tilted her mouth to his and grazed her lips with his own. "I am free, Hester. Free to marry. And I choose you."

Epilogue

Lucian had once told her that one of the wonderful things about being a duke was that one could be as unusual as one likes, and Hester was delighted to find that the same principle applied to duchesses. Or, at least, to duchesses who didn't much care what people thought of them.

"Thank you," she said, smiling sweetly at the man who held the door open for her. She strode briskly from Fitzroy Square and into the entrance foyer of the Philological Society, making her familiar way to the lecture hall and taking her accustomed seat at the side.

It was set off from the rest of the hall, her seat at least two yards from any of her male neighbours and surrounded by a velvet rope, which always amused her greatly, as though she herself was the exhibit in a museum of wonders, a museum of freaks and oddities. *Come see the philological female!*

Six months of regular attendance hadn't cured her fellow philological devotees of their curiosity—or, in some cases, their hostility. But she sat through the lectures as though she didn't notice the stares and whispers.

Afterwards, she spoke for a short while with some of the more progressive men who were ready enough to set aside her sex and discuss the lecture almost as though she was one of them. But she couldn't follow them to the nearby coffee house, where many of them retreated for deeper discussion. Instead, she left the building and entered the carriage waiting for her outside, which took her home to Cumbria House.

There was a note waiting for her in the hallway, written in Lucian's hand. It said: *232, 16,* and she smiled to herself as though it were the sweetest words of a lover, as indeed it was. In a drawer of the table on which the note lay was a familiar book with increasingly worn marbled covers. She turned to the page and line and read, *"Miss Thorogood, if I do not soon claim your lips with my own, I will go mad."* She was still blushing and smiling like a lovesick schoolgirl when the butler stepped into the hall. Hastily, she put the book away.

"Captain and Mrs Littleton await you in the parlour, Your Grace."

"Thank you, Peake."

Jane stood as Hester entered and flew as she always did to kiss her cheek. Charles took the liberty of a brother—and one who'd seen his sister almost daily these last twelve months—and stayed sitting, giving her a broad grin.

"Learn anything?" he asked, as the two women sat down near him.

"As it was my own paper being presented, not really."

"I wish I could've seen it, but we've only just this minute arrived back in town."

"The house is all settled then?"

"I can't wait for you to see it!" breathed Jane. "The sweetest stone-built cottage—"

"Cottage!" objected Charles. "It's the size of Rowlands!"

"But it *looks* like a cottage," insisted Jane. "It has that cottage *feel.*"

"Then we should have argued for a cottage *price*," said Charles, though he took Jane's fingers, and, grinning, gave them a squeeze.

Well used to Charles's teasing, Jane quickly rallied and, beaming, turned again to Hester. "And an hour from London! Even when I am confined, we'll be able to see you almost as much as we do now. Because you must visit us constantly."

"Well, I cannot wait to see it," said Hester. "I'm glad you have got it, and just in the nick of time," she added, with a smile at Jane's rounded figure. That the last few days had convinced her she was likely in the same interesting condition, she did not say. It would be Lucian's news first, as soon as he returned from the business that had taken him today to St James's.

They'd had a month's honeymoon in splendid isolation at Thornley Castle in the Lake District. But Lucian's work kept him busy, though he had, after a deal of wrangling and negotiating, managed to reduce the amount he travelled, becoming, with Hester's assistance—now approved by the powers that managed Lucian—more an agent like The Swans had been. They worked together, mostly from home, Hester on codebreaking and Lucian on the analysis of what she deciphered. She even had her own codename, though was somewhat annoyed at it being *Sparrow*.

"Did you want to be Eagle, my love?" Lucian had teased her. "Hawk, or Falcon, or even Osprey!"

"Anything but Sparrow!"

"But they happen to be my favourite birds. Small, brown, and spirited." He'd leant over her—for this conversation had taken place in bed—and looked down, smoothing her hair—sparrow brown!—back from her forehead, and grinning his familiar teasing grin. "I think it most appropriate."

Hester shook herself back to the present, realised Jane was listing all the furniture at her new home, and drifted back out again.

The newlywed Littletons had moved to London almost at the same time as she and Lucian. Society had taken to them.

The courageous young captain with his bold, easy manners, the modesty and slight air of secrecy that accompanied his Peninsular tales only adding to his interest. And his wife, beautiful enough to astonish but with manners perfectly gentle and unassuming and, much to the relief of all the unmarried ladies, safely off the marriage market.

The injury that had forced Charles from his active duty and reduced his left arm to near immobility had done little to hamper his career. A letter of recommendation from Wellington himself, and Lucian's own efforts, had secured him on the beginnings of a very promising career. This, coupled with the unexpected advantage of being brother-in-law to a duke, had done much to recommend him to Jane's parents. And though Charles—or Jane, or Hester, or Lucian—were never likely to forget their previous prejudice, everything was as harmonious as it could be between the Littletons and the Parlings.

Hester herself was accepted in town, Lucian's status and her own obvious lack of ambition or presumption protecting her from hostility. She made friends with several ladies of an academic inclination, was permitted to attend the Philological Society meetings and submit to its journals despite not being allowed to join, was currently at work on the second volume of her book, and also in the early stages of attempting to set up a language school for gifted young women.

None of this had injured her with Lucian's mother as she feared. The dowager was fonder of the handsome Littletons but sensible enough to be conscious of the benefits of the new Mrs Grey—the new Duchess of Cumbria.

"She is an intelligent girl," Lucian had reported his mother as saying, smiling throughout the account, "and well-mannered, and she is not, thankfully, the type of flighty thing to run you into debt or into scandal whom I once feared you would marry in your youth. I like her well enough."

"But, Mother," Lucian had then said, "you haven't mentioned the only thing worth mentioning. She makes me radiantly happy."

"Oh, that!" the grand lady had said. "You told me you didn't want a love match, Lucian, but now it seems love matches are becoming all the rage, and you always did like to be fashionable."

"So there you have it, Hester, my love," he'd said after recounting this story. They were in the orangery at Thornley Castle, and he'd taken her by the waist, his broad hands spanning the dip above her hips. The heat of the air and the scent of exotic leaves reminded her a little of Oporto. "You are the height of fashion. Exactly the type of wife I was looking for."

"I'm glad you approve," she had replied, very seriously, "then you'll not scold me for the thousand guineas I spent on diamond soled shoes and ostrich feathers."

"You," he'd said, starting to kiss her, "are more likely to spend it on Hessian boots and beaver hats."

"And a banyan."

"Which you wear around the house with nothing on underneath and drive me to distraction."

"That happened once!"

"Yes, when you suddenly found yourself in desperate need of checking a reference halfway through your bath, or so you excused yourself to me."

"You didn't seem to mind."

He chuckled, a low sound, his mouth moving to her jaw then her throat. "I didn't mind at all. And to think some men say they don't want a bookish wife."

The sound of the door broke into her reverie and snapped her back to the present. Her duke entered the room. His smile asked if she'd got his message. The answering colour in her cheeks confirmed it.

That same book held the question: *How does it end?* And now, at last, she had the answer.

Very happily indeed.

Thank you

Thank you so much for reading! If you'd like to sign up for my newsletter and get some free bonus content visit www.rachelrowan.com.

If you liked the book, could you help spread the love? Leaving a review on Amazon is incredibly helpful to us indie authors. We really do depend on word of mouth.

Do stay in touch to find out about new releases—follow me on Amazon, or Instagram, or join my newsletter. Or email me just to say hi! I'd love to hear from you!

Email: rachel@rachelrowan.com

Instagram: @rachelrowanwriter

Website: www.rachelrowan.com

Thank you again for reading! I hope to see you here again at the end of the next book!

Also by Rachel Rowan

More books are coming soon in my Regency Reputations series. So please sign up at www.rachelrowan.com for news!

In the meantime, I also have a contemporary romance series you can explore: Entitled Love. These books are quite a bit steamier but still feature aristocrats, stately homes, and witty banter. In fact, you might recognise some of the names – they're set in the same world as my Regency Reputations books but around 200 years later!

Engaging the Enemy

Sensible, hard-working Amelia has always had a secret crush on her neighbour—a terrible lapse in judgement given he's as arrogant as he is good looking. But when Hugo surprises her with a kiss, she makes an even worse mistake: for a moment, she believes he means it. And she really, really should have known better. At least she's now over her crush. Honest.

As the son of an earl, Hugo is used to doing what he wants, regardless of the consequences. But when his irate father cuts off his playboy lifestyle, Hugo is forced back home, where there's an unavoidable consequence right next door. Amelia. His oldest friend. Who now hates him.

OK. Maybe he shouldn't have kissed her. Even if he did enjoy it. But she could be about to make him pay: he's just discovered an ancient legal document promising enough money to free him from his father's control forever. The catch? The money is only his if he convinces Amelia to marry him.

For the first time in his life, Hugo needs to work out how to say sorry. But in his mission to gain Amelia's forgiveness, he might end up losing his heart...

Available on Amazon.

Pride and Privilege

When you're stuck sharing a flat with a man known as Lecherous Dave to save money, you'll do anything for a leg up at work—even if rumours say that requires cosying up to the boss's son. Fortunately for admin assistant Poppy, he's gorgeous. Unfortunately, she's just drunkenly laughed in his face and accused him of tax avoidance. And she's about to make it worse...

Roscoe Blackton has sacrificed sleep and sanity to land a senior role at London's biggest wealth management firm. The fact his dad owns the whole company has nothing to do with it—or so he tells himself. But he can't escape the whispers of nepotism, and his new assistant makes it horrifyingly clear everyone believes climbing *him* is the best way to climb the corporate ladder.

Desperate to prove he's more than his background, Roscoe realises Poppy might have the answer—if they can ever recover from their disastrous first impressions. She could teach him how to live without privilege, while he can give her a true taste of luxury. But as their social experiment causes their personal lives to become hopelessly entangled, keeping things professional gets complicated.

He's her boss. She's his assistant. But they're both adults. They know what they're doing. And they're definitely, absolutely, obviously not going to fall for each other...right?

Available on Amazon.

Love and Loathing

In Aubrey Ford's opinion, his best friend's little sister is a naive hippy do-gooder—a hypocritical trust-fund princess spending her father's money on lost causes. In Evie Blackton's opinion, men like Aubrey are exactly what's wrong with the world—a callous tax strategist who only cares about making the rich richer.

But when Evie's activist group targets one of Aubrey's ultra-wealthy clients, she realises the man she hates might be the key she needs to bring their target down—if she can find a way to get close to him. Luckily, she's not intimidated by tall, dark men with very stern eyebrows and ironic smiles...

Aubrey can only imagine Evie's insistence on being his fake date is her way of torturing him, but with the ex that shredded his heart back in town, maybe he needs an ally. If only Evie wasn't so young, and irritating, and determined to interfere with his broken heart. And if only she wasn't so damned attractive...

But as one fake date turns into an increasingly heated weekend away, Evie's mission comes back to haunt her. Can Evie and Aubrey separate truth from lie—and love from loathing?

Available on Amazon.

The *Entitled Love* novellas – find these first four together in The Entitled Love Collection:

Uncommon

Sparks fly in this fish-out-of-water Pretty Woman-style story in which a playboy Earl meets his match.

Unspoken

She's the only woman he's ever wanted—and the one woman he can never have.

Untouched

A socially awkward young woman asks her playboy neighbour to teach her everything about men—including how to be touched...

Unwanted

After losing his inheritance, a disgruntled viscount is forced to live with the best friend of the woman who ruined his life...

Unwrapped

A sunshine hero and grumpy heroine take a road trip at Christmas.

All available on Amazon and Kindle Unlimited. Plus, get a free short story when you sign up for the Rachel Rowan newsletter: www.rachelrowan.com

Research notes

First off, I should apologise to all linguists, philologists, and codebreakers for the liberties I took with their subjects. I sort of twisted them up, like one squeezes a slice of lemon, and only took a few juicy drops here and there, regardless of the mangled object I created in doing so.

A few nice pulpy bits of research did make it into the book though—there's a soupçon of real history hiding in this fictional froth.

Yes, correspondence really was intercepted by the Post Office's "Secret Office", based in Lombard Street, London. Coded letters were sent to the Deciphering Branch, apparently run by the Willes family, who had been cleverly deciphering things since the early 1700s. Major George Scovell, the Army Guides, and the breaking of the Great Paris Cipher are all real too. More information can be found in *The Story of George Scovell* by Mark Urban and *Regency Spies* by Sue Wilkes.

Also real, of course, is Lady Caroline Lamb, who indeed sported short hair. Troubled and fascinating, she is probably most famous for being a lover of Lord Byron. And once, apparently, disguised herself as a page boy so she could be smuggled into his rooms. As Hester might say, there is a *precedent*.

In *The Duke's Discovery*, Hester also mentions the rumour of a doctor, born female, who lived as a man. This is also inspired by fact. James Barry (1789-1865), a military surgeon in the British Army, was born Margaret Anne Barry. Their story is a fascinating one and well worth reading.

One of my favourite areas of research for this book was the Peninsular War, a subject which I previously only knew from ogling Sean Bean in the TV show *Sharpe* back in the 1990s. Not a huge amount of what I learnt made it into the final book, but I don't begrudge a moment lost to it. My main sources were the journals and autobiographies of some of the officers and soldiers who served during the war. Many of these can be found for free on Project Gutenberg—a wonderful resource.

My favourite was *Adventures in the Rifle Brigade* by Captain John Kincaid. He writes with wonderful humour—often blunt and dark—and I confess to developing a small crush on the man. But he writes so well his book is still well worth reading today.

I also used Sergeant William Lawrence's autobiography, Lieutenant-Colonel Tomkinson's *The Diary of a Cavalry Officer*, Benjamin Harris's *Recollections of Rifleman Harris*, George Simmons's *A British Rifle Man*, and the autobiography of Sir Harry Smith—Georgette Heyer fans will know his name: he's the hero of her novel *The Spanish Bride*. He was also friends with my favourite John Kincaid who appears in Smith's writing, as well as Simmons's.

Mainly I studied their accounts of Lisbon, particularly their first impressions, and so I'm afraid it's to these men that *The Duke's Discovery* owes its rather unflattering descriptions of the city. I apologise! But I went with the voices and opinions of the time. Lucian's description of Portuguese opera dancers also comes from these texts. Apologies again!

Other things I took from these texts were accounts of the battles of Ciudad Rodrigo and Badajoz, small snippets of the grim and gritty realities of the soldiers' lives, such as their buttons being tarnished black, and in general, their attitudes and loyalties—Charles's determination to see his mission through despite Lucian's temptation feels true to how many of these men would have acted in a like circumstance.

One other thing I took from these texts was the story of a young lieutenant of the 95th Rifles who suffered a bullet wound to jaw and throat. Lucian visits him recuperating in Lisbon. In reality, he died of his injuries on his way there. I took the liberty of fiction to bring him back to life in these pages. His name was Pratt, he was a friend of George Simmons, and his fate can be read in George Simmons's *A British Rifle Man* in the entry dated 1810, August 1st.

As Hester said, I wish they all could come home.

Acknowledgements

If there's any book that needs an acknowledgements section, it's this one. Not only do I doubt whether this book would ever have been published without the support of many lovely people, but I'm not sure I'd still be writing at all.

The book itself was a joy to write. The first draft flowed easily and smoothly in a matter of weeks during the summer of 2024. I spent a lot of those days chuckling to myself and thoroughly enjoying every minute spent in Hester and Lucian's company. But it was the last thing I wrote for a long time.

I got hit by a wave of imposter syndrome and authorly self-doubt. I wasn't sure if writing Regency romance was a good idea, or if *I* was any good at it, or if any of my readers would follow me in this new direction. I was worried about upsetting people or disappointing them. The release of my third Entitled Love novel, *Love and Loathing*, went quite poorly, and the book never did as well as I'd hoped. It was now autumn, and Seasonal Affective Disorder was starting to rear its ugly, dreary, repetitive head. World events were upsetting many people, especially my American friends, and people were retreating, finding it hard to stay bright and optimistic. The whole world seemed set on a course of hatred, corruption, and greed. AI was everywhere, threatening all creative industries, threatening the soul of humanity itself, and, bizarrely, humanity seemed to be welcoming it. And I was very tired. I'd been writing and publishing non-stop for a couple of years and never quite finding myself where I wanted to be. My ads were failing, my royalties plummeting, my books' ratings steadily declining, and I didn't know why or how to fix it.

Publishing is a very hard industry. I write not only because I love it—it's been my special thing since I was seven—but also because it's one of the few jobs I can fit in around the complex and changing needs of my son, who has significant special needs. I also have special needs of my own, being neurodivergent. Writing fiction allows me the social quiet, the autonomy, and the creative outlet I need to stay mentally healthy. Publishing and marketing my fiction quite often does entirely the opposite.

From around August 2024, my mental health steadily declined. I entered one of the worst depressive episodes I've had in years. Professionally, I was in crisis. No one seemed to want my stories—or not enough people for me to earn the money my family needed—and I wasn't functioning well enough to write them anyway, let alone market them. I just wasn't good enough. I decided, time and again, that I would stop. I almost deleted everything from my laptop. Almost threw away all my paperback proofs and author copies.

Why didn't I?

I think, even in the midst of that lowest of lows, there was a part of me that knew I needed to write. Telling myself to stop writing is almost equivalent to telling myself to stop living. And I can't do that. I'm a mother, a wife. My life is important to others, even when it seems unimportant to myself. But there's a line towards the end of this book when Lucian, having had to leave Hester, sees his future as nothing but a cage of time. And that's how life would feel to me if I couldn't write: just a motion to be gone through.

So I had to write, which meant I had to find a way to protect my ability to keep writing, my desire and courage to keep going.

I changed my goalposts. Success stopped being about royalties earnt or bestseller rankings or social media likes or ad conversion rates. Success became simply to keep writing. If I do that, I've not failed.

If I keep writing, I keep living—truly living. Living in a meaningful way that fulfils me, gives me joy, and lets me be the person I want to be. There will be people who hate this book. People who hate every word I ever write. There will be one-star reviews, people who scroll past this book on Amazon and laugh at the cover or read the blurb and think "meh, not for me." And that's OK—I tell myself that's OK. I've been down a very dark valley and returned exhausted, battered, and bruised but clutching a message from myself: to write is the thing. The only thing. And I'm the only one who can take that away from myself.

So where do the acknowledgements come in? Well, I wasn't alone on that journey out of the valley. I had people holding my hands, lighting my way, easing some of the burden from my shoulders. There were glimmers of brightness even in the darkness: a kind word here or there, a message of encouragement, an exasperated No you don't suck, Rachel, stop whining (more kindly put, of course, but that was the gist).

So thank you Brianna, Charis, and Libby. Thank you Jessica and the lovely people in Historical Romance Writers who welcomed me and gave me a virtual home when I was very lonely and lost. And a huge thank you to my readers, to everyone who's ever bought a book, left a nice review, or sent me a kind message. You all helped more than you could ever know. Thank you also to my editor, Chrisandra, for her skillful polishing of this manuscript.

And thank you beyond words to my husband and my children. I write for me; I live for you. You are joy and home and love. You make the fabric of my reality, the start and end of all meaning. You make me better and braver than I could ever be on my own poor behalf. I love you and thank you with every breath.

There will be more books, and it's thanks to all of you.

Printed in Dunstable, United Kingdom